THE UNFORGIVEN

The Unforgiven

JANE McLOUGHLIN

QUARTET BOOKS

First published in 2008 by
Quartet Books Limited
A member of the Namara Group
27 Goodge Street
London W1T 2LD

A catalogue record for this book
is available from the British Library

ISBN   978 0 7043 7125 5

Typeset by Antony Gray
Printed and bound in Great Britain by
T J International Ltd, Padstow, Cornwall

1

Belle saw Susie leave the barn: her sister was buttoning her blouse as she hurried towards the house, and Belle, with a sour knot of resentment inside her, knew the worst.

Ben was pulling on his jeans as she climbed the ladder to the hayloft. She caught the look on his face before he saw her, the silly, self-satisfied post-coital grin she had thought belonged only to her.

He knew he had no chance to hide what had happened. The old overalls spread on top of the hay as a makeshift blanket condemned him.

'It was nothing, it didn't mean anything,' he said, reaching for his shirt.

Belle stared at him for a moment. People say when you're drowning your whole life flashes before your eyes. Her whole future, her upcoming marriage to Ben, the life they'd planned together, exploded in a great red burst in her head, and there was nothing else she could do to save herself. She stepped towards him and he half-turned away to hide his still-open fly.

She pushed him over the edge of the loft.

He didn't shout as he fell. There was a cracking sound and a thud as he hit the flagstone floor below. Then there was silence.

Belle hung the overalls that Susie and Ben had used as a blanket on a hook on the crossbeam. She pressed her face against the still-warm cloth. She could smell Ben, and then the sickening scent of Susie's cloying perfume.

She climbed down the ladder. She didn't even glance at Ben's body. She knew he was dead. She wasn't sorry. Instead she felt at peace, the first peace of mind she'd known since the turmoil began – the turmoil of hatred and rage which had tortured her over the last three weeks since Ben came to stay and met his future sister-in-law Susie for the first time.

Belle had known what would happen. She knew exactly the way it would be; she knew exactly the impact meeting her younger sister had had on Ben because the shock of recognizing it on his face stopped her own heart momentarily. She knew too because this was not the first time she had lost a hard-won lover to Susie. It had always been the same. But she had hoped it would be different this time. Belle had hoped that Susie would let her have this one chance of happiness without wantonly destroying it. After all, it was serious with Ben and her, a lifetime commitment; he'd proved he loved her, he was going to marry her. Even so, she had tried to keep him away from Susie. But with no family of his own, he had insisted on meeting hers before the wedding and she could think of no convincing reason to refuse.

In her heart, though, Belle had known that this time wouldn't be different. That's why, though she and Ben had been together for more than three years, and engaged for ten months, she had avoided ever taking him home to meet her family. In a way, she knew it wasn't even Susie's fault, she didn't do it deliberately, it was a kind of gift she had, or a curse. Belle had foreseen precisely how it would be; how, even if Ben did not act on his inevitable desire for her younger sister, and went through with the marriage, Susie would stand between them for ever. Nothing between Belle and him would ever be the same again.

And it had happened exactly as she knew it would. That's why she had killed him. There was nothing else she could do.

Belle went back out of the barn and started to feed the pigs, which is what she had come out to do when she saw Susie buttoning her blouse as she came from the hayloft.

The pigs stared at her with their bright blue eyes, as though they knew what she had done. It was as though they were laughing at her. She gave them extra food, and felt that she was trying to buy them off. Then she went back to the house for breakfast, and Susie was there with their mother, and then Dad came in grumbling about something or other, and that was that. It was a normal morning.

Later, someone would find Ben's body on the flagstones below the loft, with his jeans round his knees, and everyone would know he had been cheating on her with someone. Everyone would conclude that he'd been interrupted and in a panic he'd tripped on his own clothes and fallen; and Susie, white-faced, would speculate with the rest of them and pretend she knew nothing about the girl who'd been with her poor sister Belle's fiancé in the hay and Belle would pretend to believe her little sister and vow to herself – again – that one day, without fail, she would get her revenge.

2

That was nine years ago, and since then that scene in the barn had haunted Belle's dreams. It still did.

She woke up with a start. Her limbs seemed to have a life of their own, as though she were trying to fight someone off. The duvet was wet with sweat and she started up knowing that she had been shouting in her sleep. She was used to this. She had eradicated the Ben incident from her waking hours, but she couldn't control her dreams. That's why she still lived and slept alone. No one had stayed overnight with her since it happened. She'd had lovers, of course, but only men who had to leave to catch the last train home, men already spoken for who couldn't push the excuse that they were working late much after midnight before their wives got suspicious.

She lay back, trying to take long, deep breaths to calm the thumping of her heart and the jangling thoughts in her head. As always, the worst thing about the dream was how real it was. It was when dreaming that she came to life. Then she smelled the sweet, dry scent of the hay, heard the sparrows, always busy in and out of the barn, start to twitter again after their deafening silence in the moments after Ben hit the ground. She saw the iridescent flash of Susie's white secret skin as she fastened her blouse over her breasts, like mother-of-pearl against her sun-burnished neck and face. And she felt the old tight, sick wrench in her stomach in the one single moment when she knew that her own jealousy had poisoned the rest of her life. Hatred and anger could never cleanse her of that poison. Night after night she knew that, but, once awake, she was helpless. Her mind refused to grapple with what she had done while she tried to soothe the wounds to her emotions with bitterness and blame as though they were some kind of balm. Dreaming, she was alive; awake, she yearned to dream again.

The damp bedclothes began to feel cold against her skin. She needed a coffee. She opened her eyes and swung her legs to the floor, reaching for the alarm clock to turn it off. But she couldn't find the alarm clock. There was a glass and a pile of books on the bedside table, no alarm clock.

She was fully awake now, trying to control her growing fear and confusion.

This was not her room. The sounds and even the smell in this room were different from her own place. She couldn't remember ever coming here. She didn't know where she was or what she was doing here.

Then she felt a man's hand grasping her from behind.

'Hey, where do you think you're going?' he asked, pulling her back on to the bed. 'It can't be anywhere near time to get up yet.'

Belle tried to remember. Who was this man?

'What happened?' she said.

The man pulled himself up on one elbow and turned on a lamp on the floor on his side of the bed. The light didn't help Belle much. He was dark, full-faced, with the sort of rosebud mouth she disliked. Why was she here? She couldn't remember who he was, where she had met him or how she had got to be here with him.

'You're shivering,' he said. He put his arms round her and pulled the duvet over her. The damp cotton felt colder than the air in the room. 'It's all right,' he said, 'it's not time to get up. You must need all the sleep you can get, judging by what you get up to in your dreams.'

His body against hers felt soft and flabby, as though he had no real bones.

Belle went rigid. 'What do you mean?' she said. 'What do you know about my dreams?'

She felt him move his hand slowly across her thigh. She heard his voice very close where his mouth, that hateful rosebud mouth, was against her ear.

'From what I heard, you'd be in jail for life if you'd really done what you dream about,' he said. He was teasing her.

'What did I say?' she said.

But he wasn't really interested. If she wasn't looking for sex, he wanted to go back to sleep.

'It was nothing ' he murmured, 'you had a nightmare. You were talking in your sleep. At least I hope it was only a nightmare. I've never been in bed with a murderess before.'

He sounded slurred now. He was almost asleep.

She asked him another question, but this time he didn't answer.

Belle didn't want to wake him. She had heard enough to bring back all the old dread. She had to think. She lay still and stared into the gloom. His heavy arm across her stomach dragged her back into the past, as though the dead weight of what she had done had returned to threaten her. Think, think, she told herself, there must be a way out.

She tried to remember what had happened last night, how she had come to be here. It had been someone's birthday at work. Sylvia's. They'd gone to the pub, some of the girls from the office. But the others had had to go home early. Sylvia had started to weep because there were just the two of them left and it was her birthday and no one loved her enough to stay with her until the bitter end.

'I'm here,' Belle said.

'But that's only because no one loves you either,' Sylvia said, with the devastating honesty of the drunk. 'You've nowhere better to go.'

Sylvia seemed to be about to start on another bout of weeping. She looked awful, her face swollen, mascara running down her cheeks, her lipstick smudged, a caricature of female loneliness. And Belle knew only too well from experience that the affliction was contagious. As far as she could remember what happened then, she had decided anything had to be better than sitting at a bar with Sylvia until the barman, in desperation, finally called a cab to take them away. So she'd set out to pick up a man, any man who would give her a reason to escape from Sylvia and her fortieth-birthday blues. He was the first man at the bar to go outside for a smoke.

'I need the loo,' she'd said to Sylvia. She followed the man outside.

He was leaning against some railings between the bar and a narrow, dark alley piled with rubbish bags. She watched him light a cigarette and draw the smoke into his lungs.

'Oh, God,' she said, 'I'm trying to stop smoking but it's no good, I can't give it up.'

'Here,' he said, offering her his cigarette, 'I won't tell if you don't.'

She remembered that, but not if she had smoked the cigarette he gave her. And after that, she had no idea. She didn't even know if he had told her his name; or if she had told him hers.

This must be the man, this stranger whose arm pinioned her to the bed, this inert and alien animal who had heard her talking of murder in her sleep.

Moving very carefully, she swung her legs to the floor and sat on the edge of the bed so that she could look down at the sleeping man. It was daylight now, and she could see him quite clearly. She used to look at Ben sometimes in the early mornings while he was still asleep, and then she would feel a great surge of love for him, as though he were her child as well as her lover. But Ben was beautiful, even in sleep, and this stranger was not. He looked like a replete pig and he smelled worse. In a queer flash of memory she saw the bright blue mocking eyes of the pigs she'd gone to feed after Ben died. She shuddered.

Watching the man, she didn't recognize him; except she did sort of remember that rosebud mouth. She had an idea that she'd wondered at the time whether Sylvia and her unlovely sobbing wasn't preferable to letting that mouth kiss hers.

Now she thought, I wish I'd stayed with Sylvia.

She looked around for clues to where she was. It was an ugly room. It smelled of cigarettes and stale sweat. What furniture there was looked cheap and second-hand. The bed was one mattress on another in the middle of the floor. The door to the bathroom was open and she could hear a constant drip of water from the cistern. Above her head there was a window which, judging by the noise of traffic, looked out over a busy road.

Belle shuddered to think of the kind of man who would choose to live like this. She picked up her clothes, which were scattered around the room. She dressed as quickly and as quietly as she could, cursing herself because she was clumsy. She didn't want to wake the man, who was now snoring slightly through those rosebud lips.

She knew that it wasn't rational, but that mouth of his made what she had to do easier. Anyway, she had no choice, she had to do it. He had heard her talking in her sleep. She couldn't let that go. She could have said anything, confessed to Ben's murder, even. She couldn't remember if she'd told him her name. She might have done. Anyway, he would remember the pub where he'd met her. It wouldn't be hard for him to find her, the woman with bright red hair and no first finger on her left hand. That missing finger was what made people remember her, and Belle suddenly resented bitterly that what distinguished her was that disfigurement. She resented it the more bitterly because that, too, was Susie's work. They were only kids. They'd been playing with Dad's tools; she was the cowboy, Susie the Indian. Susie had a hatchet, she'd swung it and cut off Belle's finger. It was an accident, Belle couldn't blame Susie; but she did, and, imagining this sleeping man using it to help the police to track her down, her anger with Susie focused on him. He would describe her and the pub staff knew her, knew where she worked. They would tell the cops and they would find her.

It was safer this way. No one knew that she had ever been here, wherever it was. There was nothing to connect her with this stranger. Only Sylvia would have taken any notice of them in the pub together, two nondescript people going out into a crowded street. And Sylvia had been blind with drink and tears.

It was as though Belle had already worked out in her head what she had to do. Perhaps when she picked up the man, she had unconsciously known what would happen. She hadn't consciously planned anything, but now she went about her task as though she'd been pre-programmed to do it.

She took her pillow and put it over the sleeping man's head. She knelt on it, taking his arms one in either hand and holding them down above his head as he began to struggle, trying to fight her off. But it was too late, his legs were entangled with the duvet and he couldn't budge her weight on the pillow. She was a very strong woman, tall and heavily built. Soon his legs stopped kicking at the duvet, she felt his arms go limp and judged that he was dead.

Belle did not move for several minutes. Her fingers, as though they had a life of their own, clenched and unclenched on the pillow, but the man was still. She had to be sure. Often enough, at home on the farm, she'd seen her mother wring the neck of a cockerel she was going to cook for supper, only for the bird to open its eyes, kick itself free and run off. She had to be sure the man could not revive when she removed the pillow from his face.

When she was sure that it was all over, she reached across for his cigarette lighter beside the bed and set light to the pillow. She watched until the flame, almost invisible, began to melt the man-made fibre stuffing of the pillow and take a hold on the bed.

Belle left there, quietly closing the door on the black fumes beginning to explore the room.

3

There were two flights of stairs to walk down, then a tiled entrance hall to the front door. There was a radio playing behind one of the closed doors on the first-floor landing, that was the only sign of life. She saw no one.

Outside, what had once been a strip of garden had been sacrificed to off-street parking. As she squeezed between two cars,

Belle knocked the side mirror askew on one of them. The vehicle alarm went off, sounding to her like the sirens of every arm of the law rolled into one. She thought, How could I be so clumsy? Her instinct was to run, to run and hide. But that was the kneejerk reaction to the shock of the sudden sound. She must keep her head, use her brain.

The din of the car alarm stopped as suddenly as it had started. No one took the slightest notice, as far as she could see, not even roused to look out of a window to see what was happening. Car alarms were probably part of the background noise in a street like this, where parking was plainly a nightmare.

Then Belle was on the pavement, walking purposefully but not so fast as to draw attention to herself. She was in a street of terraced three-storey Victorian houses, most of which, to judge by the number of bells at every door, were turned into flats. At the end of the street was a busy road. There Belle stood for a moment wondering which way lay the familiar territory of the West End.

She took a quick glance back up the residential street. In one of the gardens a magnolia tree had come into flower and suddenly Belle wanted to cry, it was so achingly beautiful in that dreary, man-made landscape. She had walked past it without even noticing it. That made her feel sad. Already she had no idea in which of these identical houses she had spent the night. She half-expected black smoke to be billowing from an upper window, to hear people shouting and see firemen putting up ladders and breaking windows. But there was nothing, no sign of that awful scene she had left behind her.

There were more people about now, all walking blank-faced like automata in one direction. Every one had a fixed gaze and avoided looking at anyone else. They were obviously on their way to work, marching to the distant drum of routine. Belle walked with them, her face as expressionless as theirs. She looked for clues as to where she was. The road names meant nothing to her, nor did the area, SW16. South of the river was uncharted territory for Belle, who worked in Victoria and shared a small house with three others in Dalston. Her flatmates would only now be getting up to go to work. She wondered if any one of them would notice that she wasn't there. They'd think nothing of it. She often left before they got up. One of them would probably make some nasty comment about her toadying to her boss by getting to work early. That would be all. None of them were really friends; they weren't interested in Belle, not as long as she paid her share of the bills and didn't take too long in the bathroom. They were not the sort of people who got noticed much.

Belle found herself struggling against growing panic. She seemed to be walking endlessly without getting anywhere. She passed small shops selling newspapers and cigarettes, or sandwiches and take-away coffee. It could have been anywhere at all. She crossed one terraced street after another going nowhere, all identical, always dragging her back to what she had done and where she had done it. Around her, other people's apparent confidence that they were going somewhere, and knew how to get there, now seemed to Belle a cruel delusion; they all began to look as lost as she was.

'Which way's Piccadilly?' she asked a young woman with a mobile phone clamped to her ear. Belle could hear herself sounding desperate. The young woman addressed seemed neither to have seen nor heard her. 'Sorry,' Belle said, and hurried on. She mustn't give anyone a reason to remember her.

Belle stopped at last at a bus stop and used the machine to buy a ticket. She didn't recognize the numbers of any of the services that apparently stopped there. It didn't matter; she would take the first bus that came, going anywhere, just to be somewhere else. But after a few minutes she couldn't bear to wait any longer and started walking again. Then she heard a bus coming, and turned and ran back to where it had stopped. She had lost her place in the queue, and the driver was shouting at the passengers to move along to make room, but she got on.

She found a seat upstairs, no longer caring where the bus was going. If it took her to some far-flung suburban terminal, too bad; at least she could make a new start from there. But she was lucky. The bus was going towards town, not away.

As the bus passed a billboard, she caught sight of herself reflected in the window. One side of her face seemed distorted, twitching like that of a cartoon villain. My God, she thought, I look like a murderer. Deliberately, she breathed slowly and deeply, trying to calm herself. It's reaction, she told herself, there's bound to be a reaction. She didn't feel anything, though – no guilt, no fear. All that seemed to matter was not to be late for work.

Rush hour had started and the traffic was heavy. It seemed hours since she had woken up in the dark in a strange room, beside a man she couldn't remember ever having seen before. Now the day seemed to be rushing past her. She started to worry about being late for work. She had hoped she could get in before anyone else arrived, then when the others came in, they'd see her there as part of the office furniture, as usual. Life would be normal again.

She glared at the other passengers on the crowded bus, as though it was their fault the traffic was moving so slowly. All of them seemed absorbed in their own thoughts, still pale and sluggish and half-asleep.

When she finally walked into the government department building where she worked, most of her colleagues were already at their computers. She tried not to draw attention to herself as she made her way to her seat. But there were catcalls and ribald comments.

'Wasn't Belle wearing that same outfit yesterday?' the woman at the desk next to hers called across the aisle to her friend.

'Heavy night at the whist drive,' someone else said.

Belle took no notice. The sight of them depressed her, but then it always did. It was all so predictable, they were like that to everyone, it was the way people who didn't particularly know or like each other were in offices, the contrived intimacy of the workplace. She wondered why they thought she was the sort of person who'd get her kicks playing whist; she was surprised that that was how they saw her.

That would have been that, perhaps, but Sylvia, who showed no outward sign at all that she had been paralytic only a few brief hours earlier, suddenly sprang to Belle's defence.

'That's all you know,' she said, 'but it wasn't like that, was it, Belle? What you see before you this bright morning, ladies and gents, is a woman who's spent a wild night of lust with a stranger.'

Belle understood that Sylvia wanted to punish her for abandoning her in the pub.

'Shut up, Sylvia,' she hissed at her through clenched teeth.

'I won't shut up,' Sylvia said, and in her voice was the malice of resentment at Belle's desertion. 'Why should you let them get away with thinking you're some kind of mousy nerd who's never got over her lover killing himself after shagging another woman? You're not like that, are you, Belle?'

Sylvia turned away from Belle to address the others, opening her arms like a stage master of ceremonies. 'What you see before you today is not the Belle of the Broken Heart we all took her for, this is Belle of the Darkness, sex siren to the vampires of the night.'

Belle tried to stop her. 'Drop it, Sylvia,' she said. 'I'm sorry about abandoning you last night, OK? But give it a rest, for God's sake.'

'No, no,' a laughing girl nearby urged Sylvia, 'you've got to tell us what happened now.'

'Nothing happened,' Belle said. 'Boring, but true. Nothing happened at all.'

Sylvia ignored her. 'Belle pulled,' she said, and there was something about the way she said it that came as a surprise to Belle. She thought, I never realized how much Sylvia actually dislikes me.

'Sylvia was very drunk, as all of you who started off the evening with us will remember,' Belle said. 'After you'd all left, and thank you very much for that, I went out for a smoke and when I came back in, Sylvia had left. That was it.'

Because that was what they really expected to be the truth, they believed her. Belle of the Darkness indeed! The eager girl who'd wanted Sylvia to tell them more tittered at the idea.

'Why yesterday's blouse, then?' Sylvia asked in a surly tone. She, too, believed Belle's explanation, but she was annoyed that the truth couldn't be less mundane.

'I wish my life was that exciting,' Belle said. 'I'll probably have to wear the same thing tomorrow. The washing machine's broken.'

Someone laughed, and soon Belle seemed to have been forgotten. It was as though, once she came into the building and got into the lift, everything that had happened since she left work last night was like a dream that had never really happened. Belle herself did not believe it was real.

Then at lunchtime, in the canteen, Sylvia joined the table where she was sitting with some colleagues.

Sylvia looked rough now. There were dark circles under her eyes, and their whites were yellow.

'I guess I was out of line earlier,' she said to Belle. 'I suppose I should thank you, really, at least you kept me company some of the time when I needed it.'

The others were embarrassed, and to divert attention they began to speculate about what kind of man would take Belle home. It was as though they were pretending not to know she was there. They were cruel, with the part-unconscious, part-challenging cruelty of young women secure in their youth towards those older than themselves. Not much older, either, Belle thought. She was only thirty-seven, less than ten years between these women and herself. But they all knew about the Tragedy, they'd been told about the way Ben died, and in their eyes this placed Belle well into past-it territory. They would never let her back over the barrier now. They were arrogant, of course, but it never occurred to them that they were hurtful.

It was Sylvia who burst into tears.

There was a horrified silence around the table. The young women looked frightened at what they had done.

'I didn't want to leave you alone on your birthday,' one of them said, 'but I had to get home to the kids. Kevin's on nights this week.'

'Don't cry, Sylvia,' Belle said, 'nobody wanted to leave, but it was late, they had to get home.'

But Sylvia turned on her. She wouldn't dare to attack the others, but Belle was an easy target.

'Don't tell me you didn't go off with a bloke last night. You didn't come back to find me. I was there all the time. I know you picked up that man, I saw him.'

'Oh, shut up, Sylvia,' Belle said, trying to make out she didn't care. 'You were so drunk you don't know what happened last night, so don't pretend you do.'

She picked up a *Standard* someone had left on the table, an early edition. She flicked through it, pretending to be interested.

And then, on an inside page, her eye caught the headline: 'Young man dies in blaze in Tooting bedsit.'

Belle tried not to show any reaction as she read the story. The body had been burned beyond recognition, but a neighbour said the victim was called Adam, though he didn't know his surname. The neighbour, from the first-floor flat, described this Adam as a man in his twenties who had lived on the top-floor at the house for only a month or two. He'd had the idea he might be from the North, but that was all he knew, except he'd had no letters, and spent hardly any time at home. He had no visitors except last night when a woman had been seen with him entering the house.

Belle felt her face begin to twitch involuntarily, but when she put her hand up to try to cover it, she could feel nothing. I've got to stop this, she told herself, it's bloody ridiculous. She looked around surreptitiously, but no one seemed to have noticed. She lifted the newspaper as if she was reading more carefully as protection.

Police suspected that the victim had been drinking, or was on drugs, and had passed out while smoking in bed. His lighted cigarette had probably started the fire, apparently igniting the mattress. The man had been overcome by smoke, and was already dead when the emergency services arrived. The body had been badly burned after death. They were trying to find someone to identify him, but so far without success. Unfortunately no one knew who the woman seen with him last night was. She was asked to come forward.

To help the police in their search for relatives, the paper had printed a photo of the dead man which had obviously survived the fire in the room.

Sylvia, unwilling to lose the attention of her young colleagues, was still intent on goading Belle. She snatched the paper from her.

'What's so riveting?' she said. 'What are you pretending to find so interesting?'

She laid the paper on the table and pointed at the smudgy photograph.

'Look,' she cried, 'that must be Belle's beau. Is he famous, Belle, or has he robbed a bank? He can't be in the paper just because he's the first man in an age to screw you.'

Belle tried to stay cool. 'Don't be silly, Sylvia. That poor young man's dead and nobody knows who he is. That's why he's in the paper, they want him identified. It's not funny.'

Sylvia glanced at the headline and looked embarrassed. But even so she was unwilling to let Belle off the hook.

'OK, OK, I didn't mean any harm. We were just having a laugh. He does look sort of familiar though, doesn't he, or is he just a common type? It could be your new conquest, couldn't it? And you could be the woman who went into the house with him. You did pick some-one up last night, didn't you,' she said. 'Otherwise why'd you leave me to go off for a smoke? I thought you'd given up smoking.'

'So did I,' Belle said. 'And after reading about that man's horrible death, I'm giving it up again.'

'We'd better get back to work,' Sylvia said. 'I'm sorry, Belle, it was a bad night, that's all.'

That seemed to be the end of it. But Belle knew that it wasn't. Sylvia couldn't seem to let it go. Belle couldn't take the risk that she would recognize the man in that newspaper picture as the same person she, Belle, had followed out of the pub. She didn't know what Sylvia had really seen, or what the wretched woman might remember when she'd got the drink out of her system. Maybe she hadn't been as drunk as she'd seemed, but used her miserable birthday as an excuse for wallowing in self-pity with anyone who would listen. That would be typical, Belle thought. In any case, better safe than sorry. Sylvia mustn't be given the chance to remember any-thing about last night. That couldn't be allowed to happen.

4

The next day was Friday. This was often a quiet time at work; the eagerness of Members of Parliament to get off early to spend the weekend in their constituencies often percolated through the administrative echelons even to the staff in the government departments.

Miss Page, the woman who had been Belle's boss for years, was leaving that day. Miss Page had worked in this office for more than twenty years, and this was the first time any of her colleagues had ever seen her upset.

'What am I going to do with the time?' she said, when someone wished her a happy retirement.

There was a pause, because it was a question no one could answer. Miss Page was part of the institution, they couldn't imagine that she had ever had an outside life of her own.

'We're going to miss you,' Sylvia said, as the silence became oppressive.

They were all gathered round a table where white plastic cups had been filled with red wine and set out on trays. The women had clubbed together to buy a cake. It was on the table too, in pride of place, in a box with the name of a famous *pâtisserie*. The cake inside was covered in white icing with Miss Page's name written in dark capitals, then the dates of her service with the department, and under that RIP. It was Sylvia's attempt to lighten the occasion, but now, because Miss Page plainly wasn't looking forward to her retirement, no one wanted to open the box and signal the beginning of the end.

Belle's phone rang. Grateful for the diversion, she left the group to answer it.

She knew at once that something was wrong. Her father's voice sounded odd, as though he was fighting for breath.

'It's your mother,' he said. 'She's not well. Can you get down to see her? She's been asking for you.'

'What's the matter, Dad? Have you had the doctor?'

'Yes, yes, but the stuff he gave her doesn't seem to be helping much.'

'What's wrong with her?'

Belle felt ashamed, even while she was doing it, at sounding unconvinced by the urgency of her mother's illness. She couldn't help thinking that her father was overreacting, because Mum was never really ill. She suspected that her mother had flu or something that would keep her in bed a few days, and Dad wanted someone there to look after her.

'Isn't Susie there?' Belle asked. She found it quite hard to say her sister's name aloud, even now.

'The doctor thinks your mother's got pneumonia. He wouldn't say much. We'd be better off with the vet, I think.'

'Shouldn't she be in hospital, Dad?'

'He tried to get her to agree to that, but she wouldn't go. She says there's time enough for that when she's dying.' Then he added, 'Susie can look after her. But she wants to see you.'

Something in his voice told Belle that her father knew exactly what she'd been thinking about him wanting to off-load nursing his sick wife. She felt guilty.

'I'll try to get down tomorrow.'

'We'll look forward to seeing you, then.'

Her father was bad at showing his feelings. He sounded as though he were taking a booking for bed and breakfast.

'Don't worry, Dad. I'm sure she'll be fine,' Belle said.

'Of course she will,' her father said, and gave a nervous laugh. 'See you tomorrow, then.' He put down the phone.

The group of women gathered around the still unopened cake were all staring at Belle as she rejoined them.

'What's wrong?' Sylvia asked. 'What's happened?'

Belle said, 'That was my dad. My mother's ill. I'll have to go down there.'

As they all stared at her in consternation, Belle started forward and tripped, pushing the cake box to the floor as she did so. She came down on top of it, squashing it flat.

'Oh, no,' she wailed. 'I've ruined Miss Page's cake.'

She picked it up and put it back on the table. Miss Page opened the lid.

'You bought me a cake?' she said, as though she couldn't believe it. 'Oh, I never expected a cake.'

'There was a message on it sort of commemorating your time here,' Sylvia said. 'I guess you'll have to take that as read, thanks to Belle.'

'It doesn't matter a bit,' Miss Page said; 'it's the thought that counts, isn't it?'

Sylvia handed Belle a plastic cup of red wine. 'That was a lucky break,' she said, 'but what about you? Is your mother really bad?'

'She's never really been ill before,' Belle said; 'why does she want to see me now?'

She realized that Sylvia must think she was behaving oddly. Belle couldn't explain that her feelings about Susie had made it impossible for her to have anything to do with her parents as long as they were close to her sister. Of course she knew herself that she was being unfair to them; they didn't know what Susie had done. How could they know, Belle thought, Susie hadn't actually *done* anything, she just *was*. The simple fact of Susie's existence poisoned Belle's life. Her parents couldn't understand how Belle felt about her younger sister, and had felt ever since she could remember; how Susie had always spoiled everything for her because she was prettier, more charming, more sociable. Just by being there, Susie thwarted Belle's tentative efforts to be herself. Susie did what she did quite unconsciously. If she'd set out to compete with her older sister, Belle could have fought back. But she didn't; it was her nature. And what made it worse was that Belle knew that she was being childish, still defining herself by something she should have come to terms with long ago. And perhaps she could have come to terms, if only everyone she'd ever wanted to get close to hadn't defected to Susie's side once they met her. Not that Susie even noticed them. She did not set out to impress. She made no effort to disguise her lack of concern about what anybody thought of her, it simply didn't matter to her. Sometimes, when Belle tried to define that certain something Susie had, she came to the conclusion that the secret of her little sister's magnetism lay in that self-contained quality she had, her complete self-assurance. Of course Susie was pretty, but so were lots of girls. Susie had something special.

Mum and Dad should have known how it was for me, Belle told herself, they should have taken the trouble to find out the effect Susie had on me, what she was really like. If they'd separated us, I could have escaped from her. I'd have told them if they'd asked, why didn't they ask me why I hated her so much?

At last it was time for Miss Page to leave. Soon the others followed. Sylvia and Belle were left alone to collect and throw away the plastic cups and scrape the remains of the cake into a waste-paper basket.

Sylvia put on her coat. 'Are you coming?' she asked.

'As soon as I've looked up the train timetable for tomorrow,' Belle said.

'Don't do that,' Sylvia said. She was in her element now, taking charge. She seemed to feel she owed Belle a favour for destroying that embarrassing message on Miss Page's cake. Belle wasn't going to tell Sylvia that she had not tripped deliberately, it had been a clumsy accident. Sylvia said, 'You can borrow my car and drive down tonight.'

Belle was about to refuse, but then she thought how much easier it would be to have a car at the farm. Otherwise she'd be trapped, unless someone drove her to the station ten miles away. If her mother really was ill, that would make it difficult for Dad to get away. Susie could take her, but for Belle that was out of the question.

'You can borrow my car,' Sylvia said again. 'Come home with me and you can go on from there.'

'I'll have to drop by the house and pick up a few things,' Belle said.

'You can do that in the car on your way,' Sylvia said. 'It'll be quicker than going home first.'

'Won't you need it over the weekend?' Belle said.

'No, most of the time it just sits there. I'm always telling myself it's stupid to keep a car in London, anyway, but it would make it easier for you in the country.'

Belle was surprised that Sylvia could imagine any way of life outside her own. It made her sorry that she had never tried to get to know her better. Sylvia had been sitting in that soulless office now for fifteen years or so, doing the same routine work which so frustrated Belle after less than half the time.

Belle had always assumed that that was all the two of them had in common. Sylvia had tried to make friends with her early on, but Belle hadn't even noticed. She hadn't wanted contact with anyone then. Susie had stolen Ben and Ben had betrayed her. She couldn't talk about that to anyone at all, and she had nothing else to say.

'Thanks, Sylvia,' she said. 'I promise I'll drive carefully.'

Sylvia laughed. 'You haven't seen the car yet,' she said. She turned out the lights of the office as they left. 'It's so old you can't really drive any other way.'

Sylvia lived in the ground-floor flat of a small modern house a short bus ride away from Golders Green tube station. She often grumbled about the slowness of the service on the Northern Line, and how she disliked waiting for a bus on dark evenings. She talked about finding something more attractive closer to work – south of the river, even – but the local Waitrose and, in spring, the cherry blossom in the gardens of Hampstead Garden Suburb as she walked to the tube station were more than enough to compensate for what she didn't like about the place.

'That was pretty impressive, the way you dealt with the cake fiasco,' Sylvia said, as they walked up the street. 'God knows what would've happened if you hadn't been so quick off the mark. I can't believe it but I thought she'd like the RIP joke.'

'You can never really be sure what people will laugh about,' Belle said.

Sylvia stopped to open one of the neat garden gates and led the way up an overgrown path to her front door. 'Come into the kitchen. We might as well have a cup of coffee first.'

Belle followed her down the hall to the kitchen. There were french windows opening on to a small patio bordered by a long narrow lawn which needed mowing. On either side of that, a profusion of unpruned shrubs were running riot.

'This is lovely,' Belle said. 'You'd almost think we were in the country.'

'The garden proper belongs to the upstairs flat,' Sylvia said. 'But I do sit out on the patio in the summer, if there's time when I get back from work.'

Sylvia made coffee.

'You know,' she said slowly, pushing a full mug towards Belle across the breakfast bar, 'I never thought. It seemed like a good laugh, that cake, but then when it came to it . . . '

Oh God, Belle thought, if she doesn't stop going on about that bloody cake, I'm going to have to tell her I squashed it by accident, not to save her embarrassment. But she said, 'I know, I don't think any of us had ever thought Miss Page was an ordinary human being with normal feelings like the rest of us.'

Belle asked herself, Do I have normal feelings? Am I like the rest of them?

'I can't bear to think of it,' Sylvia said. 'Poor old cow, what's going to happen to her without the job to give her something to live for?'

'I hope I never get like that,' Belle said. And she thought, That's how I'll be when the time comes. Looking back on all those empty years. Except, she thought, the years she would look back on weren't just empty, they were worse than that, they were destructive.

Sylvia was saying, 'Oh, you'll find someone and settle down and have a litter of children. You're not past it yet. You proved that the other night.' She was trying to be coy, but she looked sly. 'You can't fool me,' she said; 'you did go off with that bloke the other night, whatever you say.'

'Why do you keep on about that?' Belle said. 'I told you what happened, I went for a smoke.'

'I saw you with him,' Sylvia said.

The sound of Belle's fingers involuntarily drumming on the breakfast bar was the only sound in the room. Then Belle shrugged. 'You don't know what you're talking about,' she said.

She felt the anger stirring like heartburn inside her. She concentrated on the mug of coffee. The last thing she wanted was to look Sylvia in the eye.

But Sylvia persisted. 'You said you were going to the loo,' she said, 'and I followed you because I thought you wanted to leave and I wanted to go home too. I knew I was in a bit of a state and I was going to ask you to call a cab for me. You weren't there so I asked the waiter if he'd seen you and he said you'd gone out with a man who'd been drinking at the bar. I saw you together outside.'

'So? Why are you making a big thing of this?' Belle tried to sound offhand, but inside her head it was as though her brain had clicked into overdrive. She glared at Sylvia, who actually cringed at the hostility in her eyes.

Nervousness made Sylvia chatter. 'I can't understand why you're being so secretive,' she said. 'What are you hiding?'

Sylvia sounded puzzled, but there was something about her attitude that made Belle remember how her so-called friend had taunted her in front of the other girls in the office. It was almost as though Sylvia thought she had a right to discover Belle's secret.

Sylvia dislikes me, Belle thought, she's not to be trusted.

'What makes you think I've got something to hide just because I don't want my private life trumpeted all over Whitehall for your amusement?' Belle asked coldly.

But Sylvia ignored her coldness. 'You were looking at that picture in the paper, the one of the man who got burned,' she said. 'He looked like the bloke I saw with you. Is that it? Was that the man you went off with, and were you the woman mentioned in the newspaper?'

She seemed to realize suddenly the implications of what she had just said, and the absurdity of it struck her.

'Sorry, Belle,' she said apologetically, 'I don't know what I'm saying half the time these days. Bloody menopause.'

Belle laughed. She said, 'Honestly, Sylvia, you're going to have to watch out or someone's going to take these fantasies of yours seriously.'

She's not going to let it drop, Belle told herself, she's not as stupid as she seems, she could be dangerous.

There was a pause, then Sylvia smiled. 'God,' she said, 'I don't know what gets into me. And you're in a hurry to get on the road.'

'It's all right,' Belle said. 'Thanks to you lending me the car, I'll be there much sooner than I told my dad.'

She felt nervous now. It was because of Susie. The sooner she got to the farm, the sooner she had to face Susie. Belle felt sick at the thought of seeing her sister, at the prospect of the familiar feeling of being reduced to insignificance beside Susie. Susie who wasn't even aware of what she did to Belle.

I don't want to get there sooner; I don't want to get there at all, Belle told herself.

But there was more to her anxiety than that. Sylvia had become a threat. Belle had to put a stop to her.

And then she caught the look that Sylvia gave her, partly curious, but also triumphant, as though she had gained some sort of dominance over Belle in a subconscious battle of wills.

'Do you have a sister, Sylvia?' Belle asked.

'No, only brothers,' Sylvia said. 'Worse luck.'

'I'd like a brother,' Belle said. 'Except he'd have called me Carrots.'

Sylvia was moved by a woman's instinctive defence of another female against the insensitive male. 'You're not that kind of red-head, though,' she said. 'Yours is more red-gold.'

'Don't worry,' Belle said, and laughed. 'He'd have suffered for it!'

'I've always wanted a sister,' Sylvia said. 'You can be close to a sister in a way you can't with brothers.'

'It's not really like that, you know,' Belle said.

'Don't you get on with yours?' Sylvia was curious. She had never thought of Belle in terms of family at all. It had come as a surprise that afternoon in the office to discover that this woman she'd sat next to at work for many years had parents, let alone a sister.

'No,' Belle said.

'But how can you not get on with your sister? It's like she's part of you.'

'No, that's not true,' Belle said. 'We're completely different people. We never had anything in common. I never wanted to be associated with her, I wanted to be myself.'

'But you are,' Sylvia said. She didn't understand what Belle was talking about, but she could see that this odd colleague of hers was genuinely distressed.

'It only seems like that when we're apart,' Belle said. 'I dread seeing her, all those hateful feelings come flooding back. I can't explain. When we're not apart, she sort of consumes me.'

'You're jealous,' Sylvia said.

'I don't want to be,' Belle said.

'Is she staying with your parents now?' Sylvia asked, refilling the kettle to make more coffee. 'Will she be there?'

Belle nodded her head. She couldn't trust herself to speak. She could scarcely believe that she had said those things to Sylvia.

Suddenly she said aloud, 'That's it, then.'

Sylvia looked puzzled, not following Belle's line of thought. Belle felt a kind of comforted feeling flow through her veins like the warmth of a first neat whisky. She knew for certain what she was going to do. After that she would be completely safe. No one knew she was here with Sylvia; if anyone had seen them come into the flat together, which was unlikely because everyone else was still at work, they wouldn't think anything of it. She had never been here before.

Sylvia took it that her friend wanted to change the subject.

'I'd better warn you, there's a small problem with the car,' Sylvia said. 'There's a slow puncture in one of the back tyres. I suppose I should've said, but as long as you put some air in on the way, you should be all right.'

'Do you have a spare?' Belle asked. Sylvia's house had a garage built in, part of the ground-floor flat. Belle had seen it when they came in. Things were going to fall into place. She wanted to laugh, she felt so confidant.

'Yes, there's always the spare,' Sylvia said. 'You could go into a garage and get someone to change it.'

'Don't be daft,' Belle said, 'we'll change it here.' She seemed to Sylvia suddenly full of life, energized by the small crisis. She laughed seeing Sylvia's startled expression. 'I wasn't brought up on a farm for nothing,' she said. 'We'll do it together. I'll show you how. Do you have rubber gloves? I don't want to get covered in oil.'

'I'm always making plans to incorporate the garage into the house and make another room,' Sylvia said, leading the way through the kitchen to the door which led into the garage. 'It's really a waste of a money having a car in London, and I could do with the space.'

'Good idea,' Belle said. 'You could park in the street anyway.'

'It wouldn't be cheap, though,' Sylvia said, putting on the light to reveal the car, a dusty old red Peugeot 205 with a dent in the passenger door.

The back tyre on the driver's side was almost flat.

'It's gone down since yesterday,' Sylvia said. 'Trouble is, I don't have a pump. You'll have to take it to the garage.'

'Best to change it,' Belle said. She nudged the spare wheel slung between the back wheels with something like affection. 'The spare's fine. We had a car like this once,' she said. 'Where's the jack?'

She put on the rubber gloves and felt like a surgeon preparing for an operation.

Sylvia reached into the glove box and took out the handbook.

'Can you open the engine,' Belle said. 'I expect the jack's there. Or perhaps somewhere in the boot. I can't remember.'

Sylvia found the jack. 'Is this it?' she said.

'So we'll jack it up first,' Belle said, 'after I've loosened the nuts.'

She fitted the spanner on to the first nut, then used her foot on the arm to try to shift it. The nut was too tight.

'We need a fulcrum,' she said; 'my dad always used to say he could move anything with a fulcrum.'

'What does that mean?' Sylvia said. 'How do we get one?'

There was a pile of old piping on a bench at the back of the garage. Belle selected a length and fitted it over the arm of the jack. 'Instant fulcrum,' she said, jumping on the end of the pipe and feeling the nut give.

She loosened all four nuts in the same way.

'Now the jack,' she said.

Sylvia handed it to her. 'My God,' Sylvia said, 'I wouldn't know where to stick what.'

Belle was on her knees, fitting the jack into the socket under the car. 'Keep moving this lever up and down,' she told Sylvia, 'I'm going to release the catch on the spare wheel.'

Sylvia made hard work with the jack handle, but at last she had raised the car so that the back wheel was six inches or so off the ground.

'That's fine,' Belle said. She quickly undid the nuts and lifted the wheel off the hub. Now, she thought.

'Can you give me a hand here, Sylvia, the cradle thing that holds the spare wheel up seems to be stuck.'

Belle leaned into the boot of the car, fiddling with the nut that secured the wheel catch.

'Can you get down and look under the chassis to see what's stuck,' Belle said. Now she *was* a surgeon about to work on a patient on the operating-table. It was like doing a precise task she'd done thousands of times before, she seemed to be functioning on automatic.

Sylvia squealed: 'Down under the car you mean? You want me to crawl under the car?'

'It's jacked up, it's rock solid,' Belle said. 'Come on, I can't hold on to this for ever.'

She felt Sylvia's body moving slowly forward on the ground against her leg. 'My God, I can't see anything down here,' Sylvia said, her voice sounding muffled.

'Hang on, I'll get you the torch,' Belle said.

She stepped back, closing the lid of the boot. Then she threw all her weight against the back of the car.

The car lurched forward and came off the jack. If Sylvia made any sound as the back axle collapsed and crushed her head, it was covered by the crunch of metal.

5

Belle did not look at what she had done. She knew what was to be seen. Sylvia, wanting to use the car, had found the flat tyre. She was alone and, with the help of the manufacturer's handbook, set about changing the wheel; something she'd never done before on her own. She could see the spare in its cradle slung under the back of the car. To release it, she'd crawled under the car. But she hadn't fixed the jack properly. It shifted, and the car came down on top of her.

No one would question that Sylvia's death was an accident. Hers were the only fingerprints on the jack.

Belle went back into Sylvia's kitchen. She left Sylvia's unfinished mug of coffee but washed her own, dried it and hung it back on its hook. She used the tea towel to wipe the surface of the breakfast bar and the seat of the stool she'd sat on. Then she washed her hands in the rubber gloves, took them off and put them into the waste bin.

There was a small tabby cat at the patio door, scratching at the glass to get in. Belle caught its eye and it put back its ears and hissed at her. Belle wondered if it belonged to Sylvia. She'd never put her down as someone who'd keep a pet.

The sound of the cat's claws against the glass irritated her.

'Oh, go kill a mouse or something,' Belle muttered at it. 'You might as well start practising, you're going to be feeding yourself from now on.'

She was a little shocked at herself, the cat hadn't done anything wrong. Its green eyes reminded her of Susie, though. Belle hoped someone would find it and give it a home. If I know cats, she told herself, it won't wait around moping, it'll find a neighbour to adopt as soon as it's hungry.

On her way through the hall, Belle glanced into Sylvia's living-room. There was a *Radio Times* on the sofa, folded back to the television programmes. The remote control lay beside it. Sylvia had prepared for her evening's viewing before she left for work. If I opened the fridge, Belle thought, I bet there's a TV dinner waiting to go into the microwave.

It was weird, she told herself, standing there in Sylvia's house surrounded by Sylvia's things, which seemed to have a life of their own because they were so obviously part of her assumption that her usual routine would happen as it always had.

Poor Sylvia, Belle thought, it doesn't look like much of a life – all day doing her boring office job and then home to her pink three-piece suite to watch television until bedtime.

Belle stopped herself before she actually thought that Sylvia was better off dead, but only just.

She pulled the sleeve of her sweater down over her hand to act as

35

a glove as she opened the front door and took a quick look around. There was a certain amount of traffic on the road – mothers driving carloads of kids, the children all in dark-grey school uniform. Well, women on the school run wouldn't notice Belle; they scarcely seemed to see the other traffic. They were terrible drivers, not giving a thought to anyone else.

Belle stepped confidently out of the front door and let it slam behind her. Three teenage girls who'd stopped at the garden gate to roll cigarettes and were trying to light them mumbled, 'Sorry,' and moved away without looking at her as she reached the pavement and strode down the street.

She walked to Golders Green tube station and stood on the platform waiting for a train. The platform opposite, going north, was crowded with children on their way home. A few elderly couples were sitting on the benches with bags of shopping piled around them. So Sylvia wasn't the only one who thought it worth staying close to a Waitrose.

It all looked so ordinary. And Belle looked ordinary too, a woman of thirty-something in a dark skirt and jacket with light reddish hair and pale blue eyes who seemed to belong to any office, anywhere. Belle would never look out of place on a commuter route. Aware of this, she knew why she lost out to Susie on every level. It wasn't really that her little sister was prettier and more fun to be with. There was something distinctive about Susie, something magnetic and vivid about her which made her stand out anywhere. She attracted attention without ever seeking it. But one day, Belle told herself, Susie will be lying in an open coffin and no one will be able to tell us apart. What made the difference between them was not on the surface, it was innate, a contrast of character and spirit. Destroy Susie and you destroyed her advantage.

Now, staring up the line to see the next train coming, it was as though Belle stood apart from herself, watching an unexceptional stranger. But I've killed someone, she thought, not twenty minutes ago I killed someone, and now it's as though it never happened. Even I don't really believe I did it. She felt her face begin to twitch uncontrollably. Think of something else, she told herself, forget what happened. She thought of Sylvia's cat, wishing she could have taken it with her tomorrow to the farm. It looked like the sort of cat that would thrive there.

But even if there was no sign of it as she blended imperceptibly with the other people on the platform, Belle was exceptional, horribly exceptional. It was monstrous that she gave no sign of it, like Dorian Gray. But the terrible things she had done almost lightly must be etched in acid somewhere. If I had a soul, she thought, it would be there I'd see the testimony to what I've done.

She shivered. Once she had believed in Heaven and Hell and the existence of her soul. She'd discarded religious faith lightly, telling herself that she could always re-open the door. It all seemed so feeble, all that stuff about forgiveness and turning the other cheek. But she couldn't go back now. It was scary to know that without thinking she had slammed that door against any hope of salvation. And then she told herself, I'm better off than the Ancient Mariner, I'm condemned not to tell anyone what I've done.

She looked down at her hands, at the stump of the first finger of her left hand, and she smiled. Even if she told people what she'd done, that she had taken life, no one would believe her. They'd think she'd made it up; women with a disfigurement like that didn't kill people unless they were mad; and everyone knew that Belle wasn't mad. How could she be mad, she worked for the government?

Belle thought that was funny, but she was careful to stifle her smile. People were more likely to remember seeing someone who smiled.

6

In the train going west to Somerset the next morning, Belle pretended to read the *Guardian* while from behind it she stared out of the window at the small dramas of the countryside as fields and villages flashed past: two horses racing across the grass for the fun of it; two young boys distorting a pattern of reflected trees on a dark pond as they fished from a small boat; a cat pouncing into long grass on the verge of a farm track. What happens next? She thought, what happened then?

What had happened then, once she'd committed her crimes and moved on? It was like the Fickle Finger of Fate – no, that wasn't it, that was the catch-phrase from an old television show; she was thinking of that quotation from Omar Khayyám: 'The Moving Finger writes, and, having writ, Moves on . . . ' What she had done felt as inexorable and as impersonal as that. Those old Victorians understood about hiding guilt, and about retribution. They didn't look for public absolution, nor even explanation. They did what they did and moved on. Or that's how it seemed to Belle. No one had ever discovered who Jack the Ripper was, had they? He'd made sure there was no one to give him away. If Belle actually felt anything about what she'd done – any emotional involvement – it was simply that she was caught in a time-warp, out of sync with everyone and everything around her.

She tried to make herself wonder about the secret personal lives of the people she had put out of the way. She couldn't do it, though. She could not think of them as people – suffering, miserable, happy, hopeful people. And then she thought, It's no good, I can't think of anyone that way, I can't see other people as real.

She told herself, They're only real when they're a threat to me, and when they are, I know how to deal with them.

Belle kept her face hidden behind the newspaper. She wished the *Guardian* were still a broadsheet to give more protection in case her expression revealed her thoughts to the notice of some passing stranger. She was compelled to go back over what she'd done, the same way her mother used to check her shopping list before they started the long trek home from town. It was important not to forget anything they might need. Her mum, with her and Susie, had to walk the two miles or so to the shops then.

In Belle's head the list of the crimes she had committed resonated like a rap to the rhythm of the train's wheels: she'd got away with murder; three times she'd got away with murder; three people dead and no one suspected.

It was awesome. She knew it was and she couldn't resist a thrill of pride in her achievement. She'd read somewhere that murderers who seemed to have committed the perfect crime always gave themselves away at last because they had to tell someone about it. What possessed them? Were they looking for recognition for what they'd done? Or some sort of understanding to explain their actions. Perhaps, like trouble, guilt shared was guilt halved. Except it isn't, Belle thought, because I don't feel any guilt. Not even about Sylvia, who was trying to do me a favour.

Susie started all this, Belle told herself, it's Susie's fault. If she hadn't seduced Ben, he and the other two who got in my way would still be alive. Or half alive, Belle told herself; you couldn't describe Sylvia's life, or, apparently, that of the man in the Tooting bedsit, as more than half-lives. In a way, I may've done them a favour, she thought, though they probably wouldn't thank her if they could.

She nearly laughed out loud, and then remembered not to draw attention to herself. Fellow passengers seeing a woman laughing at nothing would think she was certainly mad.

The train entered a tunnel and Belle saw her own face mirrored in the window. She looked gaunt in the dark reflecting glass, lacking only a black hood to represent the image of the Grim Reaper.

She smiled and the Face of Death smiled back at her, sharing her private joke. Belle shivered. In less than twenty minutes now the train would be stopping at her station. And then there would be Susie, either sent to meet her or at home.

She tried to remember exactly what Susie looked like. She couldn't bring any kind of image to mind. She hadn't seen Susie since the day Ben's body was found. Her little sister had kept out of her way, and then she'd left so suddenly herself. Belle wondered now what Susie had felt then. She asked herself, Did she feel guilty? Did she miss me? She'd always confided in me, she wouldn't have had anyone to talk to. Serve her right, she thought, all our lives she never gave a thought to how much I didn't want to hear her silly confidences.

The train was slowing down. Until then, Belle had assumed that her dad would meet her, but now she realized that was probably wishful thinking. If her mother were really ill, he wouldn't leave her even for an hour to drive into town. But surely he wouldn't send Susie, he couldn't do a thing like that. He might not know why Belle had cut her sister out of her life, but he understood that the hatred his elder daughter felt for her younger sister was implacable, something he could not change by forcing them together.

No, Belle thought, Dad won't send Susie. For a moment she loved him so much, and so longed to see him again, that she wanted to weep because nothing was ever going to be the same as it used to be.

She saw her father standing on the station platform as the train stopped. She saw him, and then she wasn't sure that it was him she saw. That stooped, grey old fellow wasn't her father, it was someone else, an ancient man in a battered tweed jacket meeting a stranger off the train. He was looking towards the last carriages and hadn't seen her. There was no sign of anticipation on his face.

But as soon as she got off the train and started to walk back up the platform towards him, she recognized him as her dad. It had been a queer insight, though, to see him as someone she didn't know, a weary old man weighed down by worry. He's aged so much, she thought.

'Dad,' she said. She was afraid to call him too loudly in case he did not recognize her voice. At least if he didn't respond now he could pretend he didn't hear her.

But through the din of the station platform he did know her voice and turned towards her. He smiled and waved, but the joy she had hoped for on his face was not there. His expression was of overwhelming relief.

He held out his hands to her and she clasped them. They did not hug, they never did.

'Oh Dad, it's been too long,' she said.

'I never went anywhere,' he said. 'You've always known where to find me.' He sounded sad. He withdrew his hands and said, 'You're here now, that's the main thing.'

Belle bit her lip and then asked the question she knew she should have asked at once, but couldn't bring herself to. 'How's Mum?'

Her father shook his head. 'She'll be so happy you got here in time,' he said.

Oh, God, Dad, don't cry, you've still got me, Belle thought. And then she too was fighting tears, because she could see in her father's face that her mother was not going to get better. The mum who had always been there, who loved the old-fashioned ways of doing things, who had sung folksy songs as she churned the butter in the dairy, who had told her when she was fifteen years old that one day she would find someone who would love her for herself, someone who wouldn't even notice Susie when he was with her, Mum wouldn't be around any more. Had her mother believed it when she said that about Susie? Belle wondered.

She followed her dad to the old Land-Rover parked outside the station. He started the engine, then hesitated before moving out into the queue of traffic waiting to cross the main road.

'Belle,' he said, carefully not looking directly at her, 'there's something I've got to ask you. I know it's a lot to ask, but while you're here, could you try to get along with Susie? It would mean so much to your mother if she thought you'd made peace with her.'

Belle was silent for a moment, then put her hand over his as he gripped the gear lever.

'I'll try to,' Belle said. 'I didn't come here to fight with her, anyway.'

Her father nodded. He said nothing, but looked relieved.

'She's been a real tower of strength since she came,' Dad said. 'She's been a great help to Mum.'

There was a pause, then Belle asked, 'How long's she been staying?'

'Two weeks,' Dad said. 'Mum took a turn for the worse and I rang her. She had to do a bit of juggling to get the children sorted but she came as soon as she could.'

'You should have called me,' Belle said, 'I'd have come at once.'

'I thought it would be easier for her,' he said.

He didn't want to be drawn into any kind of argument. He sounded defeated, worn out.

Belle watched him as he drove through the town. She loved his face, bony and sun-burned, always seeming about to burst out laughing. But he'd got so old; there was more grey than black in his hair, and the sparkling blue eyes which had always looked the colour of the sea in sunshine looked now as lifeless as a glass of tap water.

'Dad, I'm so sorry,' she said. He didn't ask her what she meant. He was embarrassed by attempts at intimacy, he always had been.

'I don't see what you've got to be particularly sorry about,' he said. He changed the subject, 'At least your train was on time.'

Susie came out into the yard to meet the Land-Rover.

How odd that I couldn't remember her face, Belle thought, she hasn't changed.

It had always been the same when Belle saw Susie after an absence. For a brief moment, at first sight, she seemed so ordinary, not even particularly pretty, a nice, healthy girl with a lot of shaggy tawny hair, a little overweight but just tall enough to carry it, nothing special. And Belle always thought, as she thought now: What's all the fuss about? She's no threat, it's all in my head.

And then Susie smiled and moved forward and it was as though she'd been touched by magic and was transformed with the allure of some compelling secret. Inside herself, Belle felt as though she had begun to shrivel and fall apart. All the lightness went out of her body and she knew herself to be plain and awkward and unwomanly.

'Hallo, Belle,' Susie said, 'it's been a long time.'

7

Susie looked at Belle and thought, She hasn't changed much since I last saw her.

That was the day her older sister had left the farm without a word to anyone. True, there'd been a postcard about a week after she left, addressed to Dad, asking that her things should be sent to somewhere in London where a friend would store them until she found a place to live. After that, as far as Susie was concerned, Belle disappeared.

And now she was back, seeming smaller and slimmer than when she went away. But that, Susie told herself, was because she herself had been younger then, closer to the childhood years when Belle had always loomed larger than life, big and tall and dominating. Now Susie looked at Belle's face and wanted to weep because all the years hadn't softened that hard expression in her sister's eyes.

When did Belle start looking at me like that? Susie asked herself.

She only remembered how, when they were children, she was always wanting to tag along with Belle, and her big sister had given her that long, hard stare to get rid of her. It went back as far as Susie could remember. But I didn't realize she meant it, Susie thought, I didn't know she really hated me being there.

Not till Ben died, Susie told herself, then I knew. I wanted to talk to her, but she shut me right out. She's my sister, for God's sake, my only sister, I'd have done anything to get her back.

At least, she'd hoped, she and Belle could have put everything else aside for Mum's sake. Surely Belle couldn't hold Ben's death against her, not now. She must know it wasn't her fault he'd fallen from the hayloft the way he did.

Susie wanted desperately to make peace with her sister. Maybe Belle had always found her a nuisance and wished she'd leave her alone, but Susie had looked up to her, had desperately wanted her approval. She missed her.

Susie had known from the moment she came to the farm to look after her mother that Belle would have to come sooner or later. Mum kept asking for her, and finally Dad telephoned to ask her to come. Apparently he'd known for years where she worked in London and he'd rung her at work. Susie guessed that because it was the first time Dad had ever not made light of any illness, particularly Mum's 'female complaints', Belle would travel down at once.

Susie had awaited her sister's arrival all morning with mixed feelings. She still felt the old guilt about seducing Ben, and dreaded having to face the part she herself had played in what had happened afterwards. When Belle went out of their lives so suddenly, it had been easy enough for Susie to avoid confronting that. Belle's return would bring it all back. But, deep down, Susie believed that everything they had shared as children could overcome the gulf that had opened between them.

And she was also curious to see her sister. What was Belle like now? Was she happy? Had she made a life for herself so that they could meet now on some sort of equal terms, as two grown women who could build on the past and perhaps even become friends?

Susie wanted that to be true. She didn't realize until Belle gave her that hard look that her sister had never really liked her, even though they were the same flesh and blood. It had never occurred to Susie that anyone disliked her, why should they? She took that impossibility for granted because of the way it had always been. Now she began to understand that Belle didn't really know why she felt as she did either, but her antagonism was a primitive part of her. And, Susie thought, perhaps her sister had latched on to the Ben

45

episode as a justification for her dislike. She had sometimes wondered if Belle knew that it had been her with Ben in the hayloft before the accident. But how could she have known? Susie asked herself, and then she thought, Belle would suspect me anyway; she always blamed me for everything.

Oh well, Susie told herself, it doesn't matter now. I've got my own life now.

She felt homesick for her nice modern home on a tree-lined street close to the shopping centre in a commuter-belt town on the Surrey-Berkshire border. She missed her husband, John, and the two kids. John had taken leave from his work as a detective inspector in the police to look after the children while she was away, and when he was not available, his mother was only too eager to help out. Susie rang John every day, ostensibly to check on how he was coping but in fact because it gave her something to look forward to, which helped her get through days which were not only painful because her mother was ill, but because living in her parents' Somerset house again brought back memories of farm life and farm life was something she had always hated. Hearing John's voice on the telephone, and the background noise of traffic and some sort of roadworks going on in the road outside the open window of her cheerful, comfortable suburban home, Susie could comfort herself that her return to the farm was no more than a blip in her happy existence of the school run, regular visits to the hairdresser, soft hands with manicured nails, and gossipy coffee mornings with her friends.

Susie knew she was lucky. She loved John, she loved her children, she loved her suburban life, she loved being happy. She had overheard her mother once tell her father that Susie was blessed with the secret of happiness, and that she had a gift because she would always be loved for bringing sunshine into other people's lives.

That had been years ago, she'd only been about ten, but she could still remember how sad her father had sounded when he'd said, 'Not like Belle, I'm afraid.' And her mother had said, 'Poor Belle, she doesn't have an easy nature.'

Susie surprised herself that she remembered that now. At the time, she'd felt pleased and proud that she had such a gift to make her special. Particularly because it was something Belle didn't have, something her elder sister could never take away from her.

But then of course she'd had to go and boast about it to Belle. Susie had never learned that when she tried to impress Belle, to make Belle take notice of her, her sister would always find some way of putting her down.

Susie couldn't remember what Belle had done then; probably startled the pony so that he shied and tipped Susie off. Susie had never been any sort of a rider, she was hopeless with animals, hopeless at sports and games and outdoor things. But Belle wouldn't help her ride the pony, although she was a brilliant horsewoman. They were meant to share the pony, take turns at riding him, but Belle would have none of it. Sometimes she would ride out on her own, ignoring Susie's pleas to wait for her, to let her come too. Susie, in tears, would tell her parents what Belle had done, and Dad would scold Belle or send her to her room, but it made no difference to Belle.

'You said I could have a pony of my own when I was twelve,' she'd said.

And Mum and Dad had explained that they could only afford one pony and they must share him.

'But I'm older than she is,' Belle had said. 'Can't I ever have anything of my own? Why can't she wait until she's my age?'

Belle knew how to look after the pony, how to put on the tack and pick his hooves, but she wouldn't have anything to do with it if it wasn't hers, and she wouldn't show Susie. Dad had to do it.

Remembering that old quarrel, Susie had said something about it the other day when she was sitting with Mum after supper. Mum had difficulty eating, and she'd choked over the food. She was exhausted but she'd seemed glad to talk to Susie about old times.

'Why did Belle hate me so much when we were kids?' Susie asked.

'She was jealous,' Mum said. Her voice was weak.

'But what did she have to be jealous of?' Susie said. 'She was so good at everything. I couldn't even compete with her. She was always Dad's favourite, too.'

Mum sighed. She looked so tired, Susie thought, so worn and old.

'That wasn't true,' her mother said; 'it was just that he thought he understood Belle because she was such a tomboy. Men like your father never know what to do round really feminine women. But he loved you. In a way he loved you more because he'd created something so perfect.'

'Perfect? Me?' Susie didn't understand.

'He thought so. Poor Belle was too like him, he knew she wasn't perfect.'

Mum closed her eyes and lay back against the pillows. Susie thought she wanted to sleep, but her mother suddenly said, 'Just be grateful you've got a boy and a girl. It's murder having two girls close in age.'

She shook her head, clearly not wanting to talk about it any more. Susie picked up the book she'd been reading to her in the evenings and opened it at the marker. She could never remember what she'd read the night before; she found it hard to concentrate when her mother lay so still against the pillows and looked so ill.

Suddenly her mother interrupted her reading.

'I want to see Belle,' she said. 'I want you to get Belle here.'

Susie dropped the book.

'But Mum, it's been years, not since Ben . . .'

48

'I don't care, I need to see her now, before it's too late.' The sick woman was clawing at the duvet, twisting in the bed in distress.

Susie stood up. 'Of course we'll get hold of her, Mum,' she said, taking her mother's hand to reassure her. 'She'll be here soon. I'm sure she will.'

Susie felt shaken by the panicky way in which her mother was asking for Belle. It had not occurred to Susie until then that her mother was actually afraid that she was going to die, but that note of panic crystallized Susie's fears.

She ran downstairs to the kitchen, where Dad was asleep in the armchair beside the Aga. He woke up when Susie burst in and pretended he had been reading the paper.

'She wants to see Belle,' Susie said.

Dad looked shocked. He, too, seemed suddenly aware that his wife thought she was going to die.

'Do you think she'll come?' he said to Susie.

'I don't even know where you can get in touch with her,' Susie said.

'I know where she works,' Dad said.

Susie was surprised. 'I thought she'd left without a trace,' she said. 'After Ben. But was it just me she never wanted to see again?'

Her father looked sad. 'She gave the farm as her address for a job she applied for, before she got herself a place in London,' he said. 'She didn't hear about that job, but when she did find somewhere, she gave me the number in case the other firm got in touch. She said she'd rather work there.'

'Everything is always so complicated with Belle, it always was,' Susie said. She sounded resigned.

'Will you ring her and tell her about Mum?' Dad asked.

'No,' Susie said. 'I can't. You'll have to do it. It's better coming from you, anyway. The moment Belle heard my voice, she'd put the phone down.'

Dad nodded. 'I'll do it tomorrow, then,' he said. 'It'll have to be during office hours.'

There was silence between them for a while. They were painfully aware of the sound of the old dog, Benson, snoring on his blanket by the Aga, which reminded them both of the breathing of the sick woman upstairs.

Suddenly Dad said, 'Susie, I'm sorry to ask you this, but it's important to me to know what happened. Did you sleep with Ben?'

Susie didn't answer at once. She stared at the old dog on the floor and she looked sad.

'Yes,' she said. 'Once. In the hayloft. The same day he died. He was fine when I left him.'

Her father wasn't listening to what she was saying, not after the initial 'yes'. 'Why did you do it?' he asked. 'You knew how much Ben meant to Belle, why did you have to do it?'

Susie looked down at her hands, and the image of Belle's hand with the missing finger came into her mind. Her voice faltered as she said, 'I wanted to see if I could. Like a test, to see if he really loved Belle as much as she thought he did. He obviously didn't, and I was pleased. I felt like we were even after that.'

'Even? Even for what?'

'For Belle always trying to shut me out. As far back as I can remember, she always wanted everything to herself.'

'But you weren't going to tell her, were you?' Dad looked puzzled. He said, 'Susie, how could you, you knew how she felt?'

'No, Dad, I swear I wasn't going to say anything. I'd never have told her, and I knew he wouldn't. I did it for myself. It just seemed so harmless then.'

'But it wasn't harmless, was it?'

Her father sounded old and tired and very sad.

8

Belle climbed out of the Land-Rover and took her bag out of the back.

'Hallo, Susie,' she said. 'How's Mum?'

'She's looking forward to seeing you,' Susie said.

Belle was immediately on the defensive, though she told herself she was being absurd. But she thought, Mum can tell me that herself; since when did Susie become my mother's spokesperson?

'I came as soon as I could after Dad called,' she said.

'I didn't mean that,' Susie said. 'I simply meant she's looking forward to seeing you.'

Belle looked at Dad's face, disappointed and resigned. She made an effort. She forced herself to give her sister a tight little smile. She said, 'I know you did. I'm sorry. I've been working in a big office in London too long. There's always some kind of hidden agenda behind what people say there.'

'You and Belle go on up,' Susie said to her father. 'I'll put Belle's bag in her room. You don't want to keep Mum waiting.'

'I'll follow you up, Belle,' Dad said. 'It's you she's been asking for.'

Belle had the feeling that her father wanted an excuse not to go with her. She understood that he must dread seeing Mum as she was. It was more than that, though; Belle realized that her father dreaded seeing the shock on her own face when she first saw the state her mother was in. That's when Belle knew that her mother was dying.

Her mother looked very small in the big old bed. The curtains were half-closed because the daylight hurt her eyes, and there was a stuffy, sickly smell in the room.

Belle took a deep breath and went to the bed. Her mother's eyes were closed and the half moan of her breathing was the only sound in the room. Belle took her hand and was frightened at the brittle feel of the bones through dry skin. Her own hand felt like a bludgeon.

She had always found it difficult to know what to say to her mother and it was no easier now.

'Mum,' she said softly, 'it's me. Belle.'

Her mother opened her eyes and managed a weak smile.

'I love you, Belle,' she said in a hoarse whisper that Belle had to strain to hear.

'I love you, too, Mum,' Belle said. She thought, There's so little time left, and so much I never said when I should, and now I can't think of anything to say that means anything.

'But I love Susie, too, Belle,' her mother went on in her croaking, unrecognizable voice. 'Susie's my child too, whatever she did to you.'

'I know, Mum, don't worry about it, it's all right.'

'No, it's not all right.' Mum seemed to struggle to raise her head, but she was so weak she couldn't move. She was finding it hard to breathe. 'For my sake, forgive her. Try to love her.'

Belle would have let go her mother's hand, but the sick old woman would not loosen her grip on her daughter.

'I can't, Mum,' Belle whispered. 'I'm sorry.'

'You must,' the hoarse voice whispered. And then, 'If only . . . '

'Mum?'

The harsh breathing had stopped.

Belle heard her Dad come into the room behind her.

'Dad, I think she's gone,' Belle said, putting her mother's hand carefully on the bed and pulling up the duvet to cover it.

Her father pushed her aside and embraced the body.

'Mary, come back. Don't go, don't leave me now.' He was shouting.

Belle was shocked because he sounded so angry, not sad at all. He was red in the face and there were beads of sweat on his forehead.

He turned on Belle then. 'What did you say to her?' he shouted. 'She was fine till you came.'

'Dad,' Belle said.

'Leave us alone,' he said, in a voice she could scarcely recognize. 'I love her and we want to be alone.'

9

That evening, Belle faced Susie across the table in the kitchen.

The afternoon had been a blur of people coming and going; the doctor, the funeral director, the vicar, an endless stream of people Belle didn't know who had been the dead woman's friends. None of it had seemed to Belle to have anything to do with her mother. Mum's sister Kirsty, her only close relative but recently widowed herself, was unable to travel from Scotland.

During all this Belle had scarcely been aware of Susie.

Now, though, there was no escape. Dad had shut himself in the bedroom once the funeral men had taken the body away. He refused to come out, or answer when Belle pleaded with him through the door at least to have something to eat and drink.

Belle ran her hand over the well-scrubbed surface of the kitchen table. It seemed to her to have more to say about her mother than anyone or anything that day. That table attested to decades of toil. It was like an extension of her mother's person, the table and then her pots and pans, her kitchen tools, her bowls and jugs, the washing-up cloths hanging on the Aga rail with the red-striped hand towel and the tattered blue oven gloves.

'It's weird being here without her,' Susie said.

'Yes, it is,' Belle said.

Belle knew that Susie had almost said, 'How would you know, you haven't been near the place for years?'

'All my childhood's tied up in this place with Mum,' Belle said, answering Susie's unspoken question.

'Me, too,' Susie said.

Belle didn't answer her.

Susie had made a pile of sandwiches and tea in the old brown pot. No one Belle knew apart from her mother still made tea in a teapot like that. Belle felt resentful that Susie so easily slipped into her mother's ways, but that was ridiculous. What else could Susie do? Belle thought, I've enough against her already without getting all offended about stupid things like the brown teapot. The thought of her accumulated childhood justification for hating Susie was like a comfort blanket.

The silence between them grew oppressive.

'Are you still in the same job?' Susie asked at last. 'Dad says you work for the government.'

'Yes,' Belle said, 'still the same job.' Then she added, 'It's really boring, actually.'

Susie nodded. There was nothing more to say on that subject, she felt. She said, 'John will be here tomorrow.' She was making an effort to sound bright.

'Your husband?' Belle asked. She remembered that Dad had said something ages ago about Susie getting married, but he hadn't mentioned the man's name.

'Yes, John Smart. I'm Mrs John Smart.' Susie suddenly looked bleak. 'Didn't anyone tell you?'

'I don't suppose I asked,' Belle said. 'I'd more or less lost touch with them.'

'It wasn't their fault,' Susie said.

'Do you think I don't know that?' Belle made no attempt to hide her bitter tone.

There was a long pause. Susie poured herself another mug of tea. Her hand was shaking as she added the milk. Belle could hear the tiny rattle of the jug's spout against the rim of the mug.

There was another long pause, then Susie said, 'John and I've got two kids, a boy and a girl. Jonty and Kim.'

'Is John bringing them with him?'

'No,' Susie said. 'His mother says she'll come to stay in the house and look after them, so they don't miss any school. She lives quite close to us anyway.'

'Oh, of course, I suppose they're old enough for school,' Belle said.

'Yes,' Susie said.

That seemed to exhaust the subject of Susie's children.

Belle told herself, If Susie thinks being an aunt is going to make me interested in her brats, she's going to be disappointed. I don't want any part in her family.

There was yet another long pause.

'What does your husband do?' Belle asked.

'He's a policeman,' Susie said.

Belle laughed. 'You married a cop?'

Susie went on the defensive. 'Why not?' she said. 'It's a good job and he's good at it.'

'Sure it is,' Belle said, 'but it's a bit humble for you, isn't it?' She was smiling, but Susie had no doubt that Belle was making fun of her. 'I thought you'd get hitched to a millionaire and divide your time between homes in New York and the South of France,' Belle said.

'I married for love,' Susie said. She sounded defensive about that, too, and Belle was pleased, sensing a weakness in her sister's perfect life. She thought, The little gold-digger's disappointed that she's not rich.

'Oh, you don't have to be ashamed of that,' Belle said. 'Don't forget, I was going to marry for love myself, once.'

She looked Susie in the eye and knew that, for a moment, Susie didn't know what she was talking about. Her sister looked surprised, as though the thought of Belle marrying, let alone for love, had never occurred to her. It seemed to Belle impossible that Susie had forgotten, even for a moment, about Ben, forgotten that Belle and Ben were getting married, that their marriage was the reason they had come down to the farm to meet the family at all. Ben had no family of his own and he'd wanted to meet her parents and her sister. She hadn't been able to refuse.

Belle watched as enlightenment dawned on Susie's face.

'Of course you were!' Susie said. 'You were going to marry that guy who got killed falling out of the hayloft.'

Something felt as though it was exploding inside Belle's head. She clenched her hands round her mug of tea to keep herself from grabbing Susie by the throat and throttling her there and then. There must have been a crack or some weakness in the mug because she felt the china shatter in her fingers and the hot tea spill on to the table, but she didn't feel it scald her palms. She couldn't speak. Only in her head she kept repeating to herself, That's the end, there's no way back now, if I don't destroy you, I'll die.

It was impossible. Susie had demolished Belle's future when she took Ben from her, and she'd forgotten all about it. It had meant so little to Susie that she hadn't even remembered that she'd played her own part in his death, the death she dismissed as an accident. She never even questioned that.

Belle thought, She's probably even blanked out what she did; no doubt she's convinced herself by now that Ben was in the hayloft having sex with a village girl, which is what everyone else believed. Susie knows what she did, except she's forgotten it ever happened.

Susie was mopping up the spilt tea.

'The mug must've been cracked,' she said. 'I'm sorry, I didn't mean to open old wounds. I didn't think. I probably expected the millionaire and all that myself, but John and I fell in love and that was it for me. Do you want something for your hands? That tea must've hurt.'

'No,' Belle managed to say.

Susie made another pot of tea and put a new mug on the table in front of Belle.

'Thanks,' Belle said.

Susie sat down again and leaned across the table towards Belle.

'I'm really sorry,' she said.

'Why? Why should you be sorry? I broke the mug.'

'Oh, stop it, Belle. You know that's not what I mean.'

'I've no idea what you mean,' Belle said.

'I know you know. I've always known.'

Belle felt as though there was a lump of ice forming inside her brain.

'What do you know I've always known?' she asked, and her voice was cold.

'I know you know that I was having sex with Ben that day. I know you know it was me he'd been with in the hayloft before he fell, not some scrubber from the village. I've always known you knew. You must've known.'

Belle gave her a long, blank stare. Then she laughed.

'Did I know that? What makes you think so?'

'The way you cut me out of your life, I suppose. There had to be a reason for it.'

'You were born, that's when I cut you out of my life,' Belle said.

'Why? Why do you hate me so much. Apart from Ben, what did I ever do to you?' There was a note of hysteria in Susie's voice.

'Why does it have to be about you?' Belle said, and then paused to control the anger she could hear in her own voice. She went on, more calmly, 'You had nothing to do with it. There wasn't anything here for me once Ben was dead. I had to get away. I had to make a life for myself. And you and me, Susie, we weren't ever close. I don't see that I cut you out of my life, you just weren't in it once I was in London.'

Susie shook her head. 'It was more than that,' she said. 'I could feel it between us.'

'Then why did you have sex with Ben?' Belle asked.

'To get even.'

Susie was shouting in her frustration.

Belle stared at her. 'To get even?' she repeated. 'Even for what?'

Susie sat staring at her hands clenched on the table. She was very aware of the first finger on her left hand, the finger which was missing on Belle's.

'Oh,' Susie said, 'for everything.' She put her hands out of sight under the table top and looked quickly up at Belle and then down again. She hadn't really answered Dad when he asked the same question as Belle, but now she tried to explain.

'You were always first,' Susie said. 'You were Dad's favourite, you did things with him on the farm. You drove the tractor at haymaking and harvest time, and he took you to market and you sat up with him at lambing and I was always left out of the real things and told I'd mess up my dress or I wasn't strong enough or old enough.'

'You hated things like that,' Belle said. 'You used to cry when you got your feet wet.'

'I wanted to be part of things,' Susie said, and wished it didn't sound so feeble.

'I didn't know,' Belle said. She didn't sound sympathetic. 'Are you sure this isn't hindsight?'

'You must've known I was jealous,' Susie said. 'You can't not have known that.'

'Honestly, it never occurred to me,' Belle said. 'Why should it? I didn't want to think about you at all. Anyway, it seems to me that you were the one who took everything away from me.'

'You had everything I wanted,' Susie said. 'So I took what I could, which wasn't much. One quick shag with Ben, that's all.'

'If you tell me that screwing Ben didn't really mean anything, I'm going to kill you here and now,' Belle said. She spoke very quietly, but the venom in her tone was obvious to both of them.

Susie looked shocked, then her face cleared as though she had suddenly seen the light. 'My God,' she said. 'Did you kill Ben?' There was a note almost of awe in her voice.

10

From upstairs, their father started to shout for Susie. She got up from the table quickly, without glancing at Belle, and went to the door.

'What is it, Dad?' she called.

'I'm cold,' he shouted back. 'I'll come down for some soup.'

Why did he shout for Susie and not me? Belle thought. I'm the eldest, he should call me first, not her. She's taken Dad away from me.

Susie went to the Aga and lifted the hotplate cover to make toast to go with the soup. 'I'll open a tin,' she said. 'He likes Baxter's Royal Game. We can all have some.'

'You don't have to tell me that,' Belle said. 'He's my dad too. It always was his favourite.'

'Yes,' Susie said. She wasn't really interested.

It's because she's got kids, Belle told herself, he knows where he is with her because she's a mother. And a wife. Well, so would I have been if Susie hadn't done what she did with Ben.

Belle tried to stifle what she was thinking then. I can fix her, she thought, and then she felt frightened by herself, tried to tell herself that there was a line she couldn't cross. But she couldn't make herself believe it.

She watched Susie opening a tin of soup, and the old sick feeling was sour in the pit of her stomach. Her sister's grace was obvious even doing something so mundane. Where did it come from, that way Susie had of making everything she did seem full of warmth and joy, as though however tedious it was, she was glad to do it?

'It was an accident,' Belle said, in answer to the question left hanging in the air. 'You know it was. He must've heard someone coming.'

'I know,' Susie said, emptying soup into a saucepan. 'Of course you wouldn't kill him. I just suddenly had to ask.'

'Yes,' Belle said. 'But it was an accident.'

'I wonder what would have happened if he hadn't died,' Susie said, and for a moment the hypnotic rhythm of her stirring was broken.

Belle was so angry that she almost sprang at her sister to try to throttle her then and there. There was blood on her palms where she had dug her nails into her flesh in the effort of containing her fury.

'I wouldn't have married him, if that's what you mean,' she said. She couldn't stop her voice quivering, but Susie didn't seem to notice. 'I wouldn't have had anything to do with him once he'd been with you.'

Susie appeared to have no idea that she was playing with fire. She clearly thought it was a step forward that she and Belle were reminiscing about old times they'd shared when they were different people.

'Of course you would,' she said lightly. 'He'd have told you it didn't mean anything, he'd been an idiot, and you'd have had a good time making up and you'd be married with several kids by now.'

'No,' Belle said.

'Balls,' Susie said, and grinned at her with a familiarity she seemed to regard as part of the rights of sisterhood. Then her eyes suddenly looked shrewd. She added, 'After all, getting married would've been all the proof you needed that he chose you above me, wouldn't it? Wasn't that what you always wanted?'

Susie might have been joking, but Belle heard a spiteful undertone in her voice.

'No,' Belle said, 'I never competed with you. I would never stoop that low. You had everything you wanted because I wouldn't compete with you. I didn't want to share. That wasn't what it was about. I wanted just one thing, just once, to myself. Everything between Ben and me had to be over because you'd made yourself part of it. That's the way it was for me.'

'You're weird,' Susie said. She was distracted, not really listening to what Belle had said. She set out three bowls on the table and poured soup into them. 'Give Dad a call,' she said; 'if he doesn't hurry, it'll get cold.'

Belle got up and went to the door. 'I'm not hungry,' she said. 'I'm going for a walk.'

'You could've said before I poured the soup,' Susie said.

'You didn't ask,' Belle said.

Susie followed her to the door and shouted, 'Dad, the soup's on the table.' She sounded impatient.

She's turned into some kind of control freak, Belle thought, I suppose that's what comes of having kids. Anyway, what a stupid fuss about a bowl of bloody tinned soup.

Belle walked out into the yard. It was nearly dark and the farm buildings in the dusk looked like a sinister filmset for some old French *film noir*. Or a film set in wartime maybe, for the place looked like an abandoned bomb site.

What's Dad going to do now? Belle asked herself. Now Mum's dead, how's he going to manage? She knew she should be asking herself how he and Mum had been managing for ages, how they'd scraped enough to live on out of this seedy smallholding. Has he even got a pension? she wondered. He'd never have put anything aside to buy the National Insurance stamp, and now he'd be far too proud to look to the State for help. He'll have to sell up to give himself enough to live on. If he could flog the land for development it would be worth a fortune. But he'd rather die. He'll cling on as long as he can, she thought.

And then she told herself, Once I've dealt with Susie, I'll make sure he's all right.

It had been a warm day for the time of year, but now as dusk fell the wind got up and it was suddenly cold. There could even be a frost later, Belle could feel it in the air. It was like the old days – she'd been able to smell rain coming, felt the bite of overnight frost long before the forecasters and known from the heavy ache behind her eyes when there was thunder in the offing. She hadn't lost it, then, that bred-in-the-bone country girl's instinctive relationship with Nature. It had to do with understanding the cycle of life and death, a knowledge way beyond the sentimental grieving of those who could never conceive of themselves as being simply part of the process of decay and regrowth.

It wasn't just belonging to the country, it was more than that. It was a sort of surrender to something secret and inevitable of which most people, it seemed to Belle, were unaware. Susie, who had shared her childhood, wouldn't know what she was talking about. There had always been too much happening on the surface of Susie's life, too many things to do and places to go, too many friends and activities. Susie and her life were always full of clatter; she had never learned to listen not only with her ears but with something deep inside her. Only those who knew how to be alone could understand how to tune in to the subliminal undercurrents of Nature's life force.

A newborn moon, a nail-clipping of silver light, slipped into the dark sky from behind a cloud. I can't kill Susie, she thought, it wasn't her fault. She didn't know what she was doing. I should blame Ben, not her – except he's dead already and that's not enough. And anyway, Ben was just the excuse. What Susie's done to me goes much deeper. It *was* her fault, everything was her fault; from the moment she was born nothing could ever be perfect for me because of her.

Belle knew she wasn't making sense. She couldn't explain even to herself her grudge against Susie. All their past years seemed to reverberate in her head with clamouring voices: 'Susie's older sister . . . '; 'she came with Susie . . . '; 'Susie asked if she could bring her . . . '; 'You'd never think she was Susie's sister . . . '

I've always been in her shadow, Belle told herself, she was always the one who mattered, she has always defined my whole life. And then she thought, If I stopped hating her, I'd have nothing left to live for. I wouldn't exist. Destroying her will be a kind of apotheosis for me. It must be the one perfect thing she can't spoil for me.

Belle felt very weary, as though she had been walking for hours, not just a few hundred metres from the farm. But it had been a long day. It was almost dark now, the deep, dense darkness of the country-side. Belle could see lights in the far distance on the coast of South

Wales over the invisible sea.

The night and the distant coast and the small sounds of the wild around her brought Belle a kind of peace. She knew what she had to do and then she could move on. She must destroy the poison in her life that Susie was.

But then Belle remembered Susie's face across the kitchen table, that silly tinkling laugh of hers as she'd made light of what she'd done with Ben. The horrible sick, hot, rush of hatred rose from the pit of Belle's stomach and surged through her heart and head.

Out of the night and into the darkness, the words chimed from nowhere in her head, without meaning, without purpose. I have to destroy her, she told herself. It's part of natural lore, I can't escape.

11

At last Dad came down for his soup. Susie had already poured it back into the saucepan to keep warm, and she was irritated enough to let it boil and grow lumpy. She told herself she was upset by her mother's death and she resented the way she felt she was being taken for granted. But it wasn't that. It was Belle. Her older sister had always been able to unsettle her, make her blame herself for something she didn't know she'd done.

But then Susie saw the expression of relief her father didn't try to hide when he saw that Belle had gone out, and she wanted to go over to him and hug him and tell him he needn't worry, she would look after him, and she'd protect him from Belle. She had no idea what she thought Belle would or could do to hurt either of them, but she understood that her father felt the same vague trepidation around her sister that she did.

Susie wondered what it was about Belle. When she looked back over their childhood, it seemed to her now that there had always been something alien about her sister. No, alien was too strong a word, they'd both been children, after all. Freaky wasn't quite right either. But Belle hadn't been like the other girls at school. She hadn't been interested in what interested Susie and the rest of them. She had been detached from them, never joining in, never going out with friends, never actually making any friends. Never, never, never, it was always so negative. But that was Belle.

Mum and Dad thought that their elder daughter was shy. Then they said that she was academic, and the impression was that the other girls weren't good enough for her. Susie remembered how she had tried to involve Belle in having fun, but Belle had made it clear that Susie's idea of fun did not interest her. After that, Susie had tried to keep out of her way. Susie's domain had been the house, doing indoor things, and other people; Belle occupied the out-of-doors, and there she repelled all would-be boarders.

Dad had been Belle's constant companion on the farm. He had made a point of boasting to friends and visitors about how strong she was, how skilful with the tractor and the stock. He'd been trying to boost her confidence. But in Susie's eyes it had never been confidence that Belle lacked. Susie believed that Belle despised them all.

But now, seeing her elder sister again after all these years, Susie wondered if she had been wrong about her. Now she asked herself, Is Belle quite right in the head? Has she always been a bit mad and we never noticed because we were so used to it? And she thought: Is she all right? Does she need help?

Susie knew there was nothing she could do now to change the past. Nor did she want to worry Dad about Belle's sanity now, not when he had so much on his mind. And anyway Belle herself had dealt with her problems. She had made a life for herself in London, with a good job. As long as she was far away from her family, she was fine. There was no reason to think that she wasn't happy. Thank God she's got that, Susie thought, she'll go away and I won't have to worry. She was a little ashamed of her relief.

'How do you think Belle is?' Susie asked her father when he had finished eating.

'She seems fine,' Dad said. The way he said it, he seemed to want to leave it at that. Then he added, 'Don't you think so?'

'Yes,' Susie said. 'She seems to have made a good life for herself in London.'

If Dad doesn't want to talk about it, I'm not going to force him, Susie thought.

'Are you two getting on?' Dad asked.

'Sure we are, Dad,' Susie said. 'Don't you worry about that.'

After supper, Dad went back upstairs. Susie left the saucepan of soup on the top of the Aga in case Belle wanted it when she came in, and then she, too, went to her room. She didn't want to have to see Belle again that night.

In her bedroom, she rang John on her mobile phone. She burst into tears when she heard the sound of his voice.

'Darling, what is it? What's wrong?' he asked.

She told him about her mother's death, and he was all sympathy. But she couldn't tell him that that wasn't why she was crying now. She would weep for her mother later, with her head buried under her pillows and the duvet pulled up over her face. She couldn't explain to John that his voice, so ordinary and strong and full of life, had made her painfully aware, in contrast, of how thankless was the life her parents had lived, how humble and pathetic their expectations and their inevitable failure to be happy. And what she found so heart-rending now was the fact of how Dad's life had been – and was now – ingrained in poverty which he and Mum had accepted without rage or bitterness. And now she was reminded that this was the life she came from, the life that wanted to reclaim her; John's voice on the phone was like a lifeline she couldn't grasp.

'John, I love you so much,' she said in a voice full of urgent emotion.

He was taken aback. 'I love you too,' he said. 'I'll be down as soon as I can.'

She couldn't explain how terrified she was that something would stop him coming.

'You will come, won't you?'

He was calm and firm. 'Of course I'll come. My mother's taking the kids. Do you think I'd abandon you in your family's hour of need?'

He was teasing her, and she felt comforted. 'I'm sorry. I don't know what's got into me. I think it's because of Belle.'

'Your big sister? The one with the high-powered job in London? Don't let her intimidate you.'

'I suppose seeing her after all these years brings back painful memories,' Susie said.

'She works for one of the government departments in Whitehall doesn't she?' John said. 'There's a story in the paper today about a woman in one of those jobs who killed herself changing the wheel of her car. Hadn't fixed the jack properly. They had a picture of her, poor woman. She looked like I imagine your Belle, one of those middle-aged spinster career women with spectacles and no make-up.'

'You seem to be able to tell a lot from a newspaper photograph. Belle's not really like that at all.'

'Do you think your sister might've known her, though?'

'I don't see why she should. There are thousands of people working in those government places, aren't there?'

'Yes, of course, it just seems like a coincidence, that's all.'

'You, my darling, have an unnatural interest in death and the manner of people's dying.'

'Sudden death makes very ordinary people associated with it seem interesting,' John said. 'Any death, to a certain extent. Isn't that what's happening now to you and your father? And, presumably, Belle?'

'I don't know about Belle,' Susie said, 'she dislikes me too much for me to tell.'

12

Belle did the milking on her own next morning because, for the first time in all the decades since he started farming, her father didn't get up at dawn and start the routine of fetching in the cows from the meadow to start the slow, orderly procession through the milking parlour. So Belle was the one who sponged the cows' udders and attached the black rubber teats to each cow in turn, while those who would take their places as soon as they'd been milked out waited patiently for their turns.

Belle hadn't done the milking for years. But she'd been brought up doing it. She used to help her father with it before going to school. In those days there were far fewer cows, and for a time they'd milked by hand, hands covered in a cream called Udsal to lubricate the cows' cold, cracked teats. Things had changed, the milking parlour was like a small factory now. The animals' names were still the same, though. They were written on boards above each stall: Rosie, Cowslip, Bluey, Buttercup. Belle remembered their grandmothers and great grandmothers, family resemblance ran like a thread through the generations. How can anyone think all cows look alike? Belle thought. They're just as different from one another as humans. She asked herself, Would I recognize Susie's kids if I saw them in the street? Is the girl – Kim, isn't it? – is she another Susie? No, she can't be. She may look like her, but there's only one Susie.

Belle sent each cow out through a gate at the far end of the milking shed to wander down a short track back to the pasture. When the last had lumbered away, she turned on the hose and sluiced the concrete floor.

As she finished and coiled the hosepipe ready for the evening milking, she heard a car pull up and then Susie's excited voice. John had arrived.

Belle lingered in the cowshed as long as she could. She was curious to meet Susie's husband, but dreaded, too, the look of disappointment he wouldn't be able to hide when Susie introduced her. She'd always been an anti-climax for Susie's friends, who expected Susie's sister to be someone as bright and vibrant and as much fun as Susie herself.

But there was no help for it, she had to go and watch Susie and her policeman together, as happy as she and Ben might have been once. Belle felt more than ever an outsider in her own family.

'You must be Belle?' a man's voice behind her said.

She turned and saw him outlined against the open door.

'Yes,' she said, 'and you must be Susie's husband.'

She didn't move and he came towards her across the wet concrete. Susie didn't marry just for love, then, she thought, he's incredibly good-looking.

'I'm John,' he said. 'I'm glad to meet you at last. I've heard a lot about you.'

Belle was disconcerted; if she'd ever thought about it, she would have expected that for Susie out of sight was out of mind. She was pleased that she had been on her sister's mind. Perhaps Susie did feel guilty about Ben after all.

'Don't believe what anyone in this family has told you about me,' she said, 'we've never been really close, and we've had very little contact for years.'

John laughed. 'Don't spoil the images Susie gave me of an idyllic childhood, the two of you as kids here with your animals and the woods to run wild in. Wasn't there really a woodpile you pretended was a ship and fought the pirates on the Spanish Main? Or the secret tunnel through the blackthorn thicket where you and Susie hid out when the grown-ups wanted you to do something you didn't want to do?'

Belle gave him a closer look. He was just as good-looking as all Susie's conquests; of course he would be, Susie would never have married a man who wasn't handsome. But he wasn't good-looking in the wrong way, he wasn't one of those sophisticated glamorous creeps with lots of money that her little sister used to favour when she was single and carefree. This John of hers looked thoroughly nice, with a craggy sun-tanned face and unruly dark hair. One of the best things about him was the expression in his deep-set brown eyes, which gave the impression that he perhaps found life amusing. Belle looked into those eyes with their mocking gleam and found it hard to break away from their hold. She thought, I feel he's reeling me in like a fish. I feel sorry for criminals trying to lie to him. Then she added to herself, Particularly the women.

Belle was excited.

She smiled. 'Do you know, I'd forgotten all about those childhood games,' she said. 'We did have a ship we called *Hispaniola* and we used to go treasure hunting in the Caribbean with a table-cloth for a sail. And yes, we used to hide out in our secret tunnel. Imagine Susie telling you all about that.'

What had Susie said? Did she tell him about the old drinking trough which Belle launched on a pond in the woods behind the farm buildings? She had punted to a muddy island across the water and claimed it for her own. Susie had begged to be allowed to go with her; she'd shouted and threatened and finally burst into tears but Belle had ignored her. And then she'd gone and told Dad and he'd taken the trough away and made her promise never to do anything so dangerous again.

No, Susie wouldn't have told John about that. Belle smiled and said, 'I suppose as childhoods go it was idyllic.'

'Oh, yes,' he said, 'and talking of Susie, she sent me out to tell you breakfast is getting cold. I suppose that should be is cold by now, so she'll be mad at me. Do you think I should hide in the secret tunnel till she gets over it?'

'You're far too big, even if the blackthorn hasn't grown over it,' Belle said. 'It's nasty stuff, blackthorn. It only has to give you a scratch on your skin and the wound will go septic.'

She thought, That's like what happened to my childhood, it poisoned me. Susie was like the blackthorn and she poisoned my life, long before she took Ben away from me. She cut off my finger and I've been infected by her ever since.

'You might get blood poisoning and have to have your hand cut off,' she said to John, trying to sound flippant to hide what she was really feeling.

'I'm not sure I wouldn't rather face that than Susie in a bad mood,' he said, and laughed so she'd know he didn't mean it.

Belle thought, She didn't tell him about cutting off my finger, either. If she had, he wouldn't have said that without getting embarrassed.

They came into the kitchen together like old friends, and Belle watched Susie to see her reaction. She knew only too well how she would have felt in Susie's place, and she was a little disappointed that it plainly never occurred to Susie that Belle might be trying to take the gorgeous John from her. But then, Belle asked herself, Why should Susie think any such thing, no one ever gave me a second glance once they met her. And she thought, If I can, I will. She can't stop me trying.

Anyway, Susie was preoccupied with Dad, who had not come down to breakfast although she'd called him several times.

'What are we going to do about him?' she asked John, not Belle. 'He's falling apart.'

'Give him a chance, sweetheart,' John said. 'Your mum only died yesterday, and they were together for decades. He's shocked and frightened of the future and he needs time to come to terms with it.'

'That's all very well,' Susie said, 'but what about the farm? He can't just sit around and mope, the farm can't look after itself.'

'At least let him get the funeral over,' John said. 'We can keep things going till then, can't we?'

'Yes, but suppose he doesn't snap out of it?' Susie said. 'I've got to get back to the kids, I can't be in two places at once.'

'Thank God for that,' Belle said. 'You've no idea how to cope here, you never had.'

Susie looked surprised that Belle spoke, as though a stranger had interrupted her private conversation.

Belle went on, 'But I can, and I will if I have to. I'll look after the farm. You get back to the kids as soon as you like.'

'But what about your job?' Susie said. She made no attempt to hide that she suspected Belle of some sort of ulterior motive. 'They'll give you a few days grace because of Mum dying, I suppose, but you'll have to go back as soon as the funeral's over.'

'I was going to give in my notice in any case,' Belle said. 'It's a dead-end job, and it bores me to tears. I'll find something better when the time comes. I'll like looking after things here for a bit. I don't suppose it'll be for long, anyway, Dad'll be back in harness in no time.'

Susie protested, but it was obvious that she wanted to go along with Belle's willingness to take over. She hated to be away from her children, and suspected that John's mother would be doing everything wrong. She tended to spoil the kids, and let them get away with things she shouldn't. They'd get out of hand if Susie was away too long.

'Well, if you're sure,' Susie said. 'It's probably the best way to get Dad back on his feet, he'll hate having to depend on you.'

Belle and John both laughed at that, but Susie didn't understand why.

'I could stay on a few days after the funeral and help get things back on track,' John said. He explained to Belle, 'I took annual leave when Susie came down here when your mother first got ill. I thought I'd have to look after the kids, but then Mum offered to take over so I could be with Susie.'

'What use would you be round the farm?' Susie said. 'You've been a townee all your life.'

'That's all you know,' John said. 'We used to spend the summer holidays in the country when I was a kid. And much as I hate to offend your feminist principles, I'm a big strong man, I can do any heavy work that needs doing, and I don't need special skills for that.'

'Fine,' Susie said. 'At least I won't feel so bad leaving Belle to cope on her own.'

She's amazing, Belle thought, she thinks everything revolves round her.

And, of course, it did. It always had. How could Susie know any other way to be?

'I must say it would be a help, just for a week or so after the funeral,' Belle said. 'I expect there's a lot that needs doing we could do together. Things difficult for one person, like fencing and moving the slurry. I noticed last night Dad hasn't got round to that yet, and it's almost too late to get it on the fields.' She asked John, 'I don't suppose you can drive a tractor?'

John said, 'I've driven mechanical diggers and forklift trucks, I can probably manage a tractor. And if I'm in a field, it's not as if I can do much damage.'

Belle laughed. 'Don't kid yourself,' she said, 'you can do a lot of damage to a field.'

'If you're sure?' Susie said to Belle.

'Of course I'm sure,' Belle said. 'I'll ring the office today.'

'Well, thanks.' Susie sounded grudging, but she was never going to refuse Belle's offer. 'Well,' Susie went on, 'that's put my mind at rest.' She touched John's cheek in gratitude that he was prepared to do this for her.

Belle could see that Susie was glad that she would not have to leave her sister in sole possession of their father and the farm. She thought, she's afraid I'll turn Dad against her, perhaps persuade him to make a new will leaving the farm to me and not her. Susie sees John being here as a way of protecting her interests. She can't wait to get her hands on the money when the farm's sold. Belle looked at Susie and John together, engrossed in one another, and she told herself, John's never going to earn enough to give her as much as she wants. She thinks he'll stop me turning Dad against her. Well, I'll take care of her concerns, with him or without him.

And Belle said to herself, Let the game begin. Now I know how to start getting my revenge.

13

Belle wasn't sure how long she had been asleep when she became aware of someone knocking on her bedroom door. Long enough to be disorientated when she was suddenly awakened, anyway.

She started up, not knowing for the moment where she was. She had been dreaming; someone had been knocking in her dream, but she couldn't remember the context. She reached out for the bedside light, but her sleep-sodden hand simply clawed at the air.

Then she heard Susie's voice, urgent and sounding frightened. 'Belle, wake up, let me in. I've got to talk to you.'

Belle rolled out of bed and stumbled to the door. 'Go away,' she said, 'leave me alone.'

'I can't,' Susie said, 'there's something I've got to tell you. Something you need to know about Mum.'

'I don't want to know anything you've got to tell me,' Belle said.

Susie said, 'No, you're right, but you've got to listen.' There was a pause, then Susie was pleading. 'Let me in, Belle, even if after this we never speak again.'

There was something about her voice which made Belle hesitate, then open the door to let her sister come into the room.

Susie turned on the overhead light as she shut the door behind her. She was wearing a shimmering satiny nightdress in a shade of peach which was almost exactly the colour of her skin. She looked naked, like a slim mermaid gliding across the room. Belle felt peculiar, seeing her sister as John did when they were alone together.

Belle got back into bed and pulled the duvet up to her face. 'Well?' she said.

Susie, once in the room, seemed to be wishing she could escape.

'You can sit on the bed,' Belle said. 'Whatever it is you think's so important you've got to tell me in the middle of the night, it's probably easier if you don't have to bellow at me from across the room.'

It was a clumsy attempt to put Susie at ease, but Belle's sarcasm didn't help. Susie seemed about to burst into tears. She perched on the edge of the bed, twisting the shimmering cloth of her nightdress between her fingers. Then she took a deep breath and managed to say, 'There's something you should know about Mum's illness, Belle. There's no easy way to say it, and I don't know if I'm doing the right thing telling you, even. But you've got a right to know.'

'Pneumonia?' Belle said, puzzled. 'Isn't that what she died of? It was on the death certificate.' Belle could see nothing mysterious about pneumonia. She was getting irritated with Susie.

'She had Huntington's chorea,' Susie whispered.

Belle stared at her. 'What are you talking about?' she asked, and as she spoke her tongue seemed to have turned to stone in her mouth and she couldn't form the words properly.

'Oh, she actually died of pneumonia,' Susie said. 'Thank God. People with Huntington's chorea often do die of an infection like that.' Susie swallowed hard before she went on. 'There's no cure. The brain wastes away. It's a degenerative genetic disease. It passes from parent to child.'

'Yes,' Belle said, 'I know what genetic means.' She's making this up, she told herself, it's her way of getting back at me.

Susie said, 'The children of a sufferer have a fifty-per-cent chance of developing it.'

She was silent for a moment. Then she said, 'Can you imagine how Mum must've felt, waiting to see if we developed it? And facing what was going to happen to her, too?' Susie seemed anxious to pre-empt Belle's blaming their mother.

Belle stared at her sister. She still wasn't convinced that Susie didn't have some hidden agenda in making up this preposterous story. And yet such terrifying lies were surely beyond Susie's imagination, particularly since they implicated her own kids.

Belle snapped at her with words intended like a slap in the face to a hysteric: 'She'd have been better making sure she didn't get pregnant,' she said harshly, 'knowing what she might be saddling us with. Think of your kids, too. Why didn't she tell you before you got married and had children? It was unforgivable of her.'

'It wasn't like that,' Susie said, and her voice quivered. 'She didn't know. Mum didn't develop any symptoms till after she'd had us. She hadn't any idea, and when she did know, it was too late.'

'Well,' Belle said, 'what are the symptoms?' She sounded to herself like a contestant in a TV contest waiting for the announcer to milk the tension before announcing the winner.

Susie said, 'Odd jerking movements in the legs, arms and face, clumsiness, restlessness and fidgeting, hallucinations, paranoia, psychosis, loss of judgement, confusion, irritability, inability to interact with other people – injuring others or oneself . . . '

'You sound like a medical encyclopedia,' Belle said. 'It seems to me that those symptoms could apply to almost everyone.'

'I know,' Susie said, 'that's what makes waiting to find out if you've got it worse; you keep seeing signs in yourself that you've got it.'

'Gran or Grandpa must've had it, if its genetic,' Belle said. 'I know Gran died young, but Grandpa must've known.'

She was trying to take in the implications of what Susie was saying, but her first thought was to find someone to blame.

Susie said, 'Gran died in an asylum. They found out afterwards that she'd had it. She killed herself. They thought she was an alcoholic and then that she was crazy so they locked her up in a loony bin. She hanged herself. They didn't diagnose that she had Huntington's chorea till it was too late, we were grown up by then. Mum didn't have any symptoms to speak of. Or at least no symptoms which seemed significant at the time. She got depressed and she sometimes thought her brain was softening, she said, but nothing that couldn't be explained by constant worrying about money and her time of life. She thought it was the menopause. She didn't think anything of it.'

Belle thought, I've got symptoms like that which don't seem significant.

Susie was saying, 'This thing doesn't usually show until people are at least in their mid-30s.'

'Like us,' Belle said.

'Yes.'

There was a long silence, then Susie began to babble. 'It's caused by a genetic defect on one of the chromosomes which repeats itself much more often than normal in the DNA.'

She leaned towards Belle, suddenly urgent. 'There's a test. It's not certain that because one of your parents has the defect, they'll pass it on to all or any of their children. And if the child doesn't inherit it, they can't pass it on to *their* kids. It doesn't skip a generation.'

Belle was watching Susie with a kind of detached curiosity. Why was Susie so calm, knowing that she might have condemned her own children to something so hideous?

Belle asked, 'Don't you hate her for this? Don't you hate all of them down the generations who didn't put a stop to this?'

Susie slowly shook her head. She was remembering how she had felt waiting to hear if she herself was going to inherit this hateful disease. The worst part of it was knowing that she might inadvertently have condemned her precious children to a blighted life.

'She loved us so much,' she said.

'*Loved* us? You call that love? I've always known she never really loved me, anyway. And now I know why.'

Susie said slowly, 'When I didn't know if I was going to get Huntington's chorea, I found it hard to be natural with my children. For a while I didn't want to be alone with them, I felt too guilty. Everything they did reminded me of what I might've done to them. You were older than me, perhaps that's how it was with Mum, and I was too young to notice.'

Belle said, 'You've had this test.' It was a statement, not a question.

Susie nodded, and tears that had been welling in her eyes spilled as a dark stain on her peach satin thigh.

'I'm clear,' she whispered, 'me and the kids.'

All Belle's resentment against her sister welled up inside her then. Susie knew she wasn't under sentence of death. Belle thought, How dare she tell me this awful thing as though she was sharing the burden she's loading on to me?

Aloud, she said, 'I'll never forgive them, Mum or Dad. How could they do this to me? And why did they leave it to you to tell me? Dad should've said. He's the one who should have told me.' Belle knew she was sounding childish, but she couldn't find words to express how she felt.

'Dad doesn't know,' Susie said.

'How can he not know?' Belle was impatient.

'Mum didn't want him to know. Belle, you can't blame her. He'd got enough to worry about keeping a roof over all our heads. The doctor told her at first it was probably post-natal depression and she was ashamed of that because she and Dad had always wanted kids.

She ignored it as long as she could, and then when she found out she felt so guilty. She didn't want Dad to know, because of what she knew he was going to have to face. But it wasn't her fault.'

'What symptoms? I can't remember her ever being ill when I was small,' Belle said. 'She was always on the go.'

'I do remember her legs and arms sometimes seemed to have a life of their own,' Susie said. 'She couldn't remember things, and her brain always seemed muddled when she tried to think things out clearly. She was scatty. She thought other people were out to get her.' Susie paused, then added, 'She couldn't keep still, could she? Do you remember? And she and Dad used to laugh because he said she was always trying to kick him out of bed. He used to sing her that Nancy Sinatra song "These Boots Are Made for Walking", except he sang "Your Legs" instead of "These boots". Apparently not being able to keep your limbs from jerking around is part of it. It was a relief when she got pneumonia, at least she didn't have to go through things like not being able to walk or swallow or even recognize her family.'

Belle shook her head. 'She used to make funny faces,' she said, 'I remember that. When she was getting annoyed about something. I laughed at her.'

'The kids at school used to imitate her behind her back,' Susie said softly. 'I told them she was a great actress in London in her spare time and she was exercising her facial muscles to keep them in shape.' There were tears in Susie's eyes and she wiped them away with the back of her hand.

'I can't see that fooling them for long,' Belle said.

'It did, actually,' Susie said. 'They didn't think I'd bother lying to them, I suppose.'

Belle said nothing. She was trying to take in what Susie had told her, but she found it difficult to concentrate. The shock had left her confused.

'When did Mum tell you?' Belle demanded.

'About a year ago,' Susie said. 'I couldn't bear to wait and see if I developed it, I'd have been imagining I'd got the symptoms every time I got a headache. Luckily for me they found a way of testing the DNA for this genetic defect in the 1980s. Before that you just had to wait and see.'

Belle was frowning, her fingers making frenetic piano movements on the duvet cover. Susie was suddenly horribly aware of Belle's missing finger. She felt sick.

'It's almost biblical, isn't it?' Belle said. 'The sins of the parents visited on the children, even unto the umpteenth generation? It's obscene. I'm glad I never believed in God, because I can't see how anyone wouldn't lose their faith when they realized what He'd got in store for them. Just when they needed it most, too. What did John say when you told him?'

'I didn't tell John,' Susie said slowly. She seemed unsure of herself but she went on. 'I'd have told him if I had tested positive, or whatever the word is for doomed, because he'd have needed to know what would happen. But there was no point in him worrying before I was sure and there's no point in worrying him unnecessarily now.'

For a while neither of them spoke. Then Susie said, 'Mum asked me to help her die when it got too bad. But of course I could never have done that.'

'I would,' Belle said. 'She'd have been better off dead anyway. No one could face living like that.'

She was thinking, No one could face looking after someone with something that bad. Susie would have helped her die, whatever she says. Anyone would.'

Susie said, 'Well, thank God she got the pneumonia and didn't really suffer.'

How can she sound so bloody smug? Belle asked herself. Does she think God gave Mum pneumonia to make things easier for His special favourite Susie?

'How come she told you and not me?' Belle said. She sounded belligerent. She added, 'She had no right to keep something like that from me.'

'She didn't know where you were,' Susie said. 'Nor did I.'

'Dad did,' Belle said.

'But Dad didn't know about the Huntington's chorea, did he?' Susie sounded irritated. 'We hadn't any idea he'd got a number for you till Mum wanted to see you. If you were kept in the dark, you've only yourself to blame.'

Then Susie plainly thought she had gone too far. In spite of herself, she was reliving the relief she had felt when she discovered that she did not have the defective gene, but she remembered only too well how she had felt when she was first confronted by such a sentence of terrible death. All this was new to Belle. Susie reached out her hand to offer comfort to her sister. 'I could go with you to get the test?' she said gently.

Belle glared at her. 'No,' she said. 'I'd rather not know, thank you very much, I don't intend to have anything to do with it.'

She was telling herself, I do know, I don't need that test. All those incidents like tripping over nothing and crushing Miss Page's cake. And the way I can't stop my face twitching when I'm upset. And not being able to control my hands . . .

'But, Belle, if you do have it you'll need help.'

Belle gave a derisive snort. 'Counselling, you mean? Become a sort of professional invalid. No fear.'

'But – '

'There's no cure, right? So what can anyone do to make it better?'

But I can, Belle told herself, and felt something like a surge of triumph. Susie thinks she's got me where she wants me, she thought, she thinks this will wipe out the past and we'll go through this together. Fat chance of that, little sister, hell would have to freeze over before I let you off the hook.

Susie got up to leave. She couldn't think of anything to say. At the door she turned and said, 'Don't shut me out, Belle. I'm your sister, you may need me.'

'Over my dead body,' Belle muttered.

Susie tried to laugh, thinking that this was her sister's gallant attempt at bravado. She closed the door softly behind her.

1 4

Belle rang her office on the morning of her mother's funeral. The house was very quiet. Susie was doing her last-minute packing in her bedroom, and John had gone up to help her. Susie was to go home that afternoon, after the ceremony. She had prepared food and drink for the friends who wanted to come back to the farm after the church service. There were no relatives any more, except Aunt Kirsty who had never had children. Belle and Susie were the last of the line.

Their father had gone out earlier. He'd announced at breakfast that he wanted to be alone. He'd been very withdrawn for days, ever since Mum died, answering their questions in a small, neutered whisper that reminded Belle of the medium at a seance she'd once been to, who suddenly started speaking in the voice of a little girl she claimed was from the Other Side.

Belle was worried about him. He seemed to have lost all interest in the farm. She remembered how he used to be so robust about death, too. 'It's part of life,' he'd said, 'there's no point dwelling on it.' Now it was as though his passion for the farm and the animals, as well as the seasonal demands of the land that had filled his life and Mum's for so many years, had died with her. He was like a dead man himself, lost, unable to go through the motions even of an ingrained routine. The only person he was able to tolerate near him was John, but even then he seemed to be making an effort to be polite to a stranger. He ignored both Belle and Susie.

I wish he'd died instead of Mum, Belle thought. Men were so bloody helpless, and demanding with it. Mum would've been just as sad if it'd been Dad who'd died, but she wouldn't have given up on everything the way he seemed to be doing. She'd have seen it as her duty to hold everything together.

No one will have to do that when I die, Belle thought. It won't make any difference to anyone in the whole world.

For the first time, she suddenly realized that her mother was gone for ever, and she missed her with a desolation which made her double up in real pain.

'Mum?' she said aloud in panic. No answer, of course; nothing. Belle started to cry, which she hadn't done since Mum died.

The old dog, Benson, a sad-eyed Border collie, who had spent the last few days lying beside the Aga where he'd always waited in hopes that Mum would drop some titbit while she was cooking, got up unsteadily and padded across the room to lay his head on Belle's knee.

'Poor old boy,' Belle comforted him. 'You'll miss her too, won't you?'

She went upstairs to her bedroom to use her mobile to call the office.

For a moment Belle was disconcerted when it wasn't Miss Page who answered when she asked for the head of department. It was as though that last day before Dad called to say that Mum was ill had never been.

'It's Belle Adams,' she said. 'Who's this?'

'Oh Belle, this is Julia, have you heard? Something really terrible has happened.'

Julia was one of the young women who had left the pub early on the night of Sylvia's birthday. She'd had to go home to her kids because her husband was working that night. Now her voice was trembling as though she had been crying and was looking for an excuse to start again.

'What is it, Julia? What's happened.'

Belle was genuinely shocked when Julia said, 'Sylvia's dead. She's had a terrible accident.'

'Sylvia's dead?' she cried. 'What happened?'

Of course Sylvia's dead, she told herself, you know she is, how could you not realize she'd be found and it would be the talk of the office. The truth was, once it was over, Belle had never thought of the impact the woman's death would have on other people.

'It was a terrible accident, the police said,' Julia told her. 'They think it happened over the weekend.' Julia was sounding less like someone about to burst into tears as she got carried away by the thrilling enormity of her story. She sounded excited, full of self-importance. She said, 'She'd got a flat tyre on her car and she was changing the wheel and she didn't jack the car up properly. The jack slipped and she got crushed under the car.'

'God, how awful,' Belle said. 'Poor Sylvia. But what possessed her to try to change the wheel herself?'

'I know,' Julia said. 'She's the last person you'd expect, isn't she? She never managed to change the ink in the printer on her own. But I suppose there wasn't anyone around to help at the weekend and she needed to go somewhere. They didn't find her till the Monday.'

'Who found her?' Belle asked. It seemed natural to want to know that.

Julia was enjoying herself. 'Oh, Sylvia's cat was scratching on the neighbour's window and the woman went round to complain. Apparently, if Sylvia was going away, she always asked this woman to feed the cat, but Sylvia hadn't said anything about being away so she got suspicious and called the cops.'

'Wow,' Belle said, 'how awful. Poor Sylvia.'

She thought, I always knew that cat would look after itself.

Julia said, 'The funeral's tomorrow. I can give you the address if you want to go.'

'I wish I could but I can't,' Belle said. 'My mum died. I'm ringing to say I won't be coming back to work.'

'That's awful, Belle, I'm sorry. How long do you think it'll be before you're back?'

'I won't be back. That's what I rang to say.'

'You mean you're leaving?' Julie sounded astonished. 'You're not coming back to work?'

'Exactly,' Belle said. Julia's a stupid woman, she thought, all the women in the office are. Thank God I won't have to see any of them again.

'But you can't just leave,' Julia said. 'Did your mum leave you a lot of money or something?'

'No, she didn't,' Belle said. 'Tell whoever takes over from Miss Page, will you? I'll be writing a formal letter of resignation.' Then she added, 'I'm sorry about Sylvia.'

'Yes. But what can I tell people about your leaving?'

'Tell them I said goodbye, I suppose,' Belle said, and pressed the end-call button on the phone.

No one could eat any lunch, although to pass the time before they had to leave for the church, Susie had laid out cold meat and salad.

The four of them, Dad and John and Belle and Susie, sat round the kitchen table toying with the food, each dressed in dark funeral clothes which made all of them except John look unnatural and unfamiliar.

Belle thought, Susie brought a black coat and skirt with her when she came to look after Mum. She must've expected her to die.

But then she saw herself bending over Mum's bed and hearing that hoarse whisper, 'I love you, Belle, but I love Susie too. Susie's my child, whatever she did to you.'

I wonder if Mum would've said the same thing if she knew about her bringing the funeral gear? Belle asked herself. Susie's a bitch, she thought, she dragged out Mum's last miserable hours so she could tell me that. Belle smiled then because even she could see that this particular anti-Susie theory was far-fetched. Susie would never have had the guts to help Mum to die. But what about Mum? Belle asked herself, how could Mum be so disloyal? She's betrayed me, too. She couldn't even give me her love to myself, she's forced me to share with Susie. Well, I won't. Susie can have it, I want nothing to do with it. And what, after all, had that vaunted mother-love given Belle? Some genetic inheritance you've given me, Mum, Belle thought, but you managed to withhold that from Susie. If it had to be one of us, I guess we all know which of us you'd have chosen.

She drove Dad in his old Land-Rover to the village church where her parents had got married, christened their children and buried their own parents. The weight of all those memories seemed to press down on her father, who shuffled up the aisle beside her in his too-big suit, bent as though under a great burden.

Susie and John had already taken their places in the front pew. Dad sat next to Susie, and Belle sat on the aisle conscious of the crowded pews behind her full of people she didn't know, very conscious that they all of them knew her mother better than she did. She was painfully aware of the mourners here as a community from which she was excluded. They might have known her as a child, but that child had nothing to do with the woman they saw now. Belle felt as though this faded group of strangers was staring at her, whispering about her, wondering where she fitted in. She picked up the white card with the order of service and studied it protectively. Who had chosen the readings, and the hymns? It wasn't her dad, he'd been quite out of it since Mum died. Susie must have done it. Belle didn't recognize the hymns; had Mum known she was going to die and told Susie what she wanted?

The service washed over her like breaking waves of words. They seemed to have nothing to do with the woman who hadn't been able to love her elder daughter enough, the woman who's name was printed in Gothic script on the front of the order of service: Mary Felicity Adams, born 2nd March 1942, died 14th April 2007. She'd died quite young, really. Dad was ten years older than she was, but he was still going strong. He'd worn her out with the farm and everything else he'd taken for granted.

So who was this Mary Felicity Adams? She had failed as a mother to Belle, but Susie wouldn't see it that way. In her eyes, Mum was everything a mother should be. Apart from that, though? Being a mother was only part of her life, there must have been so much more that her children could never know about her. What had she wanted to do with her life? Where had she wanted to be? Had she been happy? What books had she read that made her see the world through other eyes? What had she hoped for, for herself, and for them? How had she ended up scraping a living from a dilapidated smallholding with Dad, bringing up two children? Such a life couldn't possibly be the sum of a person's dreams. Belle thought, I should feel sorry for her, that she wasted her life, but I don't.

Susie whispered to John, who sat between her and Belle, 'Poor

Mum, I can't help feeling she'd be disappointed that this is what it's come down to, all her hard work and love for us.'

John took Susie's hand. Belle was suddenly angry with the two of them. In the circumstances, she resented their sentimentality.

She hissed, 'She wasn't "Poor Mum", she was selfish. She shouldn't have had children when she'd nothing to give them except drudgery and a terminal illness.'

Belle felt John stiffen beside her and he gave her a startled look.

'What?' Susie said. 'I didn't hear. What did she say?'

'Something about how your mother lived for you two children,' John muttered. 'I think that was the gist of it.'

Susie's eyes welled with tears. 'Yes,' she said to Belle across John, 'didn't she always put the family first?'

Belle was about to say something but she met John's eyes and changed her mind. She wished she had kept quiet.

No one wanted to come back to the house after the service. They were all asked, but one after another they made their excuses. Belle thought it was because of her that they didn't want to come to their dead friend's house. She was a threat to the memories they treasured, an alien presence that offended their rituals of grieving.

At the church gate Susie said, 'I've got to go, if I get caught in the rush-hour traffic it'll take me hours.'

John opened the car door for her and she kissed him goodbye. 'Look after Dad,' she said. 'I'll ring when I get home.'

The vicar, a military-looking man with a little beard that Belle assumed was a small gesture of defiance against the dusty image of penurious religiosity, came up to speak to Dad.

'You look as if you could do with a pint, Tom,' the vicar said. 'And I'd like to drink Mary's health.'

It was an invitation that excluded Belle and John. The vicar smiled at them. 'It'll do him good, a few drinks with some of his and Mary's old friends. Just people from the village, you understand? Don't worry, I'll drop him home later.'

'That's kind of you,' Belle said. 'I've got to get back to do the afternoon milking, but a few drinks with old friends will do Dad good.'

She thought, I sound like a school matron or a prison guard. 'What about you, John, Dad would like to have you along.'

'Not today,' John said. 'I think today's a time for remembering old times.' He added to the vicar, 'But another time . . . '

The vicar smiled and shook hands.

Susie had taken their car, so John climbed up beside Belle on to the bench seat of the old Land-Rover.

'Do you want to drive?' she asked. He looked to her like the type of man who didn't like being driven.

He seemed to read her thoughts, and laughed. 'I'm a cop,' he said; 'my sergeant's a woman and she does most of the driving. She's the best driver I know, far better at it than me.'

'Sorry,' Belle said. She was embarrassed because he must think her old-fashioned. In passing, she noted as odd that it mattered to her what John thought. Perhaps it's because he's Susie's husband, she told herself, but she knew that wasn't it. She wanted to impress this man. She liked him.

She drove badly, crashing the stiff gears, seemingly unable to help herself. 'Sorry,' she kept saying.

When they reached the farm at last, he jumped down and opened the Land-Rover door for her, handing her out.

'Thank you, kind sir,' she said, suddenly feeling as though she were much younger and two stone lighter.

He followed her into the house. Susie had laid out the plates of sandwiches and trays of drink on the table in the dining-room, a dining-room which was scarcely ever used. The stuffy smell of a shut-up room conflicted with the sharp tang of ham and sliced tomatoes.

'I'm starving,' John said, 'I feel as if I haven't eaten for a week.'

'Me too,' Belle said. 'Ham sandwiches and whisky – just what the doctor ordered.'

But they took their food and glasses of whisky through to the kitchen. There was something unwelcoming about the formality of the dining-room. And all that food laid out for guests who hadn't come was a painful reminder of what day it was. In the kitchen they could relax. Belle fed Benson pieces of her sandwich, and John offered him a drop of whisky in a saucer.

'Thank God that's over,' Belle said. Then she thought she sounded hard-bitten. John was probably sentimental about death and dying. 'I mean the ceremony,' she said, 'all the trappings of death; they don't seem to have anything to do with the person who's gone.'

'Going through the motions helps a lot of people,' John said. 'But I know what you mean.'

Belle started to get up from the table. 'It'll be time for milking soon,' she said. 'I must get changed.'

'I'll help with the milking,' he said. 'Just tell me what to do.'

So they sat on for a while in a companionable silence, listening to the sounds of the old house settling around them.

Belle said suddenly, 'I'm sorry about what I said in the church, when you lied to Susie for me. I don't know what got into me.'

'Think nothing of it,' John said, 'we all think grief's simple, but it takes people in different ways. Any paramedic will tell you of times when someone dies suddenly and the wife – it's usually wives, not husbands – isn't overcome with grief, but furious with the dead person for abandoning her.'

'They're scared of being left to fend for themselves, I expect,' Belle said. 'Women's lot is not a happy one.'

'I'm afraid you may be right,' John said. 'Women over a certain age, anyway,'

'Well, that's not why I'm angry,' Belle said. 'I think I feel guilty, but I don't know why.'

'I think Susie does too.'

'Does she? I don't know why she should.' Belle didn't want to talk about Susie.

There was silence for a while. Belle was suddenly aware of the ticking of the grandfather clock in the hall. She wondered if her dad had remembered to wind it on this day of all days. Probably Susie had done it, it was the sort of thing she'd do to try to make everything as normal as possible.

John said at last, 'Can I ask you something?'

Belle nodded.

'What happened to your hand?'

She stiffened, then took a swig of whisky. She didn't answer for so long that John thought he had offended her.

He started to say, 'I'm so sorry, I didn't mean . . . '

'No, it's all right,' she said. 'Most people don't ask, that's all, so you took me by surprise. Susie did it. We were kids, playing cowboys and Indians, and she got an axe and cut my finger off.'

'My God,' John said, 'what a terrible accident. Susie must've felt awful.'

'Well, I know I did,' Belle said. 'I've never liked the sight of blood since. We were only kids, and Susie was always a bit of a drama queen. I think she thought it was rather interesting.'

'Well, I suppose a child thinks as a child; she can't have had any idea what she'd done, really,' John said.

Belle wished she hadn't made him feel he had to apologize for Susie. 'I don't suppose she did,' she said, 'and since she's never really grown up, I think she still doesn't.'

John looked taken aback by Belle's tone. Before he could defend Susie, Belle went on, 'Susie's never had to take the consequences of anything she's done,' she said, 'she's always been protected from that. First it was Mum and Dad, and now I suppose it's you. Everyone forgives Susie, whatever she does.'

Belle knew she sounded bitter, and that this was a mistake. John stared at her in surprise, and she knew he thought she was disloyal to her little sister. Belle asked herself, Where did that assumption of loyalty come from? Why did people expect their close relatives to support each other, whatever they did?

And then she thought, Why does Susie impinge on everything I do, even on John and me now, two friends having a drink before we go out to do the milking? I can't even tell her husband about how Susie disfigured me without her getting the sympathy. It's not fair, no, not at all bloody fair.

15

It was late the day of the funeral. Belle and her father had long ago gone upstairs to bed, leaving John alone in the kitchen. He felt too weary to drag himself upstairs. It had been a long day. The old man had been drunk when the vicar brought him home; he'd been cantankerous, looking for an argument. Then Belle said she'd had enough and went to her room. After that, her father had had nothing to say. He declined John's offer of help and stamped upstairs.

John stretched out his legs in front of the Aga and felt that he belonged in this place, something he had never felt before on previous visits. He kicked off his shoes and his stockinged feet began to steam from the heat of the stove. Then Benson got unsteadily to his feet and went to the back door, asking to be let out. John pulled on his shoes and got up to go out with the old dog into the yard.

The air was clear, but not cold. It was refreshing after the heat of the Aga in the kitchen. John walked slowly across the yard breathing in deeply the night air scented with the sweet smell of animals and clean straw. He could hear the gentle grumbling of chickens in the darkness as the sound of his footsteps disturbed them.

'It's all right,' he said softly, 'I'm not a fox.'

He leaned against the gate into the field where earlier that evening he and Belle had released the cows to make their way to their pasture after milking. Now John looked up at the sky and was astonished at the number and brightness of the stars. The sight struck him with genuine surprise. At home in the suburbs the sky never looked vast like this, vast and romantic, the stars like millions of diamonds sewn on to black velvet.

He wished that Susie were here with him. He had left his mobile in the house or he would have rung her to involve her with him in the magnificence of the night. Even as a young copper on night duty, he had never realized that the sky was a landscape of it's own, a secret world normally hidden behind the sun.

And then he wondered if Belle, who had left all this to go to the city, felt the same awe he did; if now, on her return to her family home, she looked out of her bedroom window to see the fantastic world of the night.

John was glad to have met Belle at last. He had long been curious about her because the family seemed to make such a mystery of her. Over the years since he and Susie had been together, he had gleaned very little about the sort of person Belle was. It was as though Susie didn't know her at all, although she and Belle had grown up together. Indeed, it had been ages before he even knew that his wife had a sister. Susie never volunteered any information about her, and if he asked the odd direct question, she fobbed him off with vague answers. All this had only fuelled his curiosity. He'd tried to imagine what had happened between them. A row, perhaps, or some silly incident that Susie had interpreted as some sort of betrayal. John loved his wife, but he knew from bitter experience in their marriage that Susie was quick to take offence. Once she'd calmed down and had second thoughts, she was eager to admit when she was wrong, but perhaps Belle hadn't given her the chance. It had long seemed to John that some old resentment festered between them.

But now that he had met this mysterious Belle, he was puzzled. She was so different from the version of her he had created from Susie's reaction to any mention of her sister. He hadn't found Belle in the least daunting or aggressive. Listening to Susie, he had expected some kind of cross between a sergeant-major and an old-fashioned school matron. But Belle wasn't like that. She was shy and unsure of herself, as though she took it for granted that people weren't going to like her. Was she like that, John asked himself, because Susie was always loved and fêted? It must've been tough when Belle was young, he thought, always to see herself as a disappointment to everyone she met.

But that's nonsense, John thought, she can't be that silly. Belle's got lots going for her, Susie's not in competition with her.

John had, from the moment he met her, taken it for granted that his wife was very beautiful. No one he knew had ever questioned it. She was slim and elegant and moved like a cat; she also had a cat's green eyes and thick tawny hair. She wasn't vain, though. She had the air always of being a little surprised at her own beauty, as though she knew it was not of her making, but that she had been specially chosen by God or Nature to display it. That modest pleasure in herself added to her charm.

Perhaps unwittingly, Susie had given John the impression that Belle was ugly. She hadn't said that exactly, but he had gathered from what his wife had said that Belle was built like a navvy and was deliberately careless of her appearance.

So he had been startled to recognize as soon as he saw Belle that she and Susie were actually quite similar to look at. True, Belle was somewhat overweight and imposingly tall, but they had the same noses, their mouths were the same shape, the bone structure of their faces almost identical except in scale. At second glance, though, the similarity disappeared, and so far John had not recaptured that first fleeting impression. He had been trying ever since that first meeting with Belle to define why the sisters now seemed to him so dissimilar. It was as though they were before and after pictures of the same person for some advertising promotion for an elixir of life. In Belle the cat's eyes were expressionless, almost colourless, while in Susie they were full of flashing emerald fire; Belle laughed and no one took any notice, but Susie's smile filled everyone who saw it with joy and a sense of excitement. Susie made even strangers feel glad to be alive; Belle did not.

But Belle wasn't ugly, far from it. She was plain because that's the way she saw herself. John told himself, Belle doesn't like herself, she has no love in her. It's Susie's soul that shines through and makes it impossible not to be drawn to her. And then he thought, If Belle has got a soul at all, she keeps it buried too deep for anyone to see it.

He liked his new-found sister-in-law though. She intrigued him. He wanted to know more about what had happened to make her cut herself loose from her family. There was something exciting about her detachment, drama in her unwillingness to pander to other people's expectations. She left him guessing about what she was capable of doing or saying. He felt that she wasn't particularly impressed by, or interested in, other people, but he guessed that the self-confidence she should have got from that was undermined because she was unsure of who and what she herself really was.

He was looking forward to getting to know her better over the coming days. And in a way he was glad that Susie would not be around. Perhaps without Susie's obviously inhibiting effect on Belle, John thought, I may discover the real person who is Susie's long-lost sister. If she'll let me, he added as an afterthought.

Benson started to bark at the back door, wanting to get back into the warm.

John turned and walked across the yard to the house. He didn't want Benson to wake Belle or her father, he wanted to be alone for a while longer. There was something about the quality of the night in this remote place under that huge impersonal sky which made him feel that he was on the brink of some sort of breakthrough in his understanding of a dormant secret he had to discover about himself.

'Silly old sod,' he said, opening the door for Benson and following the collie into the kitchen. And then he smiled because he knew that he was not talking to the dog, but to himself.

16

Belle got up early, before the alarm clock went off. She swung her legs over the edge of the bed and sat up. There was something odd going on. She looked out of the window across the lawn towards the vegetable garden where the greenhouse glass was catching the first morning sun. There were blackbirds fighting on the grass, and a green woodpecker like an automaton pecking the path.

Everything looked exactly the same as usual, but Belle could not rid herself of the feeling that there was something special about this day. After years of getting up unwillingly, and starting the day's routine as a sort of penance, today she was eager to get out into the sunshine and launch an attack on the many things that needed doing on the land. Where she was used to going through pointless motions in the office, this day held out the promise of real achievement.

This was where she belonged, as a leader getting the best out of a staff of natural things. Here she shone. And today John would be there to give her her due. Today, Susie's magnetic charms would seem like tinsel against Belle's display of practical skill and physical attainment. Belle could initiate him into the secrets of survival, expand his consciousness where Susie could never venture. Within a week, Belle told herself, he would see Susie as insipid and light-weight, a toy, merely a toy in a world that demanded real weapons.

She knew, of course, that she was day-dreaming. But all the same, she believed that she could make John take her seriously. And that, at this early stage, was what she needed.

She pulled on jeans and a sweater and went out to start milking. As she went downstairs, she heard Dad in the bathroom.

'All right, Dad?' she called.

'You go on,' he said through the door, 'I'll be with you shortly.'

Thank God, he sounded alive again. She gave thanks to the vicar and the old men in the pub last night who had apparently revived something of his will to live.

She picked up her gumboots and turned them upside down before she pushed her feet into them. Once, years ago, there'd been a mouse inside, and the memory of its sudden wriggling under her toes still made her shiver. Belle could be squeamish. She didn't see this as odd in someone who had killed three people without qualms, someone who was also planning to destroy another, this time her own sister. For a moment, she had forgotten about all that; she was aware only that today she would be with John. The hours ahead seemed full of promise.

She let out the chickens on the way to the cowshed. The cockerel burst out, trying his sideways sashay on one after another of his squawking hens.

Belle laughed. The cock seemed never to give up, although the hens kept out of his way so easily. Only from time to time when one stopped to suck a worm from the ground did he manage to jump on her and have his way.

Belle felt that someone was watching her. She suddenly felt cold because she'd let her guard drop. She couldn't do that. It didn't matter so much here, perhaps, but she had trained herself not to let it happen, ever, and for a moment it had. It was a warning. She couldn't afford to relax.

John was standing in the doorway of the cowshed. He was wearing a very old pair of men's dungarees which seemed too small for him. She recognized them as an old pair she used to wear in the old days round the farm.

'Where did you find those?' she asked as she came up to him.

'They were hanging on the back of the kitchen door,' he said. 'I thought I couldn't look more ridiculous in them than I would in my funeral suit.'

She laughed. 'Those were once my old dungarees,' she said. 'I used to be rather on the big side. I've lost a bit of weight since I last got into them.'

It gave her a buzz that he was wearing her old clothes, even a garment as unsexy as her old dungarees.

The first cows were already in their stalls, waiting for the milking machine to be fixed to their udders.

'You've done well,' she said, impressed. 'How did you know what to do?'

'I didn't, but they did,' John said. 'They made it very clear. But they couldn't tell me how to turn on the machine, so I had to wait for your help.'

She showed him what to do, and by the time her dad came into the shed, a little unsteady but looking happier than he had for ages, the cows were on their way out to the field for the day.

What right does he have to be happy? Belle found herself thinking. The wife he was supposed to be so close to knew her bloody brain was wasting away and he didn't know. And then she thought, Is this one of the symptoms, hating everyone and wanting them to suffer? She found herself glaring at her father.

'Oh, Belle, I've missed you,' the old man said, not noticing her expression. He turned to John, 'We used to milk one hundred and fifty cows every morning, Belle and me,' he told him; 'this is like the old days.'

'Except I don't have to rush off to school now, thank God,' Belle said. 'At least those days are over.'

But in spite of herself she enjoyed working round the farm again. She helped her dad start the old Ferguson tractor. He was going to roll the field he would be cutting for silage in a few weeks' time.

'Don't you make hay any more?' she asked, nostalgic for the remembered scent of herb-filled dried grass in the air.

'No one does round here any more,' her dad said. 'It's too dodgy with the weather. I don't miss that part of it.'

Belle smiled. She remembered too. Those few weeks in late June or July had been a nightmare, looking for a run of dry days to cut, turn and dry the mown grass. She remembered the blisters on her palms and thumbs from the binder twine holding the hay bales together and the sweat dripping into her eyes and down her nose.

But the drying grasses had been so beautiful, all shades of green from lime to jade; and it smelled so good, too, better than any perfume. Silage stank.

'Oh well,' she said, 'times change . . . '

She and John worked on the hedges which were supposed to protect the garden from the paddocks nearest to the house. The young heifers had broken through again and again, and done a lot of damage in the vegetable patch. Dad had tried to block the gaps in the hedges, but the heifers simply found another weak point.

Belle was good at this. She layered young elm trees into the hedge, and thinned out the overgrown hazel to weave the saplings around the stakes which John cut with a billhook and drove into the ground with Dad's old beetle.

'You know,' he said, 'meeting you has made me realize that Susie and you had really quite an unusual upbringing.'

'Did we?' Belle asked. She gave him a sideways look, wondering if her were making fun of her.

'Well, yes,' John said. 'You must admit, not many young women your age grew up in an old-fashioned place like this, living like peasants from the old days, milking cows by hand and using beetles and that sort of thing. It's like something out of the Middle Ages.'

'Oh, I don't know,' Belle said, trying to keep her voice non-committal. 'My parents were into the self-sufficiency thing. I suppose I never thought about it.'

'But you must've known other kids your age were . . . well . . . different.'

'I didn't know any other kids. I never made friends at school, partly because I went to school in the town ten miles away which made getting home in the evening difficult. So I could never stay after school for social things. Not that I wanted to, I didn't think much of the other kids. Ask Susie, she went to the local school in the village. She knew people.'

'Why did you go to different schools?'

Belle wished that John would stop asking questions, but of course he didn't. He wasn't a policeman for nothing.

'I didn't want to go to the same school as Susie,' she said in a flat voice to show that she wanted to change the subject. But it wasn't true, she didn't want to change the subject, she wanted him to make her tell him things she had never admitted to anyone else, even to herself. She added, 'I made a fuss, and in the end they let me go on my own.'

'Why did it matter so much?' John asked.

Belle again wanted to refuse to answer, but she also wanted to tell him, to explain things about herself which she was certain he would understand.

'Oh,' she said, 'it's hard to explain. And it's a long time ago.' She hesitated, then went on, 'I wanted to be a person on my own, not Susie Adams's big sister, or the elder Adams kid or whatever. I didn't want to be judged as part of a family, I wanted to stand on my own. And I didn't want to have to take responsibility for who Susie was and what she did because she was my sister, you know the way people expect in families.'

John was looking at her thoughtfully and she burst out, 'I wanted to escape from bloody Susie, OK?'

'Why did you feel like that? You were older than her, anyway, I'd have thought she'd be the one who'd feel in your shadow.'

'Maybe, but she was the one everyone measured me against. And by all their measurements, she came out on top. Except for animals and working on the farm. But no one wanted to know about that. Everyone took it for granted that I should think myself lucky to have her for a sister, but I didn't feel like that.'

'But why? She was just a kid, what made you feel the way you did?'

Belle looked at his expression. If there was a hint that he was shocked or critical of her childhood feelings, she told herself that she would never speak to him again. But he seemed genuinely interested, trying to understand the angst of a pre-teenage girl. Belle thought in passing that his Kim was a lucky kid, with a father like John. And no sister, only an older brother.

She said, trying to find words to explain, 'Oh, I don't know, it was just a fact of life for me.' She hesitated, and then the words came out in a rush. 'I was always expected to look after Susie, take her with me, make sure she was all right. I resented that. They were the ones who had her, it was up to them. I didn't want to have any part in her. They'd no right to make me into some kind of keeper for Susie . . . '

For a moment Belle was afraid she was going to burst into tears. With hindsight it all seemed so childish, but for her it was still only too real. What she was saying might make her sound horrible, or ridiculous, but she remembered clearly how miserable she'd felt at the time and she was engulfed by self-pity. She took a few deep breaths and then said more calmly, 'My parents weren't like other people, I suppose, but I didn't know that at the time. They were just Mum and Dad. They created this sort of self-contained family unit where they supported themselves off the land and raised a few pigs and sheep to eat, and they didn't want or need anyone outside. They were more than self-sufficient, they were self-contained.'

'It's the sort of life a lot of people dream of,' John said.

'Fine,' Belle said. 'Fine for them, anyway, they were totally wrapped up in each other. They never went out, or had people over, they didn't want to. They didn't want to have any kind of life outside, and they never even considered what that meant for me and Susie. We'd got each other, what more did we need? That's how they saw it.'

Belle felt the old anger boiling up inside her so that she wanted to lash out at everyone and everything. Even John, with his soothing way of asking intrusive questions as though he really cared what had happened to her.

'OK,' he said, 'but why do you blame Susie? It wasn't her fault. If anyone should be resentful, surely it should be her, if she felt they'd had her just as a playmate for you?'

Belle shook her head. 'I might have known you wouldn't even try to understand,' she said. 'I hated her because they had each other and they fobbed me off with her.'

The words were out of Belle's mouth before she had even thought what she really wanted to say. Whatever it might have been, it wasn't what she'd said.

She laughed and quickly tried to make mockery of her nonsense. At least, it seemed important that he should think it was nonsense. 'I'm talking rubbish,' she said. 'You do realize that, don't you? We'd best get back to work, I'd like to finish this stretch before lunch.'

They worked on, but in silence now. It was hard physical labour, and they were neither of them used to it. The virtuous ache in muscles she'd almost forgotten she had brought back more memories: this was how as a teenager she'd worked with Dad in the fields. She remembered the satisfaction of helping him to impose control on the chaotic exuberance of Nature. And how smug she'd felt when the two of them went home to the supper Mum always had waiting and the table Susie had invariably decorated with a bowl of flowers she'd picked from the garden. Pretty touches like that were Susie's thing, the expression of the eternal feminine; Belle felt her own superiority then, her victory over her gender, uniting the divided self that imprisoned women like Mum and Susie and chauvinistic men like Dad. And yet Dad always made a point of noticing Susie's flowers where he never said a word in praise of Belle for all the hours she'd worked with him on the land.

It had seemed so clear to her then, before contact outside with strangers in the wider world blurred those clear outlines of her teenage prejudices. Belle had never caught up with the Susies of the world after that, not once sex and work and money made nonsense of the boundaries of individual personality which still seemed to Belle should be tamed like a well-laid hedge around her psyche.

Such thoughts depressed her now. Ignoring John, she worked on in a world of her own until the sound of the tractor approaching broke her concentration.

'I reckon we're nearly there,' John said, stepping back to survey their work. 'It feels good being able to see a result like this, doesn't it?'

The sun had caught his face and his forehead and nose looked red. His T-shirt showed damp patches of sweat. There were long scratches on his arms, drops of blood like morse code written down where brambles had caught him.

Belle thought of how she must look herself.

'I must look a sight,' she said. 'It was worth it, though.'

The tractor reached them and stopped. Dad jumped down and walked up and down surveying their work.

'You've done a good job,' he said. 'That'll hold those young heifers.'

He spoke to John. Belle had to presume she was included, but at least John seemed to understand that she felt hurt.

'What a team we are, Belle and me,' he told Dad. 'She managed to make me think I knew what I was doing.'

'Yes,' he said, 'you want to have Belle on your side when things get tough.'

Belle thought, What does he mean by that? But then she told herself she was being paranoid.

John drove the tractor back to the yard, for practice, while Dad and Belle piled the hedging tools into the Land-Rover and followed.

'What did you mean about having me on your side when things get tough, Dad?' she asked. 'Was that some sort of point you wanted to make?'

He gave her a quick sideways look before the ruts in the track forced him to concentrate on where the Land-Rover was going.

'It was just something to say,' he said.

17

Belle had forgotten the irrelevance of time on the farm. Hours and dates and days of the week have nothing to do with the natural routine. Get up at dawn for milking because the cows demand it; feed animals when they are hungry; eat when the body makes it clear that food and a break will renew vigour for the next task. And shut up the chickens before dark brings out the foxes and the scavenging badgers. Badgers, so beloved by city folk, were marauding pests on the farm.

There was always so much to do that Belle was surprised when Dad said, 'It's Saturday night. Why don't you go down to the pub for a pint?'

They were finishing a meal which John had cooked. The sausages were burned black and he hadn't washed the potatoes properly, so the mash had a muddy taste.

Dad said to John, 'You could take Belle. It's not seemly for a woman to go into a pub alone, and I don't think I'm quite up to it yet. It wouldn't look right.'

'Oh Dad, for God's sake, I don't believe you said that,' Belle said. 'If

I fancy a drink I'll go in the pub and have one, whatever those old killjoys in the village think.'

'Of course you will,' John said, 'but I'd like a few pints myself after the last few days I've had, and I look forward to the slave driver buying the first round.' He smiled at Belle, then said to Dad, 'Are you sure you don't want to come? You'd make us feel less like outsiders.'

'You are outsiders,' Dad said, 'you and Belle both, in spite of her being brought up here. It's not the same as it used to be. You two will fit in fine with the Saturday night crowd they get in there, but I don't. Time enough for me to go down there when you've both moved on.'

Belle was about to protest, but John got up, scraping back his chair to distract her. 'Right,' he said, 'we'll be off. Don't want to lose good drinking time.'

He's like a bloody schoolteacher in primary school trying to divert the class bully who's about to pick a fight with some nerdy kid, she thought, and felt outraged. He thinks I'm a bully, she told herself, and was shocked.

'Don't park the Land-Rover on a slope without leaving it in gear,' Dad said. 'The hand brake's not all it should be these days.'

'It never was,' Belle said. She wanted him to know that she was still irritated with him. 'And you can do the washing-up. It's time you started looking after yourself, you can't go on being a baby for ever.'

Dad waved his hand dismissively as they went out.

You see, Belle wanted to say to John, Dad doesn't take me seriously, he knows it's just banter. Why can't you lighten up?

John laughed. For a moment, Belle thought he knew what she was thinking; then she realized that he was laughing because he understood that her father was making fun of her.

'Oh, come on then,' she said, and went out to the Land-Rover.

Belle had never been inside the pub in the village. Of course as a youngster she'd looked through the lighted windows at night to discover what went on in a place Mum and her friends seemed to think was a den of iniquity. Nothing ever seemed to happen while Belle was watching, though. There'd been a barmaid, but she was scarcely a scarlet woman, being the landlord's wife, and a plump middle-aged grandmother who's one concession to glamour was to have her hair permed in tight little rolls at Neville's in the nearest town every six weeks. Otherwise, a few old men played darts or dominoes, a local farmer or two chatted at the bar, and sometimes in the summer cricketers from the local teams went in for a pint after a match. They gave way to rugby players later in the year, and then often the sound of them singing their rollicking songs reverberated like a distant loudspeaker in the quiet darkness long after the villagers had gone to bed.

It was different now. The clientele were all from outside the village, most of them, anyway. They were mainly couples who had come to eat, not drink. They came by car, and there were CCTV cameras in the car park. Inside, the bar had been moved into a corner, and a few men in golden cord trousers and blazers sat there on stools buying each other shorts, with dry white wine for what some of them called the 'little ladies' sitting together at the tables.

There was a prominent sign banning dogs except guide dogs. The management also retained the right to refuse service.

'I wish it hadn't changed,' Belle said as they took their drinks to a table and sat down.

John said, 'Sorry, I missed that.'

'Oh,' Belle said, 'take no notice of me. It's a bit of a shock how this place has changed. Brings me smack up against my own mortality, I suppose. That and Mum dying and Dad being like something left over from another age.'

'Hey,' he said, 'we came here to have a bit of fun. It's not all doom and gloom, you know.'

'You're a cop, how would you know?' Belle said. And then she thought, He says that because he's married to Susie and they're happy.

'I love my job,' he said. 'That's your trouble, you've not found your *métier* in life.'

Belle laughed. 'Get you,' she said, 'my *métier*, eh? No, you're probably right; I'm unemployed and the world should be my oyster and I don't know what the hell to do next.'

'You'd make a good cop, I think,' John said. 'It would be something worth while. Why don't you think of that?'

Belle laughed again. She thought, Me, a cop? I've killed three people and he thinks I'd be a good cop!

'I think I'd be a better criminal,' she said. 'I used to be afraid I'd end up as a murderer. Mum always said about me that I'd get away with murder one day.'

Careful, she told herself, careful.

John met her eyes and held them although she tried to look away. 'That's as good a qualification for a policeman as any, I'd say,' he said, and smiled.

'Do many people get away with murder, do you think?' she asked. 'Is there such a thing as the perfect murder?'

She was curious to hear what he thought. He was a detective, after all, he must know the tricks of the trade. Apart from fitting people up, of course.

He took her question seriously. 'Most people are murdered by their nearest and dearest,' he said. 'That makes things easier for us. Or there's an obvious motive.'

'But what about motiveless murder, or people who are killed by strangers?' Belle insisted. 'How can they *not* get away with it?'

'Most murderers make a mistake. Most of them are stupid, I think, but even so, why would anyone kill without a reason? Anyone sane, at least.'

'Ah,' she said, 'so you think murderers who get away with it are insane? That sounds like sour grapes to me.'

John finished his drink before he answered. 'I didn't say that,' he said, 'and you know I didn't. Humans don't kill to keep in practice, we're not cats, or even foxes. What are you driving at, anyway?'

Stop this, you're being stupid, she told herself, but she could not stop.

'Perhaps people die and the police don't even know they've been murdered because there doesn't seem to be a suspect or a motive.'

John said, 'It's possible in theory, I suppose, but I don't know if it really happens . . . '

'You mean there aren't any statistics to cover it,' Belle said, and she sounded more sarcastic than she'd intended. She knew she had to change the direction of this conversation. If she carried on, she was afraid she couldn't resist the urge to hint at what she'd done, even to confess to him. She felt he was the first person she'd ever met who would understand and be impressed by the artistry of her fearful acts. Why should Susie have him to herself, he was much too good for her. Belle wanted to impress him, really wanted it as a way of expunging his relationship with Susie, rubbing out the ordinariness of love and marriage and intimacy with admiration and awe for something extraordinary, a transcendent achievement, her achievement. Never mind that what she'd done was monstrous, John at least would know that she was supreme.

'Oh, statistics!' he said. 'Statistics will prove anything.'

'They probably prove that everything about this pub is an improvement on the business in the old days,' she said sadly, 'but that doesn't make it true.'

They sat for a while watching a fat little man at the next table. He was wearing a bow tie, but before he ate he had loosened it and the two ends hung down so that every time he leaned forward to take a mouthful, they dangled in his plate and dripped red sauce like blood down the front of his shirt. He hadn't noticed.

The woman with this fat little man sat staring stonily ahead, not saying a word.

'Then again,' John said, 'there are motives and motives. Who's to say what drives people to want to kill each other?' He grinned at Belle and her eyes filled with tears because this small intimacy made her suddenly desperate for something more.

'I've had enough of this place,' she said, 'let's go home. You drive.' She didn't want to give him the chance to see her face.

18

There were no lights downstairs when Belle and John got back to the farm, though there was a glow behind the closed curtains in Dad's bedroom. He'd be awake still, reading a book. Belle remembered that. Her mother had complained that he kept her awake. He read the same books over and over again. Richard Hannay thrillers, and Sherlock Holmes. Familiarity breeds content, Belle thought, and there wasn't much in Hannay or Holmes to remind him painfully of Mum.

In the kitchen the old dog Benson looked up from his place beside the Aga and lifted his tail to greet them, but he didn't get up.

'Don't you ever lock the doors round here?' John asked.

'No one does. It's way too far off the beaten track for your common or garden opportunistic burglar,' Belle said, but then she thought, That's probably another thing that's changed for the worse, nothing's too far off the beaten track for burglars these days. Remoteness is an opportunity in itself.

John looked round the kitchen as though to make sure nothing had been stolen.

Belle flushed, embarrassed that John was thinking there was nothing worth stealing anyway. She thought how shabby the place must look to him.

But then he said, 'There are some really valuable things in here, you know. People pay a fortune for genuine oil lamps like those, and the earthenware jars. They call it kitchenalia and the interior designers go mad for it.'

'They're welcome to it,' Belle said. 'As far as I'm concerned, good riddance to the days of wringers and washboards and cooking on a range, give me washer-dryers and microwave ovens and central heating at the touch of a button. I'm not into nostalgia.'

'That's because you were brought up really using those things, you're not just trying to recapture folk memories,' John said. 'Susie was the same as you when we first married, but now she's started collecting old stuff. She's always saying, "We used to have stone hot-water bottles like that at home," or butter churns, or whatever, and she has to have them. She never uses them, but that's not the point.'

'She wouldn't know how,' Belle said; 'she never did a hand's turn round the place anyway.'

John missed the sour note in Belle's voice. He thought her sarcastic tone was affectionate. That kind of banter was exactly what he expected from sisters. He smiled at Belle as though he and she were united in indulgent fondness for Susie.

'I'm going to turn in,' Belle said. 'I'm not used to all that fresh air and exercise I had today.' Indeed she felt so stiff that she was afraid to walk away because she was moving like an automaton. After all,

John was the city boy, she was the one who was supposed to take farm work in her stride.

'Me too,' John said. 'I left my mobile upstairs and I want to call Susie. I can tell her how I've turned into a real son of the soil.'

Belle gave him a peck on the cheek as she passed him. She was as startled as he was; usually she avoided contact with anyone, except for sex.

What are you doing? she asked herself. She was shocked at how much she'd wanted him to kiss her back. She wanted him to make love to her. She wanted him.

'You sure fooled me,' she said. 'I had you down as a soft city boy.'

It was cold in Belle's bedroom. She'd forgotten how cold the house got at night, which was fine in high summer, but not now.

She remembered how, when she and Susie shared this room as children, their white breath in the freezing air had made them look like characters in cartoon strips talking to each other. They'd had narrow single beds then, with stiff ironed cotton sheets which held them flat and rigid under the bedclothes like letters in envelopes. They'd laughed at each other, pretending to be the marble effigies of Lord and Lady Tarlington laid out with folded hands and their toes turned up on their tomb in the abbey in town. One Easter Mum had taken them to a service there and they sat near the tomb, and she'd caught Susie's eye and Susie had had a fit of giggles and Mum had slapped her face. Actually slapped her face. Someone would've called the police if they saw something like that these days.

Belle got into bed and pulled the covers up to her chin. The mattress felt damp, and there was a slightly musty smell from the pink blankets. She wondered how long the bed had been waiting before Mum got ill, fully-prepared for someone to sleep in it. Not as long, perhaps, as Lord and Lady Tarlington had rested side by side on their Abbey tomb, but long enough.

What had happened to the old single beds? Had Susie taken them for Jonty and Kim, part of her nostalgia kick like the butter churn and the stone hot-water bottles. Belle remembered them, those stone hot-water bottles. She'd wrapped hers in her jumper so as not to burn her feet. Otherwise she got blisters. And, thank God, she didn't have to put on ice-cold clothes in the morning, if her jumper was still just warm from the bottle.

Somewhere in the house a door banged. Dad going to the bathroom, probably, or John. Going to bed in this house must be worse for John than for her, he'd never been used to it. He must think we're savages, Belle thought.

But at least she and John had had fun in the pub that evening. The other people had been funny, they were so awful. And John was so easy to talk to.

Belle thought, I wish I could really talk to him, tell him the truth, tell him what I've done, killing those two people I didn't even know, really. And Ben, she thought, I killed Ben too.

But Ben was different, just as one day Susie would be different. She knew that she would never be able to explain – perhaps even to herself – how Ben had wounded her by making love to Susie. He had dealt her a mortal blow and she had no choice but to defend herself against anything like that ever happening again. No, she told herself, I don't need to unburden myself about Ben, but those other two? They were a threat to me because they knew too much. But perhaps they didn't know anything that could really threaten me, she told herself, I was just afraid of what they could do to me by accident.

She thought, I wish I could tell him how miserable it makes me not to be able to feel guilty about what I've done. If I could tell him, I'd know from his reaction if the way I am is normal. He'd know that, being a cop.

And then she told herself, Even a cop wouldn't think of murder as normal. I want to talk to John like sinners confess to priests, I want to tell him that what really makes me feel bad is that killing them was so easy.

She took a deep breath and said aloud but under her breath, 'I enjoyed it. I liked doing it and then getting away with it.'

Those people, the man from Tooting and Sylvia, meant nothing to her; she felt nothing for them, no emotion at all that they were dead. It was easier to make sure they couldn't give her away by killing them than it would have been to spend the future in fear.

And now she was facing a future of fear because of some stupid gene passed on to her by a mother she'd never have chosen as a parent. And there was nothing she could do to help herself, no one she could silence to make the fear go away. Except Susie, of course, Susie who had been spared.

Or so she thinks, Belle told herself, trying to find comfort in the thought.

She tried to decide how she would feel if Susie had not been cleared, if she'd had to live in suspense, waiting for the onset of her brain's degeneration.

I'd be doing her a favour killing her then, Belle thought. I'd be disappointed.

But would she really? She felt too confused even to try to gather her thoughts.

She went to open the window and leaned out, taking deep breaths of the cold night air. It felt so clean, so cleansing, that she didn't realize how cold she was until her whole body started to judder and she had to cling to the window sill to make herself still.

When she felt calmer she closed the window and went back to bed. She thought, I just want one person in the world to understand me and that one person is John.

Why do I care what he thinks? she asked herself. Why can't I stop brooding about him? And then she thought, I'm in love with him, I didn't know what love meant till now.

It was true, she had fallen in love with him. But how was it possible? How could she be in love with him so soon. She scarcely knew him, and yet she had no doubt that this was the only man she would ever want to share her life. It was a revelation and it thrilled her.

She couldn't lie still in the damp bed, she had to keep moving or she felt she would burst. When did it happen? she asked herself. What made it happen? Why didn't I notice and stop it before it was too late? She thought, I'm in love with John and that changes everything.

She paced the room. She felt that her skin was on fire, and inside her head her brain seemed to have melted. Her thoughts were running away with her, and she could not control them. Or her feelings. I can't kill Susie, she told herself, there's no way I can arrange a fatal accident without him remembering what we said tonight. I've got to think this out. He couldn't have made it clearer if he knew what I was going to do. If I kill Susie, I'll get caught. It's not like it was with the others, I'm connected to her, I'd be a suspect because we're family. And John knows how I hate her. If I kill Susie, I lose John.

And yet what had become her life's work, destroying Susie, was more imperative than ever. Susie had to be disposed of. Except that just now her silly little sister scarcely seemed to matter. For once in Belle's life, she was absorbed, body and soul, by her passion for another human being. It didn't occur to her that John might not return her feelings. She was convinced she couldn't feel this strongly about someone who was indifferent to her. It had to be a chemical thing between them, an interaction consuming them both. For once, Belle had no thought that Susie would be able to keep him from her. She had no doubts about assuming that he was now hers. Belle did not even consider how irrational she was being. All she knew was that she must not yield to temptation and tell John what she had done. His love for her might not overcome that knowledge.

Belle had already developed a technique to stop herself thinking about the people she had killed. She'd got good at it. She pretended to herself – and she mostly believed – that what she had done had been episodes in a play. She was an actress playing a part, following a preordained script, and the people she had killed were actors, too. In her mind, once she had left the scene, they would get up and go on with their lives, disconnected with hers. So she herself had done nothing wrong; only the person played by herself as actress was guilty, and there were circumstances to mitigate her guilt because ultimately the writer and the director controlled her actions.

It had helped, this powerful self-delusion, when she had read in the newspaper about the death of the man in Tooting. Of course it had to be a scenario written by others; if she had been part of it, she would have known what happened next. And that was true of Sylvia, too. Julie at the office had told her a story, described the dramatic event of Sylvia's death with details Belle, as someone not involved, couldn't know. Even with Ben, it was the police who told her that it was an accident, he'd fallen after having sex with some village girl. That wasn't the story as she knew it, but if the police said that's what happened, she had to believe it, it was in the script.

And she did, mostly. Except in the dream. But so far she hadn't had dreams about Sylvia or the man from Tooting. And since meeting John, she hadn't dreamed about Ben.

Belle suddenly started to shiver. She went back to bed and stared into the darkness, listening to the creaks and rustles of the old house. She'd lain like this and listened like this as a child, but the sounds had been different then. Susie's sleeping breath; the secret night life of the two hamsters in a cage under the window; a vixen calling from the paddock near the hen run. Those sounds had been to do with life, life and tomorrow; now the room and the house and the land itself seemed to be decaying and dying, without a future.

She was afraid, because now she felt that she was playing a leading part and someone had stolen the script. The only certainty was the need to get rid of Susie. Once that was done, everything would be simple. She thought, I must clear Susie out of the way, and I'll use John to help me.

Her first step must be to convince John what kind of woman Susie really was, Susie his wife and the mother of his children. Love may be blind, Belle told herself, but John can't go on loving the monster that Susie is, the Susie I know, the one I'm going to make him see.

19

Dad was in the kitchen when Belle came downstairs the next morning. He was wearing overalls and gumboots ready for milking.

'I'm making tea,' he said. 'Do you want one? I've been out already, and it's brass monkeys out there.'

'It's bloody dark in here,' Belle said, switching on the light.

'Don't know what you want to waste money on electricity for,' Dad grumbled, 'you know where everything is well enough.'

It was like the old days. They were always bad-tempered with each other first thing in the morning.

'I don't know what I'm doing up at this hour,' she said, 'you can do your own milking.'

'Suit yourself,' he said.

'Well, I'm here now, we might as well get on with it.'

The early morning gloom always lifted once they were among the cows with their soft patient eyes and their sweet breath. And an hour later, as they sluiced the floor of the milking parlour and cleaned the apparatus, Dad was whistling.

'What's that tune?' Belle asked.

'What tune?'

'You're whistling it.'

'I wasn't whistling,' Dad said. 'What've I got to whistle for?' He looked distressed.

'It's OK, Dad,' Belle said, 'Mum wouldn't mind. She'd be glad. She wouldn't want you moping round the place, she'd want you to get on with the life that made you both happy.'

'She liked to hear my whistling, she said so,' Dad conceded. 'She said it reminded her of her dancing days.'

Belle felt embarrassed for a moment. There was something indecent about thinking of her parents as young and in love. All that sort of thing belonged to youth and she didn't like to think of old people that way. It made it harder for her to respect them if she had to see them in terms of youth faded and destroyed, not as experienced people serene in wisdom and know-how.

Her dad was saying, 'All that had to stop when you kids arrived. It wasn't so bad with you, with just the one of you we could take you with us and leave you in your carrycot in the room for coats, but we couldn't do that when there was Susie too.'

'That's what you were whistling, "Wake Up Little Susie",' Belle said.

'Your mother used to sing that to her when she was a baby,' Dad said.

Belle turned off the hose. 'What did she sing to me?' she asked, 'Didn't she have a song for me?'

Dad rinsed his hands under the tap and shook the water off them. 'I don't remember if she sang to you,' he said. 'With you being the first, we were always afraid of doing something wrong which would affect you for life. You know the way it is?'

'No, Dad,' she said, 'I don't know the way it is.'

'Well,' he said, and started to walk back across the yard towards the house, 'all that sort of thing's changed so much, it's quite different nowadays.'

'Like the pub is different,' Belle said.

He opened the kitchen door and stood back to let her go in front of him.

'It all started when the drink-driving laws came in. People got scared of coming out to drink. The pubs had to change or they'd have gone out of business, and that was the end of that.'

'Don't you miss it? The pub was your whole social life.'

Dad didn't answer. He banged the frying-pan on the Aga hotplate, saying, 'Give that John a call, will you? Tell him his breakfast will be on the table in ten minutes. We need to stoke him up if we're to get any work out of him today.'

Belle went to the foot of the stairs to call John, but he was already stirring. She could hear his voice from the bathroom. He was singing, 'Wake up, little Susie,' over and over again, always the same phrase.

Am I ever going to get away from being reminded of bloody Susie? Belle asked herself. And then she thought, If it was anyone else it wouldn't matter. Why does it make such a difference that it's Susie?

Belle had always resisted admitting that she was jealous of Susie. To admit it gave her despised sister some sort of hold over her and she could not accept that. I don't envy Susie, she told herself, I don't want the things she has, not really. Except John, a small voice in her head insisted. OK, she thought, but I can offer John much more than she does; all she's got is a marriage and kids. No, John's not hers, he just hasn't realized he's got a choice, but he will.

But that had little to do with the corrosive jealousy of Susie which had always and still did blight Belle's life. Her jealousy wasn't a question of wanting what Susie had; it was the fear of losing what she herself possessed, or believed she did. It's gone way beyond fear, Belle thought, it's a fact; she's taken away everything I loved from the moment she was born.

Belle felt tears of self-pity sting her eyes and pulled herself together.

'He's on his way,' she said to her father.

Dad seemed to be concentrating very hard on the frying-pan. He muttered something but Belle couldn't hear what he said.

'I can't hear you, Dad,' she said, and was ashamed to hear the impatience in her tone.

'There's something I want to talk to you about,' he said, turning to face her. 'It was when we were talking about the pub that made me think of it, and now I know what I want to do. I'm going to change my will.'

Belle was careful not to appear to react. She sat down at her place at the table and waited for a while before she said, 'Well, is that it? With Mum dying, you're going to have to, I expect.'

'As it stands, I've left the farm to Susie.'

Belle kept her voice non-committal. 'But what would've happened to Mum if you'd died first?' she said.

'It was written in the will that she could live here for her life, and then it would go to Susie and her family. I thought one day young Jonty might take it on.'

'That makes sense, I suppose.'

I don't want to know this, Belle thought, why is he telling me?

'But things have changed.'

Dad brought two plates of bacon and eggs to the table and put one in front of her. He sat down and started to eat the other at once. He seemed to be waiting for Belle to say something, but when she didn't he went on, 'I didn't expect you to come back.'

'That's all right, Dad,' she said, 'I understand.'

It's just one more thing, she thought, the last thing Susie could take from me. It's like proof of the case against her. Now I can justify the way I hate her and what I have to do to punish her.

But Dad hadn't finished. He went on, 'No, you don't understand,' he said. '*You belong here.*'

Don't, Belle was pleading with him in her head, don't do it, don't try to make us share this too. Anything but that. Leave it to her, I won't blame you.

'No,' she said, 'no, I don't. I left of my own accord, you know.'

'You left because of Susie. Something happened between you two, I know that.'

Belle tried to swallow but she couldn't. She was afraid she might start to choke. She wanted to shake the old man, shout at him about why, if he knew that, he hadn't done something then to help her?

But she simply shook her head, 'You can't turn the clock back, Dad,' she said. The words sounded bleak.

'You've given up your job, haven't you? You've nothing else in mind?'

'No,' she said. 'I'm in no hurry.'

'Don't say that,' he said, 'never let me hear you say that. There's never time to waste. I know that now.'

'I don't want to rush into anything, that's all I meant,' she said, trying to soothe him.

'What do you think about staying on here and taking over?'

She tried to take in what he'd said. 'What do you think of that, then?' he said. He looked at her with a sort of triumph, like a poker player displaying a royal flush.

'I don't know what to say,' she said.

'No,' he said, 'I don't suppose you do. But I've been thinking about it a lot. You saw at once, coming back after being away, I don't fit in here any more. Not in this village, or even in farming. There aren't many of us old guard left, and with your mother gone I don't want to hang on making everyone as miserable as I'll be.'

'But it was your whole life, it was always all you ever wanted, you and Mum,' Belle said.

'Things change,' Dad said. 'Perhaps I've changed. And without your mother . . . '

Belle wanted to tell him then that to her what he was saying seemed the ultimate betrayal. She thought, He and Mum blighted my life because they pursued their own dream without considering me; they didn't give me a chance to be a normal kid. And now he's gone back on it; it didn't work even for him and now he wants to escape and leave me as some kind of hostage to the dead past. And worse still, the dying future. She asked herself, Doesn't he see what he's doing to me?

And then she realized that she was the one being unreasonable. She was the one who was distorting the old man's intentions. She thought, Am I off my head, why do I twist everything into something it isn't?

Her father believed that he was offering her something she might want, something she could build her life around. Perhaps he was even trying to make amends for failing her as a parent. He must know he did fail, Belle thought; at least, he failed with me.

'What makes you think I'd like it any better than you do?' Belle asked, but her voice was without conviction. She wanted the farm, she wanted to do Susie out of it. She'd decide later what she would really do with it.

She thought, Perhaps John and I could make a go of it together; perhaps he'd like that.

'What are you going to do if I say yes?' Belle had to make it clear that there was no chance that she and her father could run the farm together. It had to be hers or nothing.

'I've been thinking of going up to Scotland to live with your mother's sister Kirsty. When Uncle Bob died last year she wanted us both to go, your Mum and me. She's got a nice place up there that's getting too much for her since Bob went. She'd be pleased to have me. You don't have to worry about me. It's up to you.'

Belle went on eating for a while. She heard John coming down the stairs. Another few seconds and he would interrupt them.

'Susie won't like it,' Belle said to her father.

'What won't Susie like?' John asked, coming into the room.

'Oh, nothing, really,' Belle said, and then added off the top of her head, 'Dad's thinking of going electric and getting rid of the Aga, and he wondered if Susie would like it. I said she wouldn't, she never liked cooking on the Aga, that's all. So enjoy your breakfast while you can because I think the Aga makes things taste better than anything else.'

'Oh, OK,' he said. But Belle had the feeling that he didn't believe her.

That day John helped her clear ditches that had become over-grown with hogweed and cow-parsley stems standing as hard and tall as bamboo canes. Belle drove the tractor, operating the scoop, while he got down into the trench and slashed back the overgrown banks.

They made slow progress. John looked like someone blacked up for a minstrel show and her feet kept slipping on the clutch because of the thick mud on her gumboots.

But Belle would not give in and call for a break. At last John crawled up the bank and said, 'I've got to stop, my back's on fire.'

'Are you sure?' she said. 'It may feel worse if you stop.'

Since her conversation with her father that morning, she had been driven by a strong sense that what she and John were doing was an act of regeneration, setting the land right for her to take possession. It was important to her that John contributed to this. She wanted to make Susie aware of the extent of her loss.

'I'd no idea you could be such a slave driver,' John said. He eased himself painfully upright, stretching to ease his muscles.

'Sorry,' she said. 'I'd forgotten you were a soft townee.'

'I'll take that as a compliment,' he said; 'that you forgot.'

She had brought sandwiches and a flask of coffee. There was no-where dry to sit so they stood to eat and drink, leaning against the back tyre of the tractor.

'Belle, may I ask you something personal?' John said suddenly.

'Ask away,' she said, 'but don't blame me if you don't like the answer.'

'What is it between you and Susie?' he asked.

Belle didn't say anything at first, and soon he said, 'Sorry, I shouldn't have asked. It's just I feel close to you and I can't under-stand what's between you and Susie that's set the two of you apart.'

'Have you ever asked Susie?'

'No,' he said, 'but then I didn't really know anything about you. You could've been a monster. But you're such a great girl and so's she, and I can't believe you'll go off back to London and that'll be that. We should be good friends, you, me and her.'

'No,' Belle said fiercely, and then added more quietly, 'It's too late for that, I'm afraid, and it goes too deep. I'm sorry, too, because I think we could be friends, you and I.'

125

'We are. Of course we are, whatever happens between you and Susie. But what is it? Surely you can tell me that?'

'I can tell you,' Belle said, 'but I don't think you can take it.'

'Belle, you can't say things like that and expect me to drop it. What don't you think I can take?'

'Because it's about Susie.'

John laughed. 'Of course I can take it, then. I love Susie and I know her. It can't be *that* bad.'

'It is for me,' Belle said, 'but I don't want to turn you against her.'

John took her hand. 'You won't do that, I promise. But you've got to tell me now, you must. You can't leave it like that.'

Belle felt transformed, a great tragic actress at the height of her powers convincing her audience that fiction was truth.

'I've never told anyone,' Belle said. She took hold of John's hand and clung to it. 'If I tell you, you must promise never to mention it to anyone, not even to Susie. The family had to protect Susie, I understand that now, although I did mind at the time. She's probably convinced herself by now that the story they made up about the death being an accident is what really happened.'

Belle had convinced herself. There were real tears in her eyes as he pressed her hand and leaned closer to listen to her scared whisper. 'You've heard of Ben?' she said.

He nodded. 'Wasn't he your fiancé, the one who died in an accident?'

'Yes,' she said. 'He was killed just a week before our wedding. But it wasn't an accident. He was murdered.' Belle raised her eyes and looked deep into his. 'Susie killed him,' she said. 'Susie tried to seduce him and he wasn't having any and she pushed him off the hayloft and he broke his neck on the barn floor. Ben was the only man I ever loved and she was jealous because I was happy, so she murdered him.'

20

Belle climbed up on to the tractor and started the engine.

John, who had been standing looking as though he'd been turned to salt, a sandwich halfway to his mouth, suddenly jumped forward into the tractor's path.

'No, wait, you can't leave it like that,' he said, working his way up the engine casing as though he was easing his way along the neck and shoulders of an unbroken colt he wanted to back.

Belle throttled back so the engine was just ticking over and he could hear what she said.

'I shouldn't have told you,' she said. 'I knew you wouldn't be able to take it. Everyone else put it behind them, but I couldn't.'

He seemed to be searching her face for signs that this was some kind of family joke at his expense.

'You are kidding, aren't you?' he said.

'No,' Belle said. 'You wanted to know what's between Susie and me and I told you.'

'I don't believe you. I can't.'

Belle shrugged. 'That's up to you,' she said.

'You've got it all wrong. You must've got it wrong. Susie wouldn't kill a fly.'

'That's why Mum and Dad and Susie herself have told themselves it was an accident all these years. I couldn't do that. No one talks about it, but that's why they were glad I left, because I'm sure she killed him deliberately to stop him marrying me, and they couldn't make themselves believe it was an accident as long as I was around convinced it wasn't.'

'Belle, you can't believe Susie could do anything like that?'

'I know she did. She told me she did. She said she was sorry.'

'But that sounds as though it was an accident, surely?'

'She wasn't sorry she killed him. She was sorry she couldn't get him to make love to her first.'

'No,' John said. 'No, no, no.'

'If you don't believe me, ask Dad. He'll tell you it was an accident, that he's sure it wasn't Susie in the barn with Ben that morning. He's made himself believe that, but you'll see from his face that he knows she did it.'

She said to herself, Dad won't want to talk about it, he'll gloss over the details, and John will see what I've told him to see.

She revved the tractor engine to get John to step aside. She felt an extraordinary sense of power as she looked at his face.

'They thought it was for the best if they kept quiet,' she shouted to John as she let in the clutch. 'They protected her, and I was expected to do the best I could. I was the strong one, to hell with me, I'd survive, but they knew Susie couldn't take a police investigation and then a trial and prison. Not precious little Susie. It would've broken them, too, of course. They protected themselves.'

She thrilled with righteous indignation against this fabricated perfidy. Her hatred for Susie as the murderer of Ben was like a shot of adrenalin. It didn't matter that she knew in her heart it wasn't true. She had never felt such triumph. Almost, she wished that Susie really had killed Ben so she could feel like this for real all the time.

On the spur of the moment, she had made up her mind.

'There's something I've got to do,' she shouted at John. 'I'll be back.'

She put her foot down on the throttle and the tractor leaped forward. It was like riding a bucking horse as the machine bumped across the field at top speed. Belle slewed the steering wheel and almost did a spin turn in the yard. The huge, stately rear wheel tipped and spun, then dropped back to earth.

Belle was laughing as her father came out of the barn to see what the noise was about.

'What's happened?' he cried. 'Where's John?'

He hurried across the yard towards the tractor, the colour draining from his face. 'He hasn't got trapped in that rhine, has he?'

He'd lost too many sheep in those deep local ditches across land reclaimed from the sea where, in places, the mud was bottomless and sucked in its victims like a quagmire. He was terrified.

'No, Dad, there's nothing wrong. I just wanted to tell you, I've made up my mind.'

'Made up your mind about what?' he said, grumpy because she had scared him.

'I accept your offer,' she said. 'I'll take over the farm. You can tell Aunt Kirsty you're coming to Scotland.'

She jumped down from the tractor cab and hugged him.

He was aghast. He did not know what to do. Such physical demonstrativeness was unnatural to him and, he'd always thought, to her. He had no idea what she expected from him.

'There's no need for that,' he said, pushing her away. 'I'm glad you've seen sense. It's the best thing for both of us now.'

They looked at each other, suddenly conscious that something momentous had happened between them.

'I'll get Trimble to do the paperwork,' he said.

Trimble was the solicitor who had looked after their affairs since Mum and Dad were married.

'What about Susie?' Belle asked.

'She'll have to be told. But we'll keep it from John till she knows.'

'I'll tell her,' Belle said. 'She'll be down at the weekend to take John home with her. He's got to be back at work on Monday. I'll tell her then.'

Dad looked relieved. 'Yes,' he said, 'it's better coming from you. I think she'll be relieved; she doesn't think I can cope carrying on here alone. Now she won't have to worry.'

Belle didn't like to point out that there wasn't a chance that Susie would be relieved at the news. Let Dad fondly imagine that his younger daughter was concerned for nothing but his welfare. Belle knew that Susie's first thought would be the money, that her inheritance was lost to her, and handed to Belle. The farm would be worth a great deal if it could be sold to build new houses. Belle knew that Susie had always taken it for granted that she would be rich.

Belle smiled at Dad. She knew that he thought she was happy, but really she was looking forward only to destroying Susie's hopes. Her sister was going to be gutted; Belle looked forward to telling her.

There was a short silence, then Belle turned back to the tractor and climbed into the driving seat. 'Best get back to work,' she said, 'We wouldn't want John disappearing into that ditch, would we?'

'Wait for me,' Dad said, and swung himself up behind her. 'I've finished in the barn, I'll come and give you both a hand.'

'Better still, you take over with John and let me get on with a bit of work in the house,' Belle said. She slid off the tractor seat so that he could take her place. 'We don't want Susie arriving and thinking we can't cope without her, do we?'

Belle was relieved. She hadn't been looking forward to facing John, not after what she'd told him about Susie. He'd never let her get away with dropping the bombshell she had without interrogating her relentlessly. It would be best to let her revelation about Susie sink in before she faced him alone. Let him talk to Dad about it if he must. Belle felt sure that John wouldn't just come out with what she'd told him. He'd try to tread carefully. Dad wouldn't know what he was on about, he'd trot out the old story about an accident. Of course he would, he thought it was the truth. I'd almost forgotten that as far as he and everyone else is concerned, it was the truth, Belle thought, and she smiled to herself.

'Are you sure?' Dad asked. For a moment, she wondered what he was talking about, then realized he was merely surprised that she of all people should volunteer for housework when there was outdoor work to be done.

'Yes, Dad, you go ahead,' she said, and smiled at him. 'I'd quite like to be alone in the house for a while, anyway. Maybe I'll start sorting out a few of Mum's things.'

Dad, seeing signs that she might be going to get emotional, said, 'I'll leave you to it, then.' He understood that she wanted to take stock of her new domain; Belle could be surprisingly womanish sometimes, he thought, he'd best leave her to it. Hurriedly he put the tractor in gear and moved slowly forward.

She watched his hunched figure through the gate into the field towards the ditch where she and John had been working. Poor Dad, she thought, he never understood any woman, it wasn't only me. I used to think he expected anyone female to be a less perfect version of Mum and Susie, but that didn't mean he understood them, either. He was at ease with them because he never felt threatened by them. It never occurred to him that Susie could ever be destructive. Not to him nor to anyone else. If Belle broke her heart against Susie's perfection, that was Belle's problem and she should deal with it.

Belle wondered if the kids at school had tormented Susie about her stuck-up ways as they had bullied her. Of course they didn't, she told herself, Susie always got in first. And she didn't care about them, anyway. They would never accuse Susie of being stuck-up, they accepted that she was superior. They all put her on a pedestal. Everything Susie was and did was what they wanted to be and do.

The house felt different as Belle walked into it now it belonged to her. It was no longer a masculine domain. Not so much in the kitchen, nor in the formal dining-room or the sitting-room with its battered old furniture and the remains of a log fire in the grate, left over from a winter evening when the occasional local had come to supper and sat on afterwards talking about the state of farming and the stupidity of the government. Those rare occasions were the only time her parents used the sitting-room in the winter. On winter evenings they watched television in the kitchen, warmed by the Aga. In the summer it was different; the sitting-room was luxuriously cool and peaceful when it was hot outside. Then the kitchen was uncomfortable, the Aga increasing the heat regardless. They had never watched TV much in the summer, there was always too much to do outside in the long light evenings when it was cool enough to work.

But upstairs, wandering through her mother's room and Susie's bedroom, Belle felt that at last she had taken possession of what was rightfully hers. Susie's room was full of John's things now, which was fine. Without Susie, he was only a guest.

Belle vowed to herself that once the weekend was over, Susie should never come to the farm again. This was Belle's place, hers alone. Anyone who came here now would have to know that they were her guests, their only rights the practice of hospitality. Dad was different; he was a temporary resident. But he had no future here; the future was Belle's to control.

She prepared supper that night as a gracious hostess captivating her *salon*.

'I never knew you could cook like this,' Dad said as she poured coffee afterwards.

'There's a lot about me you don't know,' she said, and smiled at him to soften her sharp tone.

John got up suddenly, his chair scraping against the flagstone floor. He had been silent all evening, scarcely noticing what he was eating.

'No coffee for me, thanks,' he said. 'Thank you for a wonderful meal, Belle, but I think I'll turn in. I'm not used to hard physical labour like you two are, and to be honest, I'm bushed.'

'What's the matter with him?' Belle asked when he'd shut the kitchen door behind him and they could hear his footsteps on the floor above. 'He hardly said a word all evening. Did you say something to him down at the ditch?'

'He's a city boy, he's probably worn himself out,' Dad said. 'He's a good worker, though, I'll say that for him.'

Belle smiled. 'He is, isn't he? And he seems to enjoy it. Not like Susie.'

Dad lit a cheroot and inhaled deeply, saying nothing.

'I thought you gave up smoking years ago, Dad,' Belle said. 'What's up?'

'Oh, I like the occasional small cigar on special occasions,' he said. 'It's not like smoking a proper Havana, I haven't had one of those since Susie's wedding day, but with these little ones I feel I'm only pretending to indulge sometimes.'

'People used to smoke menthols and tell themselves the same thing,' Belle said. 'If you want to smoke a good Havana, go ahead, it'll smell better than that.'

'I would if I could,' Dad said, 'but I can't afford things like that. As I say, I hardly indulge at all these days.'

'When something's bothering you, more like,' she said. 'Is it about John?'

Dad frowned. 'Not exactly,' he said, 'but . . . ' He looked doubtful, as though he wasn't sure of what he was going to say and thought that perhaps he shouldn't say it. Then he decided to take the plunge and said, 'There was something odd going on today. We were working on the ditch and he kept asking me questions about Susie. Did you notice anything when you were with him earlier? You don't think they're having trouble in their marriage, do you? Surely he couldn't be seeing someone else?'

'Trouble? What kind of trouble?' Belle asked. She had to make an effort to force herself to sound non-committal. She added, 'He thinks the sun shines out of her.' And she couldn't help blurting out, 'Poor sap.'

Dad took another puff and smiled. 'That's true, isn't it? I'm sure it is. I'm sure he loves her. Of course he does, everyone loves Susie. But what about her? You don't think she's . . . well, you don't think there's someone else, do you?'

'What's brought this on, Dad? What did John say?'

Dad stubbed out the cheroot but then lit another.

'It was the questions he was asking. About you, too. He wanted to know if you and Susie had ever got on. He thought something must have turned you against her.'

'Well, something did, didn't it?' Belle said. 'She seduced Ben.'

It was easier to let him believe that that was the reason she hated Susie. There was no point in trying to explain how her antagonism to her sister had grown from the moment she was born, usurping Belle's own rightful place as the one and only. It seemed too childish.

'You don't know that,' Dad said, sounding upset. 'I understand why you suspect she was the one with him in the barn. But you don't know for certain.'

'I do. She told me. And so do you. You've always known, haven't you? Why didn't you ever say so to me? It made it much worse that everyone pretended it was some stranger he'd picked up in the village. And you all knew, didn't you? You knew what Susie was like.'

'It seemed such a small thing compared to that terrible accident. Susie being Susie . . .'

Belle shook her head in disbelief. 'I can't believe you said that, Dad,' she said, and her voice was cold. Then she asked, 'Is that what you said to John?'

Dad inhaled and then slowly let the smoke go. 'I told him it was something that happened between Susie and your fiancé, who died in an accident here on the farm. I said it was a long time ago, and we've always made a point of not talking about it, but perhaps you hadn't forgiven your sister. What else could I say?'

'Nothing, Dad. That about covers it anyway, doesn't it? And I shouldn't worry about that marriage. John's a lovely guy, why would Susie look elsewhere?'

'Why indeed?' Dad said, and sighed. 'But you know what Susie's like. She's not strong and constant like you.'

21

Soon after that, Dad too went up to bed. He and Belle had tried to make conversation, but it was as though there was a barrier between them and neither could think of anything to say.

Belle washed up and then went upstairs and into the room where her mother had died.

It was a large, airy room looking out across fields to a range of hills in the distance. It had always been her parents' sanctuary, some-where out of bounds to the children unless in dire emergency. She and Susie had often sneaked in during the daytime when there was no one else in the house. Susie would use her mother's make-up and try on her best clothes, strutting in front of the wardrobe mirror looking like the madam in a low-grade brothel, while Belle checked the contents of the drawers in the bedside table.

Since Mum had been ill, though, Dad had moved into the spare room. She must have been ill for longer than Dad had let on, because there was no trace of him left; this room was now wholly the domain of a sick old woman.

Belle sat on the bed and took in the faint virginal smell of rose-water and eau-de-Cologne. The room used to smell of tobacco and the whiff of male sweat, which had made Belle screw up her nose in distaste, but was also oddly exciting, hinting at hidden dangers. She remembered now how that slight odour had made her shout at Susie, furiously telling her to stop messing with their mother's things, but it wasn't really Susie who'd made her angry, it was something else she couldn't put her finger on. Belle felt excluded, conscious of a life her parents had together which had nothing to do with her. It was her mother she wanted to shout at, not Susie, because Mum knew Dad as she herself never could. But he was hers, not Mum's; they worked together in the fields, they talked about the animals and the state of the crops. That was who Dad was, and Mum wasn't part of that. It was Belle he really needed, not Mum. And yet that horrible, magnetic smell in their bedroom told Belle that in this room, in this bed, Dad frequently betrayed her. Young as she was, she had known then as she knew now that she was jealous of her mother.

And, worst of all, Mum was never jealous of her. Belle couldn't easily forgive her for that.

Belle opened a drawer in the small chest which had served her mother as a bedside table. It was filled with bottles of pills, and small phials of cream marked with a chemist's instructions on their use.

Belle shut that drawer quickly, then opened another. It was hard to open, being stuffed with old photographs. There were snaps of Dad on the farm, Dad with a prize heifer at a local agricultural show, Dad holding babies who must have been her and Susie. There were pictures of Belle and Susie together as children, holding hands, for God's sake. When had she ever willingly held Susie's hand? Susie was in a lot of the photographs – Susie in the school play; Susie in ballet shoes and a tutu with a ribbon in her hair; Susie on the pony smirking at a gymkhana somewhere where a man in a bowler was handing her a rosette. His hand was on Susie's knee.

Belle could find no photos of herself alone. She'd never starred in a school play, or won prizes riding at shows. She'd never wanted to take part in such things. It wasn't that she hadn't been photographed; she had. But always, it seemed to her, she appeared as the stooge, the adjunct to whatever it had been that made someone call for a picture of Mum, or Dad, or a prize heifer. Or Susie. Belle was always the other little girl standing beside Susie, the one no one noticed. But Mum hadn't bothered to keep those photographs.

Belle suddenly got to her feet and pummelled the bed so that there was no sign that she had sat down on it.

'That was then,' she said aloud, 'but this is now.'

Even Dad had noticed something. He was worried that John and Susie were having trouble in their marriage. He'd even speculated that there could be someone else. What would he think, Belle thought, if he knew that that someone else is me? Dad said John talked about me. I've got under his skin, he can't stop thinking about me. Soon he'll be falling in love with me, he'll feel the same as I do.

Oh, God, she thought, please make it be true.

Belle went back to her own bedroom. She sat at the dressing-table and stared at herself in the mirror. But she didn't see her own face; she saw herself transformed because of the possibility that John's young man's lust for Susie could be incinerated in the flames of his more mature passion for herself. After all, she told herself, there's no substance to Susie, no depth to her feelings. She's like air, or flame. Real love has to put down roots, it needs earth and sustenance. I can give him that.

There was a light knock on her door. At first she wasn't sure if she had imagined it, expecting her lover in the throes of longing imagination. Then it came again, and the door opened.

John came into the room.

'I heard you come in here,' he said. 'I've been sitting in my room trying to make sense of everything and it's no good. I can't get the things you said out of my head. We've got to talk.'

2 2

For a wonderful moment, Belle thought that John wanted to talk about his feelings for her. She even started to open her arms to him to grip him in an embrace.

But she stifled the movement before she made it. It was the sudden shock of him coming into her bedroom that had confused her for a moment. She'd been dreaming of what might one day be between them, but for John the very idea could scarcely be more yet than a small voice of doubt about his love for Susie. Of course he had come to talk about what she had told him about her little sister. Belle knew exactly the effect that what she'd said must have had on him, although for a moment it had almost slipped her mind exactly what she'd said. That's the trouble with improvising, she told herself. If I'm going to get carried away like that, I'll have to take notes of what I say.

'I've nothing more to say about that,' she said.

'But you can't leave it there,' John said. He seemed to be fighting an urge to grab her and shake the truth out of her.

'I didn't want to tell you. You forced it out of me.'

'You accused my wife of murder.'

'I don't think of it like that,' Belle said. 'You asked me what there was between Susie and me, and I told you.'

'You said she killed your fiancé.'

'And I believe she did.'

'So she's a murderess?'

'Is she?' Belle said. 'You're the one saying so. There are degrees of killing people, you should know that. Maybe it was an accident. Maybe it was self-defence. All I know is, I believe she killed him and I don't really care how or why. I blame her because one way or another she destroyed the one good thing in my life.'

She turned away from him because she didn't want him to see that she had tears in her eyes.

Then he came to stand behind her and put his hands on her shoulders, gently kneading her tense muscles.

'I'm sorry, Belle,' he said, 'I didn't mean to upset you. But what you said came as a shock. I overreacted.'

'I never wanted to talk about it,' she said. 'Nobody in the family ever has. As far as I'm concerned, she did it, and of course you've got a right to know that. At least, I think you have. But what more is there to say? What do you want to do about it?'

John stopped massaging her shoulders, but he did not remove his hands. Belle thought he couldn't fail to feel how her skin burned where he touched her.

There was a short silence.

'I didn't know if you knew,' Belle went on. 'I thought she might have told you. Why do you think I talked to you about the perfect murder? I can't do anything about it if I wanted to. It's ages ago and it's her word against mine and everyone knows I hate her. It's up to you what you do now.'

She pulled away from him and added, 'You'd better not tell her what I've said, though. She might kill you to keep her secret covered up.'

'That's absurd,' John said. 'You can't believe that. She must know your dad knows.'

'Maybe she's blanked that out of her mind. But if you want to know I'm warning you, if you ask her about it, Dad had better watch out. That's what I believe.'

'She knew you knew. She never did you any harm, did she?'

'She didn't have time to, did she? Why do you think I got the hell out of here and I've never been back?'

John sat down on the bed and stared at his clenched fists. He said, 'But I love her. I know she wouldn't do anything like this. Honestly, Belle, she wouldn't. I trust her completely.'

'Of course you love her,' Belle said, and she heard the bitterness in her voice. 'Susie's more addictive than heroin.'

'She's the mother of my children,' John said. He sounded pompous. He obviously felt strongly that his kids must be protected. Like her dad. About Susie, anyway. 'I can't doubt her,' he said.

What is it with these men? Belle asked herself. And then she thought, I don't know any other men, I never have.

Belle had been with several men, but since Ben only for sex. She'd made a sort of point of never going out with the same man twice. She often didn't even ask their names because she wasn't going to tell them hers. She made contact on the internet and agreed somewhere to meet, and then when she saw them she decided if she would or wouldn't sleep with them. Even if she did, that was the end of it. She hadn't known them. Except Ben, and she wasn't sure that he'd felt anything very strongly. She thought, Two out of the three men I've known – Ben, Dad and John — isn't enough to make a statistical judgement about male pomposity, which, she added to herself, also sounded pretty pompous coming from her.

But it was John's obvious sincerity rather than his pomposity which annoyed her now. She retorted, 'You might find it easier to doubt that the children are really yours.'

That made him angry. He jumped up, his face red with fury. She braced herself, expecting him to hit her. She wanted him to hit her, she wanted the physical contact with him. But then he looked at her with something like pity.

When he spoke, he sounded as though he were reading a murder suspect her rights.'I know you hate Susie, Belle,' he said, 'but leave our children out of it. They've got nothing to do with this.'

'Oh, wake up to yourself,' she said. 'More to the point, they've probably got nothing to do with you. Considering you're her bloody husband, you don't really seem to know Susie at all, certainly not like I do. You must've known she was the local bike for years. She probably only married you because she was pregnant by A.N.Other and you were a convenient fall guy.'

She knew she had overplayed her hand then. She sounded absurd. He knew Susie well enough to believe, as she did, that her sister would have had an abortion rather than marry a sap if she hadn't loved him.

John seemed to be about to burst out laughing.

'I didn't mean that,' she said. 'I'm sorry. I was just lashing out. Talking about what happened with Ben has brought back some very bad memories for me.'

'I'm sorry I lost my temper,' he said. 'It was when you brought my kids into it, I saw red.'

There was a long pause. Then he got up and stretched. 'That ditching business is torture,' he said. 'It's time I left you in peace.'

Peace! she thought, how can I ever be at peace now, while Susie stands in the way of my love for him? But now, at last, I'm nearly there. It won't be long before Susie's going to know what it's like to have her life destroyed. And then I'll have John.

'What are you going to do?' she asked him. 'About Susie, I mean.'

He paused as he was about to open the door on to the landing. 'I don't know,' he said. 'I'll have to think.'

'You'll pretend I never told you,' she said. 'There's nothing else you can do, really, is there? You'll do exactly what the rest of the family have done all these years and pretend it never happened.'

'Yes,' he said, 'that's probably exactly what I'll do.'

Belle smiled to herself. She thought, You can try, my darling, but I'm not going to let you get away with that.

23

John, back in his own bedroom, went through the motions of going to bed. But he couldn't sleep. What Belle had said about Susie and Ben kept running through his head, and every time he closed his eyes he could see the scene in the hayloft. Susie and Ben, Ben pushing Susie away, and then Ben falling, arms flailing, being tipped over the edge of the loft on to the flagstone floor of the barn.

Of course she didn't do any such thing, he told himself, it's ridiculous. Belle may believe it, but she's crazy. Susie told me she's insane. But then he thought, Well, Susie would say that, wouldn't she? That's what she'd say if what Belle says is true? No, Belle may seem sane enough, but she must be out of her mind.

Then he thought, Is it true? Is she right? Am I going to say nothing and try to forget what Belle said? Again he thought, Yes, the woman's clearly insane, Susie should know what's she's saying about her.

But how could he tell Susie? 'By the way, sweetheart, did you know your sister's a raving lunatic?' That's what Susie had always said Belle was, he thought, she wouldn't be surprised.

The trouble is, John told himself, that's not what's worrying me. I want to hear Susie say she didn't kill Belle's fiancé, I need her to tell me she didn't. That means I'm not convinced Belle's mad. I can't ask my own wife if she murdered the wretched Ben without her knowing that I have doubts about her.

He got up and went to open the window. It was cold, but the air felt wonderful, soothing him. It was a dark night with no moon, but the sky was clear. He stared out at the glittering universe and, in proportion to that immensity, Belle's tortured imagination seemed absurd.

It's simple enough, he told himself, I'll ask her.

It took him some time to find his mobile phone. He did not want to turn on the light because he felt better able to keep Belle's accusations against Susie at bay in the darkness. In the dark he could believe he was having a nightmare and once he woke up it would go away.

At last Susie answered the phone. He could imagine her in their bedroom at home, half awake, floundering in the dark to pick up the receiver amid the clutter on the bedside table.

'John?' she said in a voice full of sleep, 'do you know what time it is? What's happened? Is it Dad? Has something happened to Dad?'

'No, nothing's wrong.' John didn't know what to say to her. He was appalled at having woken her. 'I miss you,' he said.

There was a brief pause and then Susie's voice had changed. She sounded suddenly alert, obviously suspicious. 'I miss you, too,' she said, and yawned. 'I've missed you for days, but I'll see you the day after tomorrow. Are you drunk?'

He grabbed at the excuse. 'We had a few drinks tonight,' he said. He hoped she wouldn't notice how sober he really sounded.

'More than a few if you thought I'd still be up and about,' she said. She didn't sound cross. No longer alarmed, she seemed to find his call endearing.

He wondered how he could say it. How could he ask her, 'Did you murder Belle's fiancé?'

'You and Ben?' he said, his voice cracking with tension.

'What about it?' she asked in the tone of someone trying to be patient with a small child. But at least she sounded curious, not defensive.

'Did you . . . ?' No, he couldn't say it. Better to forget all about what Belle had said. Belle hated Susie, the way sisters sometimes hated each other, not as people but simply because of the relationship. John, who was an only child, could understand that. It would have been difficult for anyone to have Susie as a kid sister, at least for someone who depended on being a bit controlling for her self-esteem. Of course Belle was going to make Susie into a villain.

Susie sounded exasperated, but she laughed. 'Oh, I see, Belle's been telling tales about what I did to her precious Ben, is that it? So I seduced him, so what? It all happened long before you and I met.'

She's laughing, John thought, she's actually laughing. She knows her sister's told me about her and Ben, and she's flippant about it. But what does Susie think Belle's told me? It doesn't bring me any closer to knowing if she did or didn't actually kill him.

He felt hopelessly confused. He had never doubted Susie before and now he didn't know what to think.

'John?' Susie said, clearly wondering what he was thinking because drunks were unpredictable.

'Oh, Susie . . .'

'You watch out,' she said. 'Belle must fancy you, if she's dragging all that up to put you against me. You be careful she doesn't try to seduce you.' He could tell from her voice that she was smiling.

John was reassured. She wouldn't make a joke about it if she'd really done what Belle said she did.

Then Susie added, 'I'm sorry I slept with her wretched boyfriend, I'm sorry he died, but really, it's got nothing to do with anything now.'

Oh, my God, he thought, if only that were true. She's as good as saying she did it and she doesn't even seem to care. Or was she really saying anything of the sort? He wished he hadn't rung her.

'John, are you still there? Go to sleep, darling, and I'll be there before you know it. I've got to go, sweetheart, or I'll be a wreck in the morning. Love you.'

She made a kissing sound and then the line went dead.

John dropped his mobile and felt his way back to the bed. He lay down and pulled the duvet up over his head. Now, after talking to Susie, he felt like a man emerging unnoticed from a long coma. He felt dazed and confused, full of dull pain.

And then, thinking that he would never sleep again, he fell asleep.

24

Susie lay down and tried to go back to sleep but she couldn't.

John's drunk, she told herself, there isn't anything more to it than that.

But she knew her husband hadn't been drunk. He'd used that as an excuse for something, but what?

That bloody Belle, Susie thought, what's she been telling him about me?

It was useless to try to sleep now. Susie turned on the bedside light and reached for her dressing-gown. Then she went downstairs to make herself a cup of tea.

She crept past the doors of the children's rooms before she remembered that they weren't there. She felt suddenly very lonely, missing them. If only they'd been at home with her in their own beds, she would have gone in to watch them sleeping for a moment and that would have made her feel better.

Even the house where she had felt happily at home for many years now seemed suddenly strange and unfriendly. It felt so cold that she overrode the heating timer. The sound of the boiler firing up and the familiar creaking in the pipes comforted her a little, as though warmth were another presence in the house.

It wasn't what John had said – or, rather, hadn't said – on the phone that disturbed her. It had more to do with the way his call had brought back all her old insecurities to do with Belle.

There was an old doll of Kim's on the kitchen table, left behind when John's mother came to take the children away with her. Susie picked it up and smoothed the doll's dress. She'd made it herself to Kim's design, but it hadn't worn well. She hugged the doll, hoping that even the hard plastic body would help her feel closer to her warm, wriggly daughter.

Belle still hates me, Susie told herself, and she wanted to weep, except what was the point of weeping when there was no one to hear her distress and try to comfort her? Some old poet had written something about thoughts which lie too deep for tears; maybe Wordsworth. It was the only poetic phrase that had ever stuck in her mind from all her years of education because that was exactly the way she'd felt about Belle then, when she was still a schoolgirl, and it was the same now. Thinking of Belle gave Susie a great ache inside, as though she was crying internally and all the bitter tears were flooding her heart.

She made herself try to remember how she herself had felt when Mum first told her about the Huntington's chorea. Belle must be going through hell, Susie told herself, and then she saw Belle's face and heard Belle's voice and she thought, She probably isn't even worried because she can't imagine a disease like that would dare to strike her, she thinks she's so strong it wouldn't dare.

Susie felt painfully sad as she imagined her sister repelling invading hordes of hostile genes, like King Canute trying to turn back the tide.

Belle would use this against her, Susie knew, she would hate her all the more for telling her. She probably doesn't believe it, she thought, she probably thinks I'm making it up to get at her or make myself the centre of attention. That's the way she thinks, she always has. She never saw how Mum was, and she's only got my word for it. She probably thinks I hate her as much as she hates me. Oh, she said to herself, poor Belle, I wish I could understand her better. I might be able to talk to her then.

Susie asked herself, Did I hope she'd got over it, that she'd forgiven me? It had been so long ago that she'd hoped, when she and Belle met again, that they could put the past behind them and start again. That's why she'd apologized for seducing Ben that one time. And Belle had seemed quite cool about it, as though she'd got over it. So what's her problem? Susie thought, Why can't she move on?

But her sister's hostility had never really been just about Ben, Susie knew that. Belle had been the same from as far back as Susie could remember. She thought, Belle always hated me, she never wanted me to be born, she would've killed me if she'd dared so she could be rid of me once and for all.

Why? she asked herself, I only wanted us to be together. I thought she was wonderful, I only wanted her to let me hang around with her. She was so strong, so sure; she stood on her own feet and never minded what people said or thought. I wanted to be just like her but whatever I did to try to make her like me, she pushed me away.

The kettle boiled, but Susie didn't bother to make tea. She went back upstairs and got into bed, pulling the duvet up over her head to cocoon herself against long ago memories of Belle's rejection.

She frightens me, Susie thought; she frightened me then and she still does.

Susie realized that she had let herself believe that Belle's hostility had all to do with Ben because that would have been easier to deal with. She had allowed herself to hope that if she could bring that out into the open and admit she had done wrong and was sorry, then she might somehow make things right between herself and her sister. It had seemed like the right time, too, with poor Mum gone and Dad so devastated. And the Huntington's chorea too, she could have helped Belle through the shock of that, she knew what it was like. It was as though she and Belle had suddenly had to become the adults, they were the ones in control. Surely they could work out a way of moving on together?

I did try, Susie told herself, but she knew that her efforts had been undermined by her helplessness in her relationship with Belle. She had tried, but only in the certainty that she would fail as she had always failed as far as her sister was concerned.

What's she up to with John? Susie wondered, as the warmth of the duvet and the central heating made her feel sleepy. Thank God, she thought, whatever she says or does, John won't be taken in. Belle will never turn him against me, whatever lies she tells. When he gets home he'll tell me and we can have a laugh about it.

She buried her face in John's pillow and breathed in the faint smell of him. I miss you so much, she thought, I love you. She felt extraordinarily blessed, secure in John's love and trust and their happiness together. In only a few days John would be beside her, the children would be home, and life would be back to normal.

Susie rolled over and pushed the duvet down off her face. Poor Belle, she thought, she'll never be happy, not like I'm happy. I'd give her some of my happiness if I could, I really would. But then, Susie told herself sadly, Belle wouldn't like that, she'd never wanted to share anything, least of all anything I could give her. Perhaps John can help her, she thought as she fell asleep, perhaps she'll let him try.

25

It was the last day that Belle and John would be working together on the farm. Tomorrow was Saturday, when Susie was coming down for the night, and then Susie and John would go home on the Sunday afternoon. Susie would cook lunch, that would be her contribution to the family get-together.

'You've the makings of a farmer yourself,' Dad said to John at breakfast.

John laughed. 'I couldn't keep it up,' he said. 'I've never worked so hard in my life.'

'You'd get used to it,' Dad said. 'I remember when I first started – '

'Yes, yes, Dad, we know,' Belle said, cutting him short, 'you had to do everything by hand, cutting the hay with a scythe and sowing the fields broadcast from a bucket.'

She knew she was being rude, but she couldn't bear the thought of Dad getting started on the old days and have John look down on him as some kind of ridiculous relic of the past.

But John gave her a hard look. 'I can't imagine how tough it must've been,' he said to Dad. 'One day, when our latter-day Simon Legré here isn't around, I'd love to hear what it was like.'

Dad smiled gratefully at John, but Belle had seen how her interruption had cowed him.

'I didn't mean it like that, Dad,' she said, but she knew it was no good. She couldn't take back what she'd said.

'No,' Dad said, 'you're right. It's John's last working day and we don't want to waste it with my ramblings.' He turned to John and added, 'I'm an old man and I tend to go on a bit. The trouble is, the past seems much more real to me now than the present, and I'm afraid young things like Belle here find me a bore.'

'It comes to us all,' John said, trying to reassure him. 'It'll come to Belle and me, but what we'll have to talk about won't be nearly so interesting as your memories.'

'The trouble is, when you get to my age, you'd much rather spend time in the past rather than the present. Everything seems to have been better in those days, we were happier then. We had some say in our own lives, at least.' Dad shook his head and stared blankly at his plate.

It was warm in the kitchen with the Aga, but Belle shivered. My God, she thought, what kind of memories will I have? I'll be half-senile and babble on about the things I've done and how I got away with murder, and no one will believe me. Worse still, she reminded herself, if little sister Susie has her way I'll be in a wheelchair and unable even to feed myself, except I'll kill myself before that happens.

She tried to laugh off this bleak prospect. 'I haven't even started creating memories yet,' she said. 'I'm going to be like Scheherazade and keep everyone fascinated for a thousand and one nights.'

She knew that what she'd said to her father had shocked John, and she wanted to appease him. 'Come on,' she said, 'there's the ditching to finish before we even start on clearing the awful old straw out of the barn. They're delivering the new stuff on Monday and if we don't, there'll be nowhere to put it.'

'I'll come with you,' Dad said, 'we'll be finished by lunchtime.'

There was nothing Belle could say. She couldn't rebuff him again, not after what she'd said. But she felt cheated, she had looked forward to being alone with John. She wanted to talk to him before Susie came and spoiled everything.

In the afternoon, Dad drove into the local town to buy rat poison and staples at the agricultural merchants. By that time, she and John had almost finished clearing the old bales of straw out of the barn.

As John carried out the last mouldering straw, Belle began to sweep the dust from the flagstones.

Probably nobody's swept this floor since Ben died, she thought, some of this debris could have been undisturbed since then. There may still be dust from drops of his blood in the dirt.

She tried to conjure up a picture of Ben in her mind's eye, but she couldn't. Even in her nightmare, reliving his death, she couldn't see his face any more. He'd been dark and good-looking, with beautiful even white teeth, but that was all she could bring to mind. She thought, My God, the only way Ben comes alive to me now is through hating Susie.

Belle became suddenly aware that she was sweating. That's true of my whole life, she thought, everything that's ever happened to me in the past has all become just a part of hating Susie. I'm not sure exactly why I hate her any more, I just do.

It seemed to Belle that this was true of everything that had gone to form the person who was now herself, of her schooling, her childhood experiences, her relationship with her parents. She couldn't think of any of these things except as evidence of the wrongs that Susie had done her. And the bad things she had done in her own right since she last saw Susie had all been caused by a kind of mission for revenge against her little sister.

But these were not the horrors that made her sweat now. What had suddenly made her skin crawl with terror was the fear that her hatred of Susie was the only thing that made her want to go on living.

Except John, she told herself, and suddenly Susie seemed unimportant, an irritation remembered from long ago. The thought of John made Belle feel that the sun had suddenly come out in her life.

She applied herself to sweeping. Moving the old straw had been hot work and John had taken off his shirt. With his dark colouring, he'd tanned easily working outside over the last ten days. Belle's arms and neck were bright red with the effort of lugging the old bales. They were both sweating, and all their exposed skin was covered with a thick coating of straw dust. Their eyes and mouths looked startlingly naked through the thick grey coating of dirt.

'I'll never grumble about police paperwork ever again,' John said at last, putting his fists against the small of his back to ease the muscles. 'That was my previous idea of hell, but this is far, far worse.'

Belle laughed. 'Oh, come on,' she said, 'you're enjoying doing some real man's work for a change, admit it.'

'Oh, you think so, do you?' John said. 'You don't look much like a man to me.'

He was teasing her, but when he looked at her, he started to laugh. 'Or a woman, either,' he said. 'You don't look human at all.'

Belle detested being laughed at. She didn't know how to respond to his teasing, but she wanted to stop him laughing at her.

She picked up the hose she was about to use to finish cleaning the barn floor and turned it on him.

He shouted and made a lunge for her, but she was too quick for him. She was laughing now, as his familiar face and torso emerged from the dust coating and he looked himself again.

She let him catch her, and felt the shock of the cold water as he turned the hose on her, soaking her. For a moment it felt wonderful.

'Stop, stop, that's enough,' she squealed.

He threw down the hose. They were both panting. Belle was suddenly aware of the drenched clothes clinging to her body. John looked at her, then down at his own wet jeans. He said, 'Now what do we do?'

'Dad's probably back by now. He'll be in the house. We can't let him see us like this.' Belle said.

John looked doubtful.

'We can't,' Belle said. 'He wouldn't understand. He'd think it his duty to tell Susie that there's something going on between us.'

'But there isn't,' John said; 'why should he think that?'

Belle said curtly, 'Ask Susie. She was the local bike, not me. That's what Dad thinks women do. Except for my mother, of course.'

She could tell that he didn't at all like that bike remark about Susie.

'He already thinks your marriage is on the rocks,' she said.

'What?' John laughed, incredulous.

'He asked me,' Belle said. 'I told him he was wrong,'

'Thanks for that,' he said. Then he added, 'If we get back to work, we'll probably dry off.'

'Hang on, I think I can do better than that. There used to be some old overalls hanging in the hayloft,' Belle said.

She didn't add that Susie kept them there in the old days because she hadn't liked lying naked on the hay, it was too scratchy against her skin. Belle certainly didn't mention that she'd hung the overalls back up there herself, after she'd pushed Ben off the hayloft. They would still be there, no one would have thought to move them. All too vividly, she remembered how the denim had smelled of the two of them, Susie's Miss Dior *eau de toilette* and Ben's aftershave mingled with fresh sweat.

John followed her up the ladder.

'There they are,' she said. 'They must've been hanging there for years.'

She took down the bundle and tossed a pair of dungarees towards John.

'Rub yourself down with some hay and put these on,' she said.

She shook out some overalls for herself.

John hesitated, the dungarees dangling from his hand.

Belle laughed. 'You're not embarrassed, are you?' she said. 'I promise I won't look. Here, do it like this.'

She took a handful of hay and twisted it into a large pad. Then she began to rub his shoulders with it. 'We used to do this with the horses when they got back from hunting,' she said. 'It gets the blood to the surface. You don't want to get cold.'

'That hurts,' he said about her vigorous rubbing. 'That's enough. I pity those poor horses. You can look the other way now.'

'What about me?' she said. 'I can't reach; you'll have to rub my shoulders.'

Reluctantly he began to rub her back and shoulders with a handful of hay.

'Hang on,' she said. She undid her sodden bra and threw it down. 'That'll make it easier,' she said.

'Belle, I – ' He stopped massaging her skin with the wad of hay. 'It's scratching you,' he said. 'I'll make you bleed if I go on.'

Belle swivelled round so that she was facing him. She pressed her naked breasts against him and felt drops of water caught in the hairs on his chest cold against her hot nipples.

'Make love to me,' she said. Her voice was low and urgent as she dropped a hand to fumble with the zip on his fly.

He tried to push her away, but she clamped a hand behind his neck and as she fell backwards on to the hay, she pulled him with her.

'Please, John,' she said, 'I want you to.'

He struggled to move away from her.

'Belle,' he said, 'Belle, please, don't do this.'

'You don't have to pretend,' she said. 'I know you want me, and I want you too.'

'No,' he shouted, 'no, no, no.'

She sat up suddenly and he rolled away from her.

'What do you mean, no?' she said. 'What's the matter?'

'I don't love you,' he said. 'I can't make love to you.'

She smiled at him and reached out to touch his cheek gently with the tips of the fingers of her left hand.

'It's all right,' she said. 'You don't have to pretend. Susie won't know. I know you can't leave your kids, but one day . . . '

'No,' he said, 'you don't understand. It's nothing to do with Susie. I can't think of you *that* way, Belle. You're a great girl, like a real sister, but I couldn't. I don't love you, I love Susie.'

'Even though she's a killer?' Belle said.

'Don't say that,' John said. 'I don't know what happened, but I can't believe she really killed him.' He saw the look on Belle's face and added quickly, 'Not intentionally, anyway. I can't believe she murdered him in cold blood.'

He got to his feet and went to the top of the ladder. 'If I gave you the wrong impression, Belle, I'm really sorry,' he said. 'I think you're wonderful, and I've had a great time working with you this last week. I thought we'd become friends, I wanted us to be friends.'

Belle leaned over and pulled on the overalls to cover herself.

John said, 'I'm going in to put on dry clothes. I'll tell your dad you pushed me in the horse trough if he asks why I'm wet.'

As he climbed down the ladder, he called back to her, 'Belle, I'm so sorry.'

Belle listened to the sound of his footsteps on the flagstones until she could hear them no longer. Then Benson barked, and she knew that John must have gone into the house.

Belle felt she was going to be sick. She started to shiver. That's it, she thought, that's the end of everything for me.

She was too hurt even to cry. All she could think to do was to become angry. But she couldn't be angry with John. It wasn't his fault. Susie had him in some sort of thrall; she'd brainwashed him. It was easy to be angry with Susie. OK, she told herself, so we'll go for Plan B. If I can't have you willingly, John, you're going to have to find out just what kind of monster Susie really is. Don't say I didn't warn you.

2 6

Belle didn't follow John into the house. She stripped off her wet clothes and put on the dungarees, which must have been Susie's because they weren't big enough for her. They would have to do. She couldn't go into the house. There was no way she could face having to speak to John as though nothing had happened, or to her father, not yet.

She walked away from the farm, like an injured animal looking for somewhere to hide.

She moved purposefully, but she had no clear idea where she was going, except that she wanted to be alone. It was late afternoon and the wind had dropped. As far as she could see across the wasteland of stony scrubland where the neighbour's sheep had grazed the salty grass down to the roots, everything seemed part of a painted landscape, suspended in time. It was unnaturally quiet. There was no sound of birds, nor even the faint crash of breaking waves against the sea wall.

The residual farmer in Belle was concerned that after the dry spring there was little sign of new growth in the grass beneath her feet. That did not bode well for next winter's keep.

Now she knew where she was going. To one side of the mudflats, no longer close to the sea, what had once been a rocky headland reared up out of the boggy reclaimed pasture now protected from the encroaching water behind a man-made bastion of rock. These vast blocks of stone had been quarried from the old headland and dumped along the shoreline.

Belle, without thinking, made for the quarry, long abandoned once the sea wall had been put in place. This was where she had taken refuge as a child, riding the pony furiously across the beach and then picking her way up the overgrown path to the edge of a great gash in the rock plundered long ago by the quarrymen. Here she had howled out her rage and frustration against Susie and all those who loved Susie and not her. No one came near to overhear her secret ravings. Only the stony-hearted walls of rock seemed to mock her despair, echoing her wails like a chorus in a Greek tragedy.

After so many years the path up to the top of the quarry had now almost disappeared beneath briars and nettles. Thorns tore at Belle's clothes, but she struggled on. She had to be alone, to think, and this was the only place she knew where that was possible. Only occasionally, in bad weather, a neighbouring farmer might come looking for a lost sheep; or, in the summer, children might find their way into the quarry to smoke illicit cigarettes and drink cheap cider in secret. It wasn't even a place for lovers; the most ardent lust could not survive those brambles or the rampant nettles.

At last she reached the top. Here there was a patch of stunted grass free of briars and even nettles. Perhaps there was too little soil for them to put down roots. It had been the same when the young Belle had come up here to be by herself. The pony had grazed on the grass, ignoring her.

As she had done then, Belle sat on the edge of the quarry with her knees drawn up to her chin. For a while, she rocked to and fro like an unhappy animal confined in a too-small space, emitting a low moaning wail because there seemed no other way to express her misery.

She did not hate John for rejecting her. Her only way of dealing with what had happened was to force herself not to *feel* anything. She had offered herself to him without reserve, body and soul, and John did not want her. That hurt far too deeply for her to be able to face it. Her overriding reaction was to fall back on the familiar, her loathing for Susie. Once more Susie had destroyed the thing that made Belle want to go on living. Belle had given John a choice and he had chosen Susie. As Ben had done, except this was worse than Ben because then she was young enough to hope for the future. Now she wasn't.

Belle thought, All I've got left is hating Susie.

She didn't even blame John, not really. He had let her down. She had thought he had more courage. She was disappointed because he had confirmed what she'd feared, that there was no hope of anything worthwhile in her life. He had humiliated and embarrassed her, but perhaps she would find a way to make him sorry for that. He was weak, his courage had failed him. He had rejected Belle to stay true to Susie. Always Susie, Susie, Susie. He had been tempted by Belle, certainly. At least, she told herself he must have been. She had felt a real bond between the two of them, him and her, a sympathy that could have turned to passion, she was sure of that. But he was a husband and father, he'd made promises, he had responsibilities, and for wife and children he sacrificed himself without question, denying himself the happiness Belle could have offered him. He sacrificed *her*.

He and I could have been happy, Belle thought, but like everything good in my life, Susie's got him for herself. She won't let him go. If he followed his heart and left her, she would take his children away from him, she'd spoil everything for him and them. Greedy, selfish bitch. She never even loved him, not really, she couldn't have. She always had too many men to love any one of them unselfishly. He can't love her any more, either, but he's like an addict, he won't break the habit.

He can't really love her, Belle told herself, not knowing what she is he can't. He believes that she could be a killer, I know he does, even if he pretends he doesn't. He made out he didn't believe me when I said she killed Ben, but he did, or at least he had doubts. He thought it possible. But she's the mother of those two kids of his, so he has to pretend she couldn't do anything so dreadful.

It crossed her mind, just for a moment, that without the kids, things might be different. If they were removed there would be nothing to hold John and Susie together, she told herself. But then she thought, It's no good, he loves those children. Without them, he'd be so broken he wouldn't be the same person. He said it himself, she thought, he said humans aren't like cats or foxes, they don't kill for practice. There'd be nothing to gain from getting rid of them.

She was surprised that she felt relieved.

Belle knew that she must force herself to face the fact that actually she didn't know what John felt or thought about anything, she had no idea. Except about his kids. But she couldn't face that yet. I'm not mad, she told herself, I'm just not like other women, at least I'm not like Susie.

Belle lay on her back on the short grass and stared at the sky. The clouds were amazing, a mountain range on the horizon. Looking up was like looking at the world from the inside of a globe, blue seas, trailing mud-coloured estuaries of great rivers, the icy white wastes of the polar snowcaps. It looked like a real landscape and it was all an illusion, the chance interaction of wind and cloud.

Belle allowed herself to think of John. Was it all over for her? When he turned her down like that, so brutally, she could have died of embarrassment and shame. And now he knew the way she felt about him, there was no possibility they could even be friends.

'I don't want to be your friend,' Belle suddenly screamed. 'I want to be everything to you.'

The rock walls of the quarry seemed to hesitate before they repeated the sound. She listened to the hysterical echo of her own voice as it reverberated, dying away on a tremulous note.

Like someone demented, Belle banged her head against her knees until the pain brought her to her senses. What's the point, after all? she thought. All I've left to live for is to destroy Susie's life; I've filled my entire life with that one thing. How sad is that? After that there's no future for me. I've got away with murder; once I've ended Susie's life, there will be nothing left. I don't want to stay on and make a go of the farm, it's pointless except to take it away from Susie. No one could make the place pay, and the money from selling the land for development doesn't mean anything to me, I've nothing I want to do with it.

Belle saw all this without emotion. It was a statement of fact. There was no way she could escape the reality of her life, that there was not, and never would be, anyone she could tell about herself; no one to whom she could reveal herself without driving them away. Without anyone or anything to love, she had nothing for Susie to steal from her. But what was left anyway? What difference would it make? If she stopped hating Susie, that was the end. Or would her hatred live on even after her sister's death? As for new beginnings, no one loved or needed Belle. Dad was an old man now, he was like a husk, not a living person. She had no lover, no children, no friends, no interests. I am the absolute definition of barren, she thought, and started to shiver.

For a brief moment, John had had the power to change the future for them all. He'd only had to choose. With him at her side, Belle could have made the farm viable. With her own life fulfilled, she might not have gone on hating Susie. In possession of John, she could have been magnanimous in victory. Her little sister could never hurt her again. We could've had a normal life, she thought, we could've been happy.

But John had said no.

She got to her feet and brushed the grass off the dungarees with her hands. She thought, So I know now what I've got to do. It's the only way.

It was growing dark, threatening, as though a vast storm was about to engulf the land, as she picked her way carefully down the overgrown path away from the quarry. The huge black clouds hunched on the horizon were lit from behind by the defeated sun, and the dark sky was full of ivory seagulls with wings like blades cutting through the gloom.

Belle told herself, I do have one thing Susie can't take away from me. When this is finished, I'll have accomplished what I set out to do. She's going to find that out for herself.

There was a sudden explosion of thunder and a searing flash as lightning struck an old tree at the top of the quarry. Then came the rain, drenching sheets of water which blotted out everything in front of her. Belle put back her head and stood, eyes closed, letting the deluge pour over her.

She thought, I wish I could pray.

27

The next day Susie arrived late in the afternoon. Belle, in her bedroom, heard the car and pressed herself against the wall so that she could watch out of the window without danger of being seen.

John must have been waiting in the barn, hoping for a few moments alone with his wife before Dad blundered in with the stock family questions about Susie's drive down, had she had lunch, did she want something to eat or drink, what about tea, Belle had the kettle boiling?

'Like hell I have,' she said aloud, and then realized that of course no one had said anything yet. Susie was getting out of the car in a bright filmy dress which clung to her voluptuous figure. She was laughing up at John, flinging her arms around his neck. She looked so happy to see him, Belle felt a painful wrenching in her stomach. John looked happy, too. He pushed away the hair blowing across her face and bent to kiss her.

'Dad, Susie's here,' Belle shouted into the house. 'She'll want help with her bag.'

She had no intention of leaving her room, but she wanted Dad to get out there quickly, to put a stop to the scene of marital bliss in the yard.

There was a crash somewhere downstairs as Dad tripped and knocked something down in his haste to greet Susie.

Belle watched as John put his arm round his wife and they began to walk towards the house. Then Dad came out, fussing over the new arrival, hugging her.

Belle looked on amazed and with a sour feeling of resentment. Dad doesn't hug me like that, she thought; we never touch each other if we can help it, we never did.

The little scene in the yard made her feel more than ever like an outsider who had no place on the farm.

And yet it's mine, she told herself, it's they who have no place here except on my terms. It wouldn't be long now before they realized that from now on she was the one who called the shots.

She heard Dad call her as they came into the house, but she took no notice. She heard Dad say, 'She must've gone out. I thought she was here.'

'She hasn't taken the Land-Rover,' John said, 'she can't have gone far.'

There was something about the way he said this that filled Belle with resentment. He made it sound as though he had special knowledge of what Belle did; what he said was almost possessive, as though Belle belonged to him, or, rather, to them, the family.

They went into the kitchen and she heard no more.

She looked around her bedroom and went to lie down on the bed. No one will look for me here, she thought, they won't dare because Dad and Susie both know that if I'm here, I don't want to be with them.

An hour or two later, though, she was hungry. Susie was cooking supper. Belle could smell pork roasting in the Aga, and her resolve melted. I'm being ridiculous, she thought, I want to see them sitting round being happy together because they don't know that what happens next depends on me.

She put on make-up very carefully, and took great care with her hair and the way she tied a silk scarf round her neck to hide the fraying on the old T-shirt she was wearing. She didn't change out of that because if she'd put on something better Susie would be bound to make some remark about who was she dressing to impress? and John would think she was doing it for him.

She found Benson in the hall and took him with her into the kitchen as though she had returned from a walk with him.

Dad and John were sitting at the table while Susie fussed over a pan on the Aga. There was a place at the table laid for her. They were all startled when she came in, as though they had not been expecting her, in spite of the place laid for her.

John stood up and pulled back a chair for her to sit down. 'I was coming to look for you,' he said. 'We couldn't think where you'd got to. No one thought of Benson.'

Susie looked over to her as though she would have said something if she could think of anything to say.

Belle ignored her. 'Something smells good,' she said to no one in particular.

There was silence.

'You're a policeman,' Belle said to John, 'you must be able to tell me. People say that when humans die in fires, they smell just like pork roasting. Is it true?'

Susie made a disgusted face.

'Stop it, Belle, there's no call for that sort of thing,' Dad said.

'No,' Belle said, 'John's the only person who might be in a position to tell me.'

'I don't know,' John said. 'I've never dealt with anything like that. Perhaps you should ask a fireman, not a policeman.'

Nobody said much during the meal. Belle found it hard to use her fork, so she stopped eating before anyone could notice. Susie scarcely touched her food. There were two spots of red on her cheeks as though she was angry, but Belle knew only too well that Susie really wanted to burst into tears because her pleasure in the perfect evening she had planned as the inheritor of Mum's place in the family had been spoiled. Susie couldn't even blame Belle, her question to John had been innocent enough. She wouldn't blame Belle, anyway; she knew how she had contributed to hurting Belle by making love to Ben that time, and she would always feel guilty about what happened. She had no right to blame Belle.

'That was a great meal,' Belle said, and when she smiled, Susie understood that her sister had deliberately sabotaged her efforts.

'Thanks,' Susie said. 'Can you make coffee for those who want it, John? I'm going to phone the kids. And you must remember you haven't started to pack your stuff.'

'I'll pack when we've finished milking in the morning.'

'When you've *what?*' Susie said. 'Did you say you're doing the milking?'

'John's been a tower of strength,' Dad said. 'He's helped Belle with the milking and they've finished laying the hedge on the ten acres.'

'And cleared the ditches on that far field near the mudflats,' John said, pleased to be able to boast of his achievement.

'You and Belle?' Susie said. She clearly did not know what to make of John's pride in his work.

'Belle's a great teacher,' John said, 'even if she did have to stand over me with a whip sometimes.'

Susie tried to smile but the effort showed. 'Well,' she said, ignoring Belle, 'perhaps sometime you'll get her to let me into the secret of how to get you doing physical labour. There's always plenty to be done at home.' She opened the door to go out and added, 'Goodnight, Dad, we'll have a proper chat in the morning. Don't be too long, John.'

'Oh, dear,' Belle said, 'me and my big mouth! I seem to have upset Little Sister Susie, and I was only trying to make conversation.'

'She'll get over it,' John said. 'I can't say the same for me, if she thinks I've turned into Action Man.'

The next morning, Belle and Dad did the milking together. There was no sign of John.

'I think Susie had other plans for him,' Dad said, and grinned. 'It's your fault. I think she's afraid he's caught the farming bug, and that wouldn't suit our Susie.'

'I must tell her about our plans for me to take over here,' Belle said. 'She'll probably be relieved about it. She wouldn't want John turning into Worzel Gummidge on her, would she?'

'He's got a good job as it is,' Dad said. He spoke slowly, as though he was thinking about something else. 'He'd make a good farmer, though, don't you think?'

'Not while he's married to Susie, he wouldn't,' Belle said firmly.

'I suppose you're right,' Dad said. He sounded wistful.

He released the last of the cows so that she could follow the others out into the pasture.

'It would be nice, though, having this place as a real family farm again,' he said. 'You'd like that, wouldn't you? You seem to get on well with John.'

Belle pretended she hadn't heard him.

Susie was in the kitchen, cooking breakfast, when Belle came in.

'I'm sorry, I forgot to set the alarm,' Susie said. 'John overslept and I didn't like to wake him.'

'Do you remember the old quarry?' Belle asked.

Susie looked surprised. She frowned.

'I used to go up there a lot when we were kids,' Belle said. 'I thought it must've been one of your secret places too.'

Susie shook her head. 'I went up there once and saw the pony there and knew you must be there. I never went back after that,' she said.

'How sensitive of you,' Belle said, and then, because she had sounded more harsh than she'd intended, she added, 'We all have our childhood sanctuaries, and the quarry was mine. Didn't you have somewhere?'

'Yes,' Susie said, 'I had a place where the rocks were piled up on the beach for a sea wall. There was a sort of cave there, except in the end I got too big to get through the entrance.'

'There's something important I want to say to you before you go,' Belle said. 'I don't want Dad or John to know. It's between me and you. Will you meet me at the quarry before you go?'

'But surely we could talk in the barn, or down the lane? Does it have to be the quarry?'

Belle filled the kettle and lifted the hotplate cover next to where Susie was frying bacon.

'Please, Susie,' she said, 'what I want to say is going to be difficult for me, and somehow it would be easier there. If you and I set off across the fields together, Dad and John'll be suspicious. They'll want to come with us, know what's going on. You can bring Benson to the quarry and say you're taking him for a walk so no one will suspect.'

'Can't you tell me now?' Susie said. 'It sounds like such a production. Is this about Huntington's chorea?'

If Belle wants to talk about that, I'll go wherever she wants, Susie thought. Maybe she wants to know how to get herself tested.

'If I'm going to do it,' Belle said, 'I've got to do it in my own way, and I feel at home at the quarry.'

Susie shrugged. 'Oh, OK, have it your own way. You always did, didn't you?'

'For God's sake,' Belle said, 'you're making such a fuss, anyone would think you're afraid I'm going to push you over the edge to your death below.

She laughed, and Susie almost laughed too.

28

'My God,' Susie said, 'why didn't you have us meet on the summit of Everest while you were at it?'

'I feel at home here,' Belle said.

'I wonder why?' Susie said. 'You must be crazy.'

Susie felt daunted by the grimness of the place. There had been rain earlier in the day and that, after a spell of dry weather, seemed to have given the brambles and towering nettles a surge of triffid-like growth. They look carnivorous, Susie thought, and shuddered. The great slabs of granite, too, seemed to have taken on a life of their own, implacable and primitive. And slippery. She wanted to turn and run.

'I feel it's mine,' Belle said.

'It looks dangerous to me,' Susie said.

'That's why I like it,' Belle said.

Susie had nothing to say to that. She was scared, but she couldn't have said what frightened her about this place. Perhaps it was Belle, and the way her sister seemed to belong there, part of the sinister and implacable brutality of those dark rocks and the rapacious weeds.

Susie knew that Belle must have been waiting at the quarry for nearly an hour. She had seen her sister set off, walking with that odd prancing movement Susie couldn't remember from the old days. She herself had intended to be late, but not as late as she was. The going up the overgrown path had been tougher than she expected. The old dog, Benson, had refused to start up the track at all. Susie had tried to make him come. She felt horribly alone when he left her.

But now, facing her sister, some instinct told her not to let Belle see her fear. She said, breathing hard from the climb, 'That's the first time I've ever felt I'm not really young any more. Is that what you wanted?'

'Why should I?' Belle said. 'I'm not likely to forget I'm a year older than you. But, come to think of it, the state you're in after climbing up here rather demonstrates the point of what I'm going to tell you. I'm certainly fitter than you.'

'Is that what this is about?' Susie said. 'I concede, I'm hopelessly out of shape, OK?' Is this her way of showing me she's not ill? she asked herself, and wished that she could tell her sister that indeed she must be clear to be so strong.

The mid-morning sun was high enough in the sky to have warmed the short grass at the quarry's edge. Susie threw herself down, shielding her eyes with raised hands as she looked up at Belle and laughed.

'Isn't it wet?' Belle asked. Sprawling in the sun like that, she thought, it's such a Susie thing to do.

But part of her wished that there wasn't always something holding her back from doing carefree things like cavorting on warm grass in the sun. She envied Susie who was so natural about it, like some glorious young predatory animal, a sportive hunter for whom all play was practice for the kill; a young leopard, perhaps, or a cub fox.

Susie was still laughing. 'At least if I'm lying down you can't push me off the top of the quarry,' she said.

'Don't be silly,' Belle said.

'You were the one who put it in my mind,' Susie said. She was teasing Belle, who had never had any sense of humour at all, especially about herself. 'I even left a note to John saying I was coming here to meet you, just in case.'

'You can't think I'd do something like that,' Belle said. She wished that Susie hadn't brought John into this. She had looked forward to telling her sister that Dad had handed over the farm to her for the pleasure of watching Susie suffer a knock-out emotional punch. Belle knew how much Susie must have been depending on the money she would make from selling the house and farmland. It would make all the difference to a greedy bitch like Susie, married to a humble policeman and with two demanding children. Belle had no doubt that Susie's children were bound to be spoiled brats. Belle wanted to be able to pity her, in a dispassionate kind of way, as Susie recognized the extent of her older sister's triumph.

But now Susie had mentioned John, with all the superiority and confidence of her possession of him, and as Belle's sense of triumph dwindled in importance, she felt the familiar relentless tightening of hatred for her sister well up inside her. She couldn't pity Susie while Susie had John.

Susie saw Belle's expression harden, and she held out her hand as if asking Belle to help her to her feet. 'Lighten up,' Susie said, 'I was joking, for God's sake.'

'Joking?' Belle said in a dazed sort of way. She ignored Susie's out-stretched hand as though she didn't see it. 'Oh, joking? So you didn't leave a note?'

'Only to tell him where we are in case I'm not back before he's ready to go.'

'Oh, yes, of course. I'd better get on with this, then.'

Susie was curious. 'You're being very mysterious,' she said. 'Is this about Mum?'

'Mum? What about Mum?'

Belle's voice betrayed that this unexpected interruption to her carefully prepared script had put her on the defensive.

'I saw your face when you came down to the kitchen after she died,' Susie said. 'She said something to you, didn't she?'

'She said she loved me,' Belle said. 'She died saying she loved me.'

Susie shook her head. 'It wasn't that,' she said. 'I think you feel guilty.'

She meant that Belle might now regret the way she had turned her back on her doomed mother when she left home, but she hadn't expected the fury in Belle's face.

'What do you mean, guilty?' Belle shouted at her. And the rocks echoed her voice: Guilty, guilty, guilty.

Susie floundered for something innocuous to say. All her old fear of what Belle was capable of doing to her made her conciliatory.

'I thought you were feeling bad because it seemed to me you didn't want to touch her. After she was dead, I mean.'

'What made you think I didn't want to touch her?' Belle asked, staring at her sister. She was thinking, How does she know that? How does she know the thought of even looking at dead people makes me feel sick?

'It was just an impression I got,' Susie said. 'Or maybe I feel guilty because I felt the same way.'

'Oh, really, did you?' Belle said. 'Well, it didn't worry me. What bothered me was Dad, the way he kissed her, it was bloody perverted.'

Susie laughed. 'Oh, God,' she said, 'you can't mean that. He loved her and he was trying to hold on to her. It was really touching.'

'Not to me it wasn't,' Belle said.

'You're mad,' Susie said.

Belle rounded on her then. 'I'm not mad,' she said, and Susie recognized real fury in her voice. 'I'm not the one that's mad. You are, if you think it's normal to try to give a corpse the kiss of life.'

'Hey, OK. I'm only trying to say that it was sad the way he couldn't bear to let her go. He wasn't kissing a corpse, he was kissing Mum. He refused to accept she was dead, he was in denial.'

Belle stared at the dark rocks and the great pit of the quarry. She was silent.

'So what do you want to say to me?' Susie asked. 'You're being very mysterious. Is this some dire secret about Ben?'

'Ben? What's Ben got to do with it?'

'He's the only thing I can think of for you to be so secretive about,' Susie said. 'Though God knows I don't know what secrets you can have left after all this time.'

She stood up. The sun seemed to set fire to her hair, and Belle could see the dusting of gold freckles where her blouse revealed her breasts.

'No, not Ben,' Belle said. 'This is about the farm.'

Susie frowned. 'The farm? What about the farm? There's no reason why Dad can't carry on as he is.' Then her face cleared, and she said, 'Oh, I see, you're worried about leaving him alone? You must be dying to get back to London and your government job and all.' Oh, God, she thought, why did I say dying? She insisted, 'You go ahead, there's no need to worry about him. I'll come over and keep an eye on him from time to time. You go ahead, you've taken quite enough time off already.'

'No,' Belle said, 'it's not that. I'm not going anywhere. Dad's handed the farm over to me. I've given up my London job and I'm taking over from him. The farm's mine.'

Susie stared at her. 'You mean you're staying with him here?'

'No,' Belle said, and she sounded as though she were repeating a simple lesson to a stupid pupil. 'No, Dad's going to live in Scotland with Aunt Kirsty. He's given me the farm.'

Susie put her hand over her mouth in shock. 'But why? He loves the place.'

'He wants to go,' Belle said. 'Apparently he and Mum were planning to retire to be near Aunt Kirsty anyway. Now he's on his own and so's she, he's going to live with her. And he wants me to take over.'

Susie jumped to her feet. Her eyes blazed and her mouth was ugly with anger. Belle watched her as though Susie were an actress making the most of her part as the murder victim in a film.

'He can't do this to me,' Susie said. 'He promised everything would come to me.'

It's fascinating to see Susie like this, Belle thought; she looks as if she'd like to kill me. Perhaps we share a murder gene in our DNA.

'You couldn't run the farm,' she told Susie, 'look at the state of you just coming up that little path. You'd sell it off to developers as soon as you could, and take the money.'

'If you had children . . . ' Susie said.

'Dad obviously doesn't think yours have the makings of farmers,' Belle said.

'That's not what I meant,' Susie said. 'If you had kids you'd know what it's like to have their future security taken away suddenly like this.' She wanted to, but she didn't add, 'Particularly when they've escaped that terrible disease.' Susie knew there was no point in appealing to Belle's sympathy.

'John's got a good job,' Belle was saying. 'There's your house, you own that. You're not hard up.'

'But John might take up farming when he comes out of the police. He's good at it. You've seen that for yourself.'

'John does like farming. But if he took over the farm with you, he'd want to be rid of you within months. You're far too girly. He wouldn't be able to stand having someone like you around. Believe me, I'm doing you a favour.'

Susie's face contorted with loathing. She attacked Belle, trying to hit her, then grabbing her by the arms.

Belle laughed, easily fending her off. She held Susie off, scratching her sister's arm as she pushed her away.

'What are you trying to do, Susie, push me over the edge?'

Susie gave up and stepped back. 'What kind of monster are you?' she said. She was almost in tears, clearly shocked at herself for what she had wanted to do to Belle. She shocked herself because for a moment she'd wanted to scream at her sister that she hoped she was going to die, that she would develop Huntington's, and of course it wasn't true.

She said,'I'm sorry, Belle, I don't know what got into me. You're my sister, for God's sake. You've got every right to a share in the farm. But so have I. You must see I can't let him get away with this, he can't just cut me out.'

'I think he can do anything he likes, but you're welcome to try to sort something out with him,' Belle said. 'But Dad told me what he wanted to do, and I thought you ought to know.'

'Yes,' Susie said.

Belle turned away to look across the quarry. 'You should get back to John,' she said, 'he'll be sending out search parties for you.'

'Does John know?'

'I don't know if Dad's said anything. I don't think so, Dad wanted me to tell you first.'

Susie turned to go. She said to Belle, 'Are you coming?'

'No,' Belle said. 'I'll stay up here for a while on my own. I hate family farewells.'

Susie looked relieved. She much preferred to go back on her own. 'Benson's at the bottom of the path,' she said. 'If he knows you're here, he may wait for you rather than come with me. Will you look out for him? He always liked you better than me.'

'I looked after him and you didn't, that's all,' Belle said. 'He was a working dog, not a pet.'

It seemed to cross Susie's mind to offer to shake hands, but she didn't. She said, 'Goodbye, Belle.'

Belle watched her sister hurry away down the rocky path, until the beacon of her hair disappeared behind a wall of brambles.

' 'Bye, Susie,' she called, and as the echo flung the words back at her from the depths of the quarry, she laughed.

29

Dad and John were in the kitchen when Susie got back to the farm.

She looked unusually flushed and dishevelled.

John said, 'What's up?'

'Let's get going,' she said. 'I've wasted enough time this morning as it is.'

'Where's Benson?' Dad asked.

'He dropped out ages ago,' Susie said. 'That mutt's not as stupid as he looks.'

'Hey, Susie, he's an old dog. What's happened, anyway?'

John was concerned. She wasn't at all her usual smiling self.

She made a visible effort to pull herself together, forcing a rather ghastly smile.

'Oh, it's nothing,' she said. 'I can't think why Belle makes such a production of everything. She pisses me off. I've ripped myself to pieces forcing my way through brambles and practically broken my neck climbing up the west face of the quarry just because she wanted to make some sort of point at my expense.'

'What point?' Dad asked. John thought he looked nervous.

'God only knows. That she's tougher than me, I suppose. Who knows what goes on in Belle's head, after all?'

Susie's tone was frosty, and she gave Dad a hard look.

'Where *is* Belle?' John said.

'Oh, she stayed behind at the quarry. It was her special place when we were kids, apparently. She probably wanted to remember old times. For God's sake, let's get going.'

'I'd have thought she'd be here to say goodbye,' John said. 'Shouldn't we wait?'

Susie thought he sounded disappointed and she felt irritated.

'She said to tell you she doesn't like goodbyes,' she said. Her tone was cold.

'I wanted to tell her how much I enjoyed being here and working on the farm,' John said. 'I hope we can do it again. We made quite a team.'

'Dad'll tell her when he sees her, won't you, Dad?'

'Hey, what's the rush?' John was puzzled. Usually Susie was so laid back.

'I guess I miss the children,' Susie said. 'And they'll be dying to see you again.'

'But they're not even at home,' John said. 'You said they're staying with my mother for the weekend.'

'Oh, John, for goodness sake!'

It suddenly dawned on John, when he saw her expression, that she'd prolonged the children's being away so that when they got home he and she could be alone in the house. He understood that she didn't want to waste any of that precious time together.

'I'm right behind you,' he said. He had already put his bag in the car. He shook hands with Dad. 'See you soon,' he said. 'Any time you want help round the farm . . . '

Dad walked out to the car with him. Susie was already sitting in the passenger seat.

'Thanks for all you've done,' Dad said to her, leaning forward to talk through the driver's open window. 'And organising everything about Mum,' he added. 'I'm not sure what I'd have done without you two.'

'Well, you've got Belle to look after things now, if you're overwhelmed,' Susie said. 'I expect she'll keep you company for as long as you're here.'

'Susie . . . ' Dad said.

'Get moving,' Susie hissed at John. As they drove away, instead of waving at Dad as she usually did until he could no longer see the car, she shut the window and stared ahead without a backward glance.

Once they were on the main road and had left the farm well behind, John said, What was all that about?'

'What was what about?'

Susie sounded so unlike herself that he pulled into the side of the road. When he turned to look at her, he saw that she was crying.

'Susie? What is it? What's the matter?'

'Belle's not going back to London. She staying at the farm and taking over.'

'But, darling, that's good, isn't it? The farm's getting a bit too much for your dad on his own. He needs someone to help him, and who better than Belle? Don't you think it might be her way of letting bygones be bygones?'

'Dad's going to live in Scotland with Mum's sister Kirsty. She's a widow. You haven't met her, she couldn't get down to the funeral.'

John smiled, and tried to wipe away her tears with his hand. 'Well,' he said, 'what's wrong with that? They're both lonely. Are you afraid they'll get hitched and he'll cut you and Belle out of the will?'

Susie was shaken by a renewed storm of tears.

John said, 'You wouldn't begrudge your dad a bit of happiness, would you? Surely you wouldn't?'

'Dad's giving the farm to Belle,' Susie said. 'That's what she dragged me up to the top of that bloody quarry to tell me. He's cut me out of the will.'

John pulled her towards him and kissed her. He was still smiling, indulging her.

She pulled away from him. 'Aren't you going to say anything?' she shouted at him. 'He was going to leave it all to me. He promised me. He'd made a will saying so, and now he's going to make a new one giving everything to Belle.'

John said nothing for a while. He was deliberately not looking at her, watching the traffic flashing past them instead.

At last he said, 'He's thinking of the farm, I expect. He knows Belle likes that kind of thing.'

'It's so unfair,' Susie wailed.

'Is it?' John turned back to look her in the eyes. 'You've got so much compared to her. You've got the kids and me and the house. A life! She hasn't got anything.'

'She's got the farm now. She's got *our* farm, she's got the inheritance which was our children's future. Don't you see what this means for Jonty and Kim?'

He hesitated. He'd had no idea that Susie expected to inherit the farm. At last, 'No,' he said, 'honestly I don't. We'll provide for our own children's future. That's what it means, being a parent. We don't need handouts, not even your dad's.'

'It's not a handout, it's my right,' Susie said. 'Don't you see?'

'You didn't mind about Belle's rights when you were going to get the whole lot,' John said. His voice betrayed growing irritation. 'Anyway, your dad's nowhere near dead yet. Perhaps you can sort something out with him. You and Belle. When the dust's settled.'

'Huh, I wouldn't put money on him lasting long once he's signed over the deeds to Belle,' Susie said. 'There are all sorts of lethal accidents happening on farms every day, it wouldn't be difficult for her to arrange something.'

She wasn't serious, just lashing out to relieve her feelings, and, listening to her, John laughed as he moved out into the traffic. He wished Susie hadn't said it, though, it reminded him that she might herself once have arranged a fatal accident for Ben.

John and Susie lived in a four-bedroomed house on a housing estate on the outskirts of a busy commuter town on the Surrey Berkshire border. It was a typical family home, close to schools and a supermarket, with a small patch of garden in front bounded by a picket fence, and a lawn and flowerbeds at the back beyond an expanse of decking with a table and chairs under a big striped umbrella. They were happy there. It was convenient for John's work, Susie's neighbours were full-time mums like her, and the children could play safely in each others' gardens.

'I'll put the kettle on,' Susie said as she unlocked the front door.

'Forget tea, I'll open a bottle of wine,' John said. He wanted her to know he was aware that she had put off seeing the kids to spend time alone with him.

'It feels funny without the children here,' Susie said.

'I feel like a teenager secretly bringing his girlfriend home when his parents are out,' John said.

'It's rather exciting, isn't it?' Susie said. 'As though it doesn't belong to us.'

'Shall we explore upstairs?' John said, putting his arm round her waist.

'Why don't you bring the bottle and a couple of glasses up with you?' Susie said. 'We might as well make the most of having the place to ourselves.'

Late that evening, they lay watching the moon through the uncurtained window. Then the telephone on the bedside table rang,

Susie twined her arms and legs around him so that he couldn't move.

'Don't answer it,' she said, and he felt her kissing his ear.

'I've got to,' he said. He struggled to free himself, and managed to grab the phone.

'You're still on holiday,' Susie moaned, 'why can't they leave you alone for a few more hours.'

But then John jerked himself upright. 'Hold on,' he said into the receiver, 'say that again.'

Susie rolled away and pulled up the duvet to cover her naked breasts.

'There's probably nothing to worry about,' John was saying. 'When did the dog get back?'

'Who is it?' Susie said. 'What's happened?'

Susie could not mistake the urgency in John's voice. Her eyes looked huge as she stared at him. He put a hand on her shoulder.

'I think you should call the police,' John said into the phone. 'Just in case.'

Susie grabbed the phone from him.

'Dad?' she said. 'Dad, what's wrong?'

But the line was dead.

'That was Dad, wasn't it?' She was already gathering her scattered clothes from the floor round the bed. 'What's happened? Belle's done something awful, hasn't she? If she's hurt him, I'll kill her.'

'Belle hasn't come home,' John said.

He looked shocked, and there was a small tic at the corner of his mouth.

Susie stopped picking up her clothes with such urgency. She said, 'Oh, she's always wandering off by herself like that.' But she sounded unsure, as though she didn't quite believe what she was saying. 'She'll be sitting somewhere at the top of that awful quarry staring at the stars and thinking about how clever she's been, coming home out of the blue and changing everything to suit herself. She'll turn up.'

And, she told herself, there was another reason why Belle might want to be alone to think. For a moment she was tempted to tell John about the Huntington's chorea, but then she thought of all the explanations and the excuses for keeping it a secret from him and she held her tongue.

'I told your dad to call the police,' John said. 'He sounded desperate.'

'God, she's such a bitch,' Susie said. 'It's her way of showing Dad who's in charge. It won't even have occurred to her how worried he must be. She's so bloody selfish.'

'We'll have to go to him.' John was already almost dressed. 'I'll get the car out. You can ring my mother in the morning about the kids.'

'Calm down,' she said, 'there's no panic. It's just Belle playing drama queen to be the centre of attention. Trust me, we don't have to go now, there's no point. What can we do?'

'You can be there for your dad, for a start,' John said.

'I'll go in the morning,' she said. 'There's no reason to rush off and then find by the time we get there that she's safely tucked up in bed and demanding to know what all the fuss is about. Belle may be able to manipulate Dad but I'm not going to dance to her tune, not any more I'm not.'

'No,' John said, 'you didn't hear your dad's voice. He's really upset. We've got to go now.'

'OK, OK,' she said, 'but I'm warning you, it'll be a wasted journey.' Reluctantly she began to dress.

Once they were on the road, John seemed to relax. Now that he was doing something, rather than talking about it, he felt that he had the situation under control. He drove fast. It was after midnight, and there was little traffic about.

'Do you really think she's just gone walkabout?' John suddenly asked.

'Of course I do. It's typical,' Susie said. She was sulking that her elder sister could still pull strings to manipulate people. Or rather, she thought, not people in general, but me.

The light was on in the yard when they drove up to the farmhouse. Before the car had come to a halt, Dad hurried out of the back door to meet them.

He went to the driver's door and opened it.

'I thought you were the police,' he said. 'They said they'd be back.'

John got out of the car and took his arm.

'Let's get back inside into the warm,' he said, 'then you can tell us all about it.'

'She was at the bottom of the quarry,' Dad said.

He seemed dazed, as though he couldn't believe what he was saying.

Susie came up to them and kissed his cheek. 'Has Belle had an accident?'

It was John she was asking, not Dad.

'The police are with her,' Dad said. 'They're getting one of those teams up there.'

'Forensics?' John said. His voice was bleak.

'I don't know,' Dad said, and they could hear hysteria in his voice. 'All I know is Belle's dead.'

3 0

Susie said, 'You'd think they thought I killed her, the way they questioned me.'

'They had to question you,' Dad told her. 'It doesn't mean anything, but you were the last person to see her alive.'

'That doesn't make me guilty of anything, they should know that,' Susie said.

'They want to know what she said, if there was any sign that she intended to take her own life.' Dad was beginning to sound as though he were quoting from a handbook of police procedure.

'Of course she didn't. You of all people should know that,' Susie snapped at him.

They were in the kitchen, drinking tea laced with whisky from a bottle which John had found in the dining-room cupboard. Every now and then, he got up from the table and began to pace up and down the room.

Benson was lying stretched out in front of the Aga. He growled when John came too close.

'You should get some sleep, Dad,' Susie said. 'There's nothing to be done now until tomorrow.'

Dad looked confused. 'I think I'd better stay around in case they need me,' he said.

'They won't now, they've cleared off until the morning,' John said. 'Susie's right, the best thing you can do is get some rest.'

'What about you two?' Dad said.

'We'll have one more drink and follow you,' John said.

'You've got your sleeping pills, haven't you, Dad?' Susie said. She wanted to be able to comfort him, but she didn't know how. Perhaps if he'd told her himself that he wanted to change his will in Belle's favour she wouldn't have felt resentful towards him, but he hadn't and she did. Susie couldn't help but feel that letting Belle tell her about the farm was a massive snub from Dad. Susie told herself that her father would have no idea how insulting it was, he didn't mean to diminish what had always seemed to his younger daughter to be the special closeness between them. It was like the night after Mum died, he seemed to want to keep everyone who tried to help at bay, as though treating her and John as strangers somehow distanced him from the tragedy. 'You'll feel better in the morning,' Susie added.

'I doubt it,' Dad said. They heard him muttering to himself as he climbed the stairs.

'Did you talk to the cops?' Susie said. 'What's going on? Do they have any idea why this happened?'

'They're not sure it was suicide at all,' John said, and she had to lean forward to hear what he said.

Susie stared at him. 'But of course it wasn't suicide. What would make her want to kill herself? She'd got what she wanted, the farm to herself. It had to be an accident; it is steep up there, and if the grass is wet, the ground's like a skating-rink.'

'They think maybe she was murdered,' John said.

His eyes were expressionless as he watched Susie.

'Murdered?' she said. She was almost whispering. 'That's ridiculous. Why would they think that?'

'Because there are marks on her arms which look as though someone grabbed her.'

'There can't be,' Susie said. 'Who could possibly have murdered Belle?'

John didn't answer. She looked up at him and met his eyes, but then she dropped her gaze. For a moment she was afraid of him. He seemed to be reading her mind and, hard as Susie tried to deny it, she wasn't sorry that Belle was dead. She felt guilty about it, but she was relieved. This wasn't simply because Dad hadn't had time to change his will, it was more than that. Susie felt that something oppressive, something that had hung over her all her life without her even realizing it, had been lifted. Belle was her sister, she had loved her automatically, without question; she grieved for her now, and for Dad, but at the same time she couldn't help this feeling of liberation. She tried to tell herself that this was because, with Belle gone, she could forget all about Mum's horrible disease. While Belle refused to get tested, there was always the possibility that she might develop Huntington's and that Susie could be forced to tell John the secret she so wanted to keep from him. She knew that even though she could tell him she was clear, he might look on her differently, almost as someone tainted. Something carefree in their relationship would be changed. Belle's death freed Susie from that suppressed but constant fear. But she couldn't meet John's eyes because she was ashamed for him to know how she felt.

John stretched out and grasped her hands in his. He looked very pale and strained, and his eyes were red and sore.

His voice was urgent as he said, 'Darling, if there's anything you want to tell me, between us, before the cops come back, remember I love you and I want to help.'

Susie looked at him aghast. She felt as though he had punched her, then kicked her in the stomach. How could he? How could he not be sure that she hadn't pushed Belle over the edge of the quarry? How could her husband, the father of her children, conceive of such a thing? Susie's expression became cold and hostile.

'There's nothing to tell,' she said. 'Belle told me what Dad was going to do with his will and we had words and then she said she wanted to stay up at the quarry on her own, and I left her there. I heard her say goodbye. She said she didn't like goodbyes, that's why she wouldn't come back with me to see us off.'

John released one of her hands and picked up his drink, which he swallowed in one gulp.

'Susie, I know.'

Susie was on the verge of tears. 'Know *what*? John, please, what is it? What's got into you? You sound as if you think I've got something to hide.'

'About Ben. That you killed Ben.'

Susie jerked her hand away from his and stood up, staring at him in horror.

'*Ben*? You think I killed Ben? Are you mad? How can you think something like that about me?'

'Belle told me you did.'

'And you believed her? You know she hates me and you believe her?' Susie suddenly looked scared. 'You think I killed Belle, don't you?' she said quietly.

'No, no, of course I don't, not on purpose, like a murderer. But it could have been a freak accident. I can imagine you pushed her and she banged her head, something like that. Is that what happened?'

'No, nothing happened like that at all,' Susie said. 'I didn't kill her and I didn't kill Ben.'

'OK, OK, there's no need to get hysterical,' John said, and then he was conscious that what he'd said was so silly he was losing control of the situation. 'I'm only telling you what Belle thought,' he said.

Susie gave him a cold stare as though he were a stranger annoying her. 'I screwed Ben once, that's all,' she said. 'I told you that. Belle was so smug about him, I just wanted to prove I could. I didn't think she would ever find out, I just wanted the secret satisfaction; but then he died and everyone knew he'd been having it off with someone, and Belle guessed it was me. I was sorry I'd done it then, I never meant it to be such a big deal.'

'But she was sure you killed him, she really was. And your dad seemed to think so too. Why would they both believe that without any reason? What would make Belle think that?'

'I don't know,' Susie said. 'Because she hated me? Don't you think that might've had something to do with it?' She bit her lip. She knew from John's expression that her sarcasm increased his disbelief. She said in a more reasoning tone, 'Because she was jealous because I've got you and the kids? Because, because, I tell you, darling, I don't know. I know we were sisters, but I hardly knew her.'

'Did you and Belle have a row at the quarry?'

'No. No, not really.'

'Susie!'

'John, remember you're my husband, stop being a cop. Why are you going on like this?'

'Because she's dead and as far as anyone can tell, you were the last person to see her alive.'

'Except the murderer,' Susie snapped. 'If there was a murderer, which I don't believe for a moment there was.'

'She told you she was going to take over the farm, didn't she? You must've had a row about that? You were really upset in the car going home. You didn't . . . ?'

'No, I didn't.' Susie pulled away from him. 'Leave me alone,' she said, 'I'm not putting up with any more of this. I'm going up to bed. You can do what you want.'

'The police are going to ask you these questions tomorrow,' John said. 'They're bound to. I'm trying to help you.'

'There's only one reason I need help and that's because the

husband I love and who I thought loved me turns out to think I'm a murderer.' Susie's voice began to get shrill as she went on, 'Not just that I'm capable of murder, mind you, but that I actually murdered my own sister for a pathetic inheritance. Having, incidentally, murdered my sister's boyfriend for . . . for what? Fun?'

Then it was as though she realized that she was becoming hysterical and she turned off some emotional tap. When she continued, she sounded as though she were talking about the weather. 'Let the police ask me questions,' she said, 'that's their job, I suppose, but I don't need your help answering them, John. I know I haven't done anything wrong.'

She took her mug to the sink and rinsed it out. Then, without looking at John, she went out of the room and shut the door quietly behind her.

31

The policemen who came to talk to Susie the next morning were called Detective Inspector Cheesewright and Detective Sergeant Miller.

Susie was in the kitchen cooking breakfast for Dad and John. She hadn't stopped to question whether anyone would be able to face food; she had simply slipped into the old routine, doing what for years past Mum had done automatically. John had gone out early to help Dad with the milking, but whether he had intended to help, or had had to make up something off the top of his head as an explanation when Dad found him trying to sleep on the sofa, Susie didn't know.

John came into the house ahead of the policemen. He felt

awkward with his colleagues, as if he was a former team-mate now playing for the opposition. He had once worked closely with Sergeant Miller, though he didn't know the inspector.

He said to Susie, 'Detective Inspector Cheesewright and Sergeant Miller want to talk to you about what happened at the quarry yesterday.' He sounded like a butler in a stately home announcing guests at a formal do, but that was because he didn't know how to make her realize that he wanted to help her. The sight of her wielding a frying-pan over the Aga made him want to seize her in his arms and protect her from everything that he knew was going to happen now.

'Cheesewright and Miller?' Susie said. 'They sound like a firm of grocers.'

'This isn't anything to laugh at,' John hissed at her in an aside. The policemen came into the room.

'I wasn't there when it happened,' Susie said. 'She was fine when I left her.'

'There are a few questions we'd like to ask you if you don't mind, Mrs Smart.'

Susie shrugged. 'Well, you'd better sit down. My dad'll be in from milking shortly for breakfast, but I suppose you can carry on regardless.'

'We'd like you to come down to the station with us, if that's all right,' Sergeant Miller said.

'Can't you talk to her here?' John said.

'We'd prefer it at the station,' Inspector Cheesewright said. He and Sergeant Miller were clearly embarrassed because John was a policeman, one of their own.

'Then we'd better get on with it,' Susie said with a sweet smile.

'Susie's my wife, I should be with her.'

'Don't be silly, darling,' Susie said. 'I don't need a chaperone. They just want to ask me what Belle and I talked about at the quarry and how she seemed when I left her.'

She smiled at her husband, but, meeting her eyes, John knew that she had not forgiven or forgotten that he had more or less accused her of murder. Her eyes said: With a friend like you, who needs enemies?

Sergeant Miller stood aside for Susie to walk out of the door in front of him.

'I'm sorry about this, John, but you know how it is,' Sergeant Miller said.

'I know you've got to go through the motions,' John said, 'but it's just so silly when you know Susie like I do. She couldn't kill anybody, let alone her own sister.'

'This must all be very difficult for you,' Inspector Cheesewright said. 'But this is a suspicious death and we have to investigate it, as you know.'

'But why are you treating it as suspicious? Surely the obvious cause of death is an accident or maybe suicide? Do you have some sort of evidence to tell you otherwise?'

'Would you say your sister-in-law was the suicidal type?' Inspector Cheesewright asked.

John thought of Belle as she had been working on the hedge of the paddock. He saw her laughing at him as he tried to move in the slime of the rhine as they cleared the ditches.

It was only when Susie was there, or even mentioned in conversation, that Belle seemed different, but still not suicidal. And Susie was going away. Why would she commit suicide when Susie was leaving?

'No,' John said in answer to the question. 'But I didn't really know her. She and my wife had been estranged.'

He saw the inspector register that. Damn, he thought, that won't help Susie. He wondered if his colleagues had seen through his protests to his own doubts about what his wife might have done. If only Belle had never told him about Ben. John knew that in those days the young Susie would have enjoyed seducing her older sister's fiancé, not meaning any real harm; but if that was true, why would Belle lie about his death? If only Belle hadn't been so obviously convinced about it.

Dad came in from the milking. He was walking with small, stiff steps like an old man. It was the first time John had thought of him as old.

'Where's Susie?' Dad asked. 'Isn't breakfast ready?'

John got up and went to put the frying-pan back on the Aga.

'It's all ready. I'll just heat it up a bit,' he said, trying to sound as though he cared if the old man never ate breakfast again. 'Susie's had to go down to the police station.'

'Those buggers and their questions. I know you're one of them, my boy, but you'd think they could call at a reasonable hour and talk to her here if they must. Badgering witnesses, I call it. She should complain. I've been out working since five, I need my breakfast.'

'Coming up,' John said, and slid bacon and sausages on to the plate Susie had left in the simmering oven to keep warm. 'They probably have to do a few tests,' he said. 'Fingerprints and DNA and that sort of routine stuff. Eliminating her from enquiries.' He had to fight to stop his voice breaking when he said that.

'Bloody government lackeys,' Dad said. 'It's nothing but tests in farming these days. too; one thing after another and most of it a waste of time.'

'As I'm sure this will be,' John said. He understood the old man's grumbling was a way of dealing with his anxiety about what was going on.

'Poor old Belle,' Dad said, staring at the food on his plate but making no effort to eat. 'I'm glad she'd sorted her problems out before this happened. Just as she'd got herself together and agreed to come back here to look after the farm, she goes and trips and falls down the quarry. She never had much luck, my poor Belle.'

At intervals all through the day John rang the station to ask what was happening. At about seven, he could stand it no longer.

'I'm going down the pub for a quick one,' he said.

'That's all very well,' Dad said, 'but what about my supper? What's Susie been doing down at that police station all day? They must know she's a married woman with things to do.'

'I'll put something out of the freezer into the Aga for us all to have when I get back. I expect Susie'll want something when she gets here. I'll call in and see if she's ready to come home while I'm at it.'

'There's no police station in the village these days, my boy. They'll have taken Susie into town. To headquarters.'

Dad was impressed by his younger daughter's importance to be treated this way.

'Don't worry, I know where it is,' John said. 'Go ahead and eat if I'm not back in time. Susie and I'll eat when we get in.'

He heard Dad grumbling to himself as he went out.

At the police station, the man at the desk remembered John, and told him that Brian Miller was taking a break in the pub.

'Same pub?' John asked.

'Some things never change,' the man at the desk said, and grinned.

Miller was sitting at the bar reading the sports pages of the evening newspaper. He didn't seem surprised to see John.

'Drink?' he said. 'I thought you'd be here before now.'

'You're holding her?'

The barman put a pint of beer on the bar in front of John and Miller signalled that he should add it to his tab.

'There's nothing else we can do,' Miller said. 'You know yourself, you can't argue with the evidence.'

'But what evidence is there really? It's only circumstantial that they were up there together and they probably had words and no one saw Belle alive after that. That's not a case, for God's sake, you can't hold her for that.'

'Of course not,' Miller said, 'but's that's not all there is.'

'What else have you got?' John could hear how resigned he sounded, in spite of himself, as though he had never expected anything else. He repeated his question, trying this time to sound as though he was confidant that Susie could disprove anything Miller and his boss could produce as evidence.

Miller felt sorry for him. They'd been good friends once. He knew he probably shouldn't, but he wanted to tell John what he knew.

'One reason we've ruled out suicide is that there are marks on the body.'

'What kind of marks? There are bound to be marks from the fall.'

'Definite marks on the upper arms where someone gripped her hard. Definite marks of fingers.'

'You'd have to do better than that. What does Susie say about it?' John tried to look Miller in the eye.

'She says Belle goaded her and she lunged at her and gripped her, but not to push her over the edge of the quarry,' Miller said. He was trying to make Susie's explanation sound plausible, but he plainly didn't think it was.

'Anything else?' John said. He signalled to the barman to refill their glasses.

Miller looked embarrassed. 'There's DNA,' he said. 'We're getting more analysis to confirm it.'

'What DNA?' John was startled.

'Traces of your wife's skin under Belle's fingernails,' Miller said. 'And scratches on your wife's arm.'

John was shocked into silence. Then he said, 'I didn't think Belle had fingernails she could scratch anyone with. They looked as though she'd been biting them for years.'

He thought, When did I notice that? I don't remember noticing her fingernails at all. Only that missing finger. Which Susie cut off.

'So what happens now?' he asked Miller.

Sergeant Miller stared into his drink. 'John – mate – it's already happened. We're going to charge Susie with murdering her sister. We haven't any choice. She had a motive. Their father was going to change his will to leave the house and farm to Belle. There's no question that anyone else was involved. I'm sorry, but you must see we couldn't do anything else. She's in custody now.'

32

The next few days passed in a blur and yet the time crawled so slowly that John felt Susie had been inside for months.

She had been remanded in custody to stand trial for murder. Later she was taken away to a prison about fifty miles from the farm. It was slightly closer to the town where she and John lived, but, with his mother looking after the children, John felt he had to stay with Susie's dad.

The old man, who had seemed to cope with Belle's death surprisingly well, was devastated now. If John hadn't taken all his holiday entitlement at once to be with him at the farm, the cows would not have been milked, and most mornings the animals would have gone hungry. Left to himself, his father-in-law would not have bothered to eat or take his blood-pressure pills.

John had been able to see Susie briefly at the police station before she was taken away.

She was sitting on the edge of the bed looking bewildered. She was so unlike the laughing, vibrant Susie he knew that for a moment he turned away from her to tell the custody sergeant he was in the wrong cell.

She looked up at him with a kind of wonder on her face, as though she'd been convinced that everyone she knew and loved had abandoned her.

He went to her and squatted in front of her, taking her hands in his and raising them to his lips.

Her face crumpled and she started to cry.

'Oh, John,' she whimpered, 'what's going to happen to me?'

'It'll be all right, darling, everything's going to be all right.'

The tears were still flowing down her face but it was as though they were incidental, like a stage backdrop. Actually, she smiled at him. 'I bet you say that to all the girls you've banged up for murdering their sisters,' she said.

At least that awful blank look in her eyes had gone. She said, 'I didn't do it, John. I swear on the lives of Jonty and Kim I didn't do it.'

'I know, I know,' he said, 'it was an accident, I'm sure it was an accident. It's a perfectly legitimate defence. She told you about the farm and goaded you and you lashed out at her and you had a scuffle and she fell over the edge. That's not murder. No one could call that murder.'

He was almost weeping now. It was intolerable seeing her in this place. What made it worse was that police cells were so familiar to him, he'd locked hundreds of people away in them over the years without a thought, except perhaps that they were in the best place for the rest of society. He'd never tried to imagine what it must be like for them.

Squatting was uncomfortable, so he got up and sat beside

her, putting an arm round her shoulders. She felt skinny under her jumper.

'She set me up,' Susie said, and her voice was full of a kind of wonderment. 'Belle set me up for her own murder. Can you believe that, that my own sister could do such a thing?'

John hugged her. 'Darling, this isn't going to get us anywhere. She can't have arranged the evidence.'

'I thought it was odd the way she laughed when she said goodbye as I walked away,' Susie said. 'She'd taunted me until I lashed out at her and I grabbed her to stop her hitting me. She knew I'd do that, she used to do just the same thing when we were kids. Even when I cut off her finger that time, it didn't stop her. Oh, when she gloated about getting the farm, I wanted to hit her. Anyone would. She scratched me deliberately so my skin would be under her fingernails.'

John said, 'Susie, stop this, it's insane.'

'Belle was insane, that's what you don't understand. Why doesn't anyone understand? She's always hated me, she's got all sorts of weird grudges against me just because she thought she was threatened by me being her sister. She blamed me because people didn't like her and she thought she wasn't attractive. Why should she blame me, it was nothing to do with me? But she did. That's not sane, is it? I tell you, she was mad. This is some sort of perverted way of getting her own back.'

'But what for?' John asked. He thought, That might be reasonable if Susie killed Ben, but if she's going to use the argument in her defence, she has to admit she murdered Ben.

'How would I know? But it is.'

John tried to look as though he believed her. At least now, arguing this preposterous theory, she was more like the old Susie. He would have said or done anything to stop her turning back into the cowed creature he'd seen when he first came in here.

196

'She didn't seem insane to talk to,' he said, as though he were considering what Susie had said. 'I know she blamed you, but it didn't seem so daft when she told me why she did, you know, Ben and that.'

'But don't you see, it was all lies. I didn't kill Ben. She knew I didn't. Can't you see it was all part of her plan. She wanted to turn you against me, to make you think I might've done something like that. And it worked, didn't it? You did think I could've done it.'

John couldn't meet her eyes.

'You still do, don't you?' Susie said softly. 'You listened to Belle and you look at the evidence and you make up your mind I'm guilty in spite of being married to me for seven years, because you're so emotionally uptight you can't trust your instincts.'

'Susie, I love you but I'm a policeman. I can't help it. Guilty people lie, but hard evidence doesn't. I'd put someone away on the case the cops have against you, except you're my wife. I want to believe you.'

Someone outside banged on the cell door.

'Time to go,' the custody sergeant said, opening the door.

John was embarrassed to embrace her in that place with the imperturbable sergeant looking on. 'I'll see you soon,' he said.

'I'd rather you didn't,' Susie said, 'it doesn't help to have the man I love argue the case for the prosecution.'

33

There was something frighteningly final about the hollow clunk as the cell door shut behind John and the sound echoed off the walls of the corridor outside. Susie, feeling more alone than she had ever felt, thought it sounded like the lid being put on a coffin in a sealed vault. She closed her fists and pressed them against her eyes to stop herself crying.

She asked herself, Why would Belle do this to me? However much she hated me, surely she'd got her revenge. She'd got the farm to herself, and she'd made John doubt me, made him believe the most incredible things about me.

Susie seemed so far removed from John. That was the worst thing, feeling the cold gulf that had opened up between them. When he'd looked at her, she'd seen something like disgust in his eyes, so unlike the way he usually looked at her with eyes full of love and trust. She felt she couldn't speak to him because whatever she said to him she was scared to face the knowledge that he was no longer sure he could believe she wasn't deceiving him.

She asked herself, Why can't I tell John about the Huntington's chorea? At least it would cast doubt on Belle's sanity. Why should it, though? Belle might not even have developed it, and her irrational jealousy predated the possibility of symptoms by years. But there was no reason not to tell him. There was no cause to worry any more; why should Susie feel she had to spare him what wouldn't concern him now? I don't want him to know I might have had it, she told herself, I don't want to look into his eyes and know he's looking at me differently, wondering if the tests were right, if the doctors were wrong and the children could develop it. John knowing about a thing like that would change everything between us; he'd see me as someone damaged, poisoned inside. It would be between us. Every time I forgot something or was irritable or got depressed, he wouldn't take it in his stride, he'd wonder, 'Is that because of the disease?' He'd still love me, but not the same way; he'd feel he had to. It's like AIDS, people think they can get it just by shaking hands with someone who has it.

Susie got up and started to pace up and down the cell. She felt she had to keep moving, to try to break through some physical impasse which would release her mind to think clearly. She thought, Before I got that test I'd have put this restlessness down to a possible symptom of Huntington's chorea. God, she thought, I'm doing it myself, I'm thinking of myself in terms of someone at risk of it.

But I'm not going to get it, and nor are my children. It doesn't have any bearing on what Belle's done to me. It's nothing to do with not telling John. It's me that doesn't want to acknowledge it. As long as I don't tell him it's as if it wasn't real, I can put it out of my mind and everything will go back to normal. Once I tell him, it's a fact and I can't escape it.

Susie stopped pacing and went back to sit on the hard bench against the wall. There was a grey blanket folded at one end and she wrapped this round her and over her head. Why did I tell Belle? She asked herself. I shouldn't have said anything. I thought she had a right to know, but now she's using it against me as if it's my fault. She blames me because I told her and now she's punishing me for it.

Susie lay on the bed and drew up her legs in the foetal position, the blanket still covering her face.

'John, help me, I'm so scared,' she kept saying aloud in a frightened whisper, but talking aloud to John as though he were there didn't help her to believe that he hadn't abandoned her.

34

Dad was in the kitchen when John returned to the farm. The old man had taken a packet of spaghetti out of the cupboard but was having trouble reading the cooking instructions. John suddenly remembered that he had forgotten all about his promise to take something out of the freezer to put in the Aga before he went out.

'I've put my glasses down somewhere and I can't find them to read what to do with this stuff,' the old man said as John came in. 'I thought you'd be hungry after seeing Susie.'

Considering the way he'd been the last few days, this was, John thought, an impressive gesture from Susie's dad. Although the thought of food made his stomach churn, he smiled at his father-in-law.

'Good thinking,' he said. 'You need to boil a pan of water first. And, by the way, your glasses are pushed back on the top of your head.'

The old man reached up and felt them. 'So they are,' he said; 'thank you for that, I didn't know what I was going to do.'

There was a short silence while he filled a saucepan from the tap and put it on to boil. John's first instinct was to do it for him, but he stopped himself. Susie's dad might be frail and elderly, but to help him would make him feel even older and more helpless. But John found it hard to sit there while the old fellow fumbled with the packet and tried to get the pasta into the pan. He managed it at last, though, and his smile of triumph made John glad he had contained his impatience.

They sat at the table while the spaghetti cooked and listened to the small sounds as the water heated.

'Did you see Susie?' Dad asked at last.

'Yes, briefly. They were taking her away today.'

'How was she?'

'She's OK, considering.' John wished the old man hadn't used the past tense. It made him feel that Susie was as dead as Belle.

'I can't take it in,' Dad said, and his voice quavered, 'I didn't think anything could ever be worse than my Mary passing away, and now Belle's dead and Susie . . . '

'Don't, Dad,' John said. He had never called his father-in-law Dad before, and it startled both of them when he let it slip out without thinking.

'There must be some mistake,' the old man said, 'the police must've got it wrong somewhere. My little Susie . . . no, it's not possible.'

'I know,' John said, 'I feel the same way. And yet . . . '

'I can't believe it,' Dad said firmly. 'A little flibbertigibbet like my Susie doesn't go around murdering people, let alone her own sister.' He broke off and then said, 'They used to be so close, those two.'

'Belle and Susie? As children? Were they?'

'Oh, yes. Susie used to follow Belle around like a little dog, she never wanted to do anything on her own without her big sister.'

'And what about Belle?'

John was trying to imagine the two little girls running off together to play among the animals.

'Oh, Belle used to keep Susie in order. I think she found having a little sister round all the time a bit difficult. She bossed Susie about a lot. Belle was a tomboy, and she liked to be in charge. But she was shy, not like Susie. Susie would talk to anyone, charm the birds off the trees, but Belle wasn't like that. Belle never wanted to mix with other children or go to parties in the village. She had to go, of course, Susie was too young to go on her own, but Belle was always glad to get home. When they got a bit older, Susie used to tease Belle about ending up an old maid.' He looked down at his knotted fists and sighed. 'Well, she did, didn't she. She was coming back here to take on the farm, you know, did you know that?'

'Yes, Susie told me.'

'I hope that's not what turned Susie . . . why she did what she did. You don't think that had anything to do with it, do you? Susie was never interested in the farm.'

John had bought a bottle of whisky on his way home. His instinct, when he thought of Susie in the police cell, or, even worse, sharing a cramped prison room with strangers, was to drink himself into oblivion. But he couldn't do that, he owed it to his wife not to do that. Still one small short might clear his head.

'Would you like a glass of the hard stuff?' he asked Dad.

Dad shook his head. 'You go ahead, lad. I think I'll go to bed.'

'What about the spaghetti?'

'I'm not really hungry,' Dad said. 'Are you?'

He shuffled to the Aga, where the boiling water was jiggling the lid of the pan.

'No,' John said; 'to tell the truth, I think eating anything at all would choke me just now.'

Dad moved the saucepan and closed the lid of the Aga hotplate. He walked slowly to the door, dragging his feet, then turned to say to John, 'Don't think I'm not grateful, my boy. I know how much you've had to do and I appreciate it. There just doesn't seem anything to say about anything any more.'

'I've been glad of something to do,' John said. 'See you in the morning.'

Dad nodded and shambled away down the hallway to the stairs. He didn't say goodnight; they both knew that neither of them would be able to sleep.

John poured himself a whisky but he didn't drink it. It didn't feel right, somehow. He wasn't used to drinking alone, only in the pub with colleagues from work, or with Susie sometimes in the evening at home.

In the end, he went upstairs and into Belle's bedroom. He felt that he had to try to feel closer to those two little girls dancing up a farm track hand in hand, two little girls who were alive in his imagination as they'd probably never been in reality. But even if they weren't the children he imagined, the sisters, Belle and Susie, had been real once. They had existed here, and they'd learned somehow here to hate and fear one another. It seemed to him important to try to understand. But it all seemed so elusive to him because he felt that he didn't know who those little girls were, and what they had become. In spite of all the years of marriage to Susie, he felt he actually knew less about her now than he ever had. And the empathy he'd felt with Belle was just as unreal.

What's the point, anyway? he asked himself. I can't change anything now, it's too late.

I must look deeper, he thought, what else is there for me to do?

Belle's things were still scattered around the room. There was a paperback novel on the bedside table, and a clock with the alarm set to go off at five-thirty. There were clothes on a chair by the window, and a few face creams on the dressing-table. There was a hair-dryer on the stool in front of the dressing-table and, on a small writing-desk near the bed, a pad of paper.

It was so different from the room he and Susie shared at home, where there were always Susie's underclothes spilling out of the chest of drawers, and a mess of her make-up and scarves and jewellery in front of the mirror. Belle's room was austere as he imagined a nun's would be, the bedclothes rigidly tucked in, no pictures on the walls, no colour, nothing frivolous at all.

John shivered. If he had to imagine the woman who might choose to live in a room like this, he could believe that, if she wasn't a religious, she might be a murderer. In Susie's room, he couldn't conceive of such a possibility.

Which just goes to show how wrong instincts can be, the policeman in him thought. But he didn't convince himself.

Now that Susie had put into his head the monstrous proposition that Belle had manipulated her sister into serving a life sentence in jail for murdering her, John had been nagged by doubts. He remembered a conversation with Belle in the pub when he first met her about the perfect murder. Could whatever he'd said then, which he didn't remember, possibly be taken as a challenge to an unhinged mind? He thought he'd said something about no murder being motiveless, something mundane and glib, no doubt, but of course Belle did have a motive to destroy Susie's life. Not one that anyone sane would recognize, but what if Belle were really mad? Revenge. Rightly or wrongly, Belle had wanted revenge because Susie seduced her fiancé.

Surely, though, that couldn't be enough to justify what Susie was now facing? Of course Belle believed, too, that Susie had killed Ben. Or did she? Was that part of the set-up? Was Belle really willing to die to make Susie pay for her own unhappiness?

And Susie, too, had a motive for murder: Belle had stolen her inheritance. Mundane, perhaps, but not without precedent; whereas Belle's . . .

And then John remembered how that conversation with Belle had started. He remembered a fat little man at the next table, with his bow tie undone and the two ends dangling in his food, and the expression on Belle's face as she watched him. And he'd said something about how she'd have made a good cop, and she'd said, 'I used to think I'd end up as a murderer.' He'd thought she was kidding, but perhaps she wasn't. Perhaps she really was afraid of what she might do, that she might be insane.

John began to walk slowly round the room, touching Belle's things as he went, trying to understand how her mind had worked.

On the little writing-table beyond the bed, an uncapped biro lay beside the pad of paper. The top was close by, as though someone had been writing and then broken off and left in a hurry. The paper was blank, but when he picked it up and tilted it towards the light, John could see the impression of writing. All he could make out for sure was his own name: Dear John.

Why would she write to him? Was it something to do with the pass she'd made at him in the hayloft? He'd rejected her quite roughly because he'd really been tempted but he couldn't do anything to hurt Susie. But was that enough to make her want to take her own life? Surely not.

Who am I kidding? John thought. I'm not the kind of man women kill themselves over, I'm just an ordinary guy.

But she had written something, though when and why he'd never know now. Almost absent-mindedly he rummaged through the waste-paper basket by the dressing-table.

And there he found what he was pretending to himself he wasn't looking for. An envelope, addressed and stamped, now torn into sixteen neat squares.

He laid the pieces on the writing-table, and made out the name of the person the letter had been sent to. Detective Inspector John Smart, and the address was the police station where he worked.

35

She had mad handwriting, John thought. The letter looked like the work of a child trying to get as much as possible into the space, but when he tried to read it, it was like trying to decipher medieval script in miniature. He told himself, if she'd used green ink, no one would doubt that she was a crazy woman.

He took the pieces out of the torn envelope and laid them out on the writing-table before trying to fit them together. He was lucky, there were only two pages. If Belle had written more, he might have given up before he began.

It took him a long time to put the page together.

Dear John [Belle had written] – By the time you read this, if I don't change my mind and decide not to send it, I will be dead and Susie will be charged with murdering me. It's what I know will happen because that's what I've planned.

Everything was so straightforward until I met you and we worked together on the farm. The last deliberate act of my life will be to take my revenge on Susie, and leave her to a long and lingering fate. That lovely young girl you first fell in love with, the girl with the laughing face and the beautiful bright hair, she isn't going to survive a long sentence, John. She's going to come out a bitter, sour-faced bitch. Lovely, sweet little Susie will get the face she deserves. They say we all do, which is one reason I'm glad I'm not staying around to find out for myself.

If only I hadn't fallen in love with you, John. That's what changed everything, and why I'm writing you this letter. I want you to know I never intended you any harm, only in so far as you are part of Susie's life, which is what I'm happy I'm destroying. It has always seemed to me that her happiness was at my expense. I've felt like that all my life, but now more than ever. Now I can't bear it any more. You shouldn't have turned me down when I asked you to make love to me. You've always believed Susie when she's told you that sort of thing doesn't mean anything. She has told you that, hasn't she? She must have done, when she's had it off with every bit of rough she fancied. That's what she told me when she screwed Ben. And you're still with her, so you must've believed her. Why not me, then, John? Why couldn't you do it with me, even if you didn't think it meant anything?

It's not going to make you feel better now to know that Susie didn't kill me. At least, I don't think she did. She may surprise me when the time comes, but I don't think she will. I've planned it so that it looks as if she did, though, evidence and all. There'll be proof she did, and no way of proving she didn't. Do you remember we talked once about the perfect murder? Well, I've achieved it, and it's all the better that Susie's sentence for murder will be a living death. Actually, for the record, I've achieved two perfect murders before this which no one ever suspected weren't accidents. No, three, actually, including Ben. One was some bloke who died in a fire somewhere in Tooting. I spent the night with him and talked in my sleep about killing Ben He made a joke about it, so he had to go. And then there was Sylvia from the office. I crushed her under her own car. She asked too many questions about the Tooting man. I suppose it'll shock you, but I could get a taste for arranging fatal accidents. It's quite a buzz, if you ever find you can't stand another second of little sister Susie. Don't say I'm mad, though; no one who's got away with what I've done deserves to be called mad. Genius, perhaps, but not mad.

Don't kid yourself, John. I'm not dying because you rejected me, or even, really, because I've nothing left to live for if you're not in my life. I'd rather go this way than the long miserable death I'll face. I'm pretty sure I've inherited a particularly horrible genetic disease which will waste my brain away. I looked it up on my laptop and it might take me twenty years to die. A lot of sufferers commit suicide, apparently. I haven't had a test, which, incidentally Susie has and she's clear. Well, long may she enjoy it, that's all I have to say to her. I only heard about this disease when Susie told me the day of Mum's funeral, so this has nothing to do with what I've always felt about her. One of the symptoms, though, is inappropriate sexual advances, so if it makes you feel better you can put my efforts to seduce you down to that. I don't. It's the only thing I feel sad about, that I didn't have sex with you.

So when it comes down to it, I don't want you and your kids to have to pay for what Susie did to me. She trashed everything I ever valued, including Ben. I killed Ben. I had to wipe him out of my life after she had sex with him. It wasn't that he was unfaithful, it was because it was Susie.

But I think I loved you with all my heart, the way normal people talk about so nonchalantly. I want you to have the farm, which Jonty or Kim may one day take over. And look after Dad, even though he betrayed me by loving Susie more than me.

If you had loved me I wouldn't want to die. But now I've nothing to live for. There'll be one perfect moment after I jump off the edge of the quarry and before I crash on to the ground when I will be free of Susie, the way I believed when I was little that life would make me.

I don't know if I shall actually post this letter. If I do, I suppose you'll use it to get Susie freed, but if you ever for a moment doubted her innocence, she'll never forgive you. You and she are over, whatever happens. I'm glad; you deserve better.

I think we talked once, though, about how someone who commits the perfect murder is supposed to have a compulsion to tell what they've done. You're the one person I've ever wanted to tell. It's ironic, isn't it, that if I succumb to temptation and send this letter, I'll spoil the most perfect murder of them all. I haven't decided yet.

That was it. There was no signature. John sat slumped in the chair and stared unseeingly at the scraps of paper on the writing-desk. He felt as though someone had bludgeoned him in the chest and driven all the breath out of his body.

All he could think was that Belle was crazed. She was beyond evil, she couldn't have known what she was doing. But she had known exactly that. She'd plotted and planned and controlled everything that had happened.

Even though she was dead now, and he'd seen her body with his own eyes, John felt afraid that such malice could exist in a woman whom he'd liked and with whom he'd empathized. What made it worse was that in the end Belle had refused the small chance of redemption that exonerating Susie might have offered her. She had torn up the letter; she'd deliberately chosen to condemn Susie to a living death.

What was she thinking as she wrote the letter? he asked himself over and over again. How had she felt? He tried to put himself in her mind as she sat at this same writing-desk that day and put down on paper the revelations which would condemn her. And having done that, having shown how far she was prepared to go to get revenge, she tore up what she'd written. Belle, in spite of wanting him to know how clever she had been, clearly didn't want Susie ever to escape the fate she had arranged for her. John tried to feel the hatred towards her that she must have felt for Susie. He couldn't do it. It seemed absurd.

John wished that he believed what the churches taught about good and evil and the immortal soul. Then Belle would rot in hell.

Maybe there is a God, he told himself. He'd found the letter, hadn't he? In spite of all Belle's efforts. Perhaps, after all, there was no such thing as a perfect murder.

36

John was on his way to bring Susie home from prison. He tried to tell himself that she hadn't really been in jail, because she hadn't been tried, but it was no good. Remand or custody or whatever you called it, it was prison. However often he told himself that she was innocent, and he himself was the one who had proved it, he couldn't get it out of his head that because the police had had an open-and-shut case against her, at some point in the process she had been judged guilty. He was a policeman, he thought like a policeman, and even now his joy and relief at her release was marred simply by the fact that she had been put in jail.

He tried to imagine, too, what Susie had gone through worrying that she might develop Huntington's chorea. How had he never known how afraid she was? He felt ashamed that he had never noticed that she was suffering. I spend too much time at work, he told himself, I've drifted away from her because of the job. But she knew I was always there for her, surely she did? Why didn't she tell me after she was cleared?

When John had shown Inspector Cheesewright Belle's letter, Cheesewright had made no bones about what he thought about it.

'This isn't any sort of evidence you can use,' he'd said when John took it to him.

It was clear that as a policeman the inspector had no system for dismantling what he saw as a proven case. John understood that. He knew he should have taken the letter to Susie's lawyer, not the police at all. But with his colleagues he felt at home, whereas lawyers put him immediately on the defensive.

'Of course it's evidence,' John said. 'It's a bloody confession. She says it was suicide. She'd got Huntington's chorea.'

'She *thought* she had. And anyway there's a vast difference between intention and performance. You're not going to convince a jury with that, not with the evidence against Susie.'

'Belle admits she set Susie up.'

'But there's no evidence she wrote the letter at all,' Inspector Cheesewright said.

'Her fingerprints are on it,' John said. 'That proves she handled it.'

'So are yours,' Cheesewright said.

'Of course they are, I pieced it together and read it,' John said.

'You could have written it. You must see how it looks. You wrote it as a desperate ploy to get the case against your wife dropped.'

'Then why are Belle's prints on it? If I'd done that, it was after her death.'

'You say you found the letter in her room? If you'd written it yourself, you probably did it there, using her writing paper. She could've handled that paper any time before the letter was written.'

'Oh, my God,' John said, 'don't you think I can see all that? But I know I didn't. What do I have to do to prove it? Don't you see, this proves what Susie said, but in the eyes of the law . . . ?'

Inspector Cheesewright nodded. 'Of course I see. But you need something more.'

'Well, isn't it her handwriting?'

'Possibly it is. Probably it is,' Inspector Cheesewright said. 'But it's not definite. Obviously if it's genuine she was in some sort of emotional turmoil when she wrote it, and that could account for any discrepancies. But a jury might think it was a clever forgery.'

John suddenly shouted, 'There's DNA. No one can question that.'

Inspector Cheesewright sounded excited. 'DNA? Are you sure?'

'The letter was in a sealed envelope. She must've licked the envelope. That's where you'll find DNA.'

'Why didn't you say there was an envelope?' Cheesewright said.

'I thought the letter was the important thing,' John said. 'But when I found it, the pieces of the letter were still inside the envelope. It can be pieced together.'

'Don't get your hopes up,' Cheesewright said. 'It might've been one of those self-seal envelopes.'

John understood that his colleague wasn't being obstructive, he simply wanted to avoid disappointment. Cheesewright liked Susie. He and Brian Miller had hated taking her in, but in the face of the evidence there was nothing else they could do.

They both came to tell John the news. They were as pleased as though they had cracked a case against a real murderer. There were definite traces of Belle's DNA on some of the scraps of the envelope, where she'd licked the gum to seal it. Hers and no one else's.

'My God,' Miller said to John, 'what kind of a woman was that Belle? Imagine killing yourself and then framing your sister for your murder. I don't think we've ever had a case like this before. I don't suppose anyone has. It's unique.'

'It's crazy,' John said.

Inspector Cheesewright showed his relief with an attempt at levity. 'I'd be bloody glad there weren't more sisters if I were you, John, at least if they were all like Belle and had it in for Susie,' he said.

But later John wondered, would any of this have happened if there weren't just the two of them, Belle and Susie? But Belle would still have been a monster, John thought. The Huntington's chorea gene didn't determine what a person was, and the symptoms didn't usually begin to appear until middle age. Belle's unreasoning hatred of Susie went back to when they were both little kids. Belle couldn't escape responsibility.

None of that matters now, he told himself, Susie's coming home. He wondered how she was feeling at this moment, cut off behind those thick grey walls waiting for him to come for her, and he asked himself whether he should have brought the children after all. He'd told them Susie was looking after her father; the last thing he'd wanted was to have to tell them the truth. But at least if they'd been with him, they would have dispelled any awkwardness she might feel. However relieved she was to be released, she was bound to be incensed at the monstrous way Belle had made her suffer. She would be angry at the police, too, that colleagues of her own husband had been so convinced by the case against her. She was bound to feel betrayed, it was only natural.

John was also painfully aware that he was worried about her feelings towards him.

He thought, I won't think about that, we'll talk about it later, when all the fuss has died down. For the time being, she's free, and she knows it's down to me that she is.

He spotted a car leaving a meter ahead of him, and drove into the space as the other driver edged into the line of traffic. Finding somewhere to park so easily seemed to him a good omen. He was surprised at how nervous he was. I feel worse than I did before I picked her up on our first date, he thought. I feel that I'm meeting her for the first time.

The prison stood at the end of the street where he was parked. He put money in the meter and started to walk towards the main gate. His feet felt as though they were weighted with lead. He couldn't believe that he wasn't moving at top speed, walking on air at the thought of seeing Susie.

Then a small door opened in the wooden gates hiding the prison from the prying eyes of the public. Susie stepped out into the street, turning back to say something to someone unseen who then shut the door behind her.

John wanted to shout out to her, but when he opened his mouth, no sound came out. And still his feet, which his head told to run towards her, dragged at a snail's pace.

Susie stood for a moment in the street looking around as though she wasn't sure what to do or where she was. Then she seemed to make up her mind and turned to walk briskly away from John.

Then the spell was broken, and he shouted out her name and began to run after her.

She stopped and turned back towards him. She stood and waited for him, but made no move in his direction.

'Susie,' he cried, 'why didn't you wait for me?'

She stood as unresponsive as a lamp-post within the circle of his arms as he embraced her.

There were tears in John's eyes as he said, 'Oh, darling, thank God we've got you back. Thank God it's all over.'

'You think it's all over?' she said. They started to walk towards the car.

'You can't imagine how awful it's been without you,' he said.

What should I say to her? he asked himself. What is there to say?

'The children are so excited,' he said. 'Kim's made you a card saying Welcome Home.'

'I bet you haven't told them their mum's a jailbird,' she said, and laughed. He hadn't heard her laugh like that before; it had a harsh, unamused note to it. It reminded him of Belle. She had a laugh like that.

He tried to laugh with her, but there was something about the way she was looking at him that worried him.

'Don't say that,' he said. 'They think you were looking after your dad because Belle died. They can't wait to see you.'

They reached the car and he opened the door for her to get into the passenger seat.

He started the car and then turned off the engine.

'You must've got out early,' he said. 'Why didn't you wait? Surely you knew I'd pick you up?'

She looked down at her hands in her lap, playing with the strap of her bag. 'I wanted to get away before you came,' she said.

John was aghast. He stared at her, but could not read the expression on her face.

'But why, Susie? Why didn't you want to see me? Is it because it's a prison?'

She laughed again with that new unamused sound.

'You think I'm embarrassed by what's happened to me? Let me tell you, embarrassment doesn't come into it. I didn't want to see you because I didn't want to have this conversation with you, not yet.'

'What are you trying to say?' he said, but the expression on his face showed that he suspected already what she meant.

'It's no good, John, we can't just go home and carry on as though nothing's happened. I don't want us to be together any more.'

She looked him straight in the eyes as she said this, and he knew that she meant it.

'No, Susie, no, don't say that. We can work through this.'

She shook her head. 'I can't,' she said. 'I can't forgive you. Ever.'

'But, darling, what have I done? I've never stopped loving you.'

She looked as though she couldn't believe he'd said that.

'Do you honestly think it could ever be all right between us?' she asked. 'You believed I murdered my sister. And Ben, for God's sake. How can you say you love me when you believed something like that? And even if you do love me, what does that mean? How can you say you care about me when you obviously don't know the first thing about me?'

'You shut me out, how could I? You didn't talk to me. You didn't even tell me about that genetic disease which could've destroyed your whole life and mine, but you never said a word.'

'This is nothing to do with that,' Susie said. 'This is about you believing Belle's *fantasies* about me.' Susie couldn't think of a word strong enough to describe her sister's malicious lies. She said, 'You've made a mockery of our love and our family and our commitment to each other. You didn't trust me, and now I can never trust you again. I can't.'

John started to protest but instead said nothing. There was nothing he could say in his own defence and it was best not to try. This was not something they could argue through.

Susie went on, 'I'll never be able to get over that. Even if I ever forgive you, because I suppose it wasn't altogether your fault – I do know what Belle could do – I can't get over it. I don't want to.'

There was a long silence while he stared down the sad grey street under the prison walls. How much despair had passed along that windy pavement before today, and how many heartbroken people would follow him and Susie in the future?

'The kids are waiting,' he said, 'we can't keep them waiting.'

He started the car and waited for a break in the traffic.

He drove in silence until they were clear of the city centre and then he asked, 'What happens now? What do you want to do?'

They had reached the suburbs. Trees lined the streets, and the terraced Victorian houses were set back behind front gardens which had now mostly been concreted over to provide a standing for a car. Susie stared out of the window at some children playing football on a side street.

'I'll take the kids to stay with Dad. They won't suspect anything; it'll fit in with what you've already told them.'

'What about school? And they've got friends at home.'

'I'll get them in somewhere near the farm for the time being. And once you've sorted something out for yourself, I'll bring them home.'

She seemed so businesslike, as though she were planning their holidays. But perhaps she was feeling something behind that hard-headed front, John told himself. He felt his heart was breaking, but he knew he must seem wooden and detached.

'Right,' he said, 'whatever you say. I'll drive you down to the farm tomorrow.'

'No, I don't want you to spend the night in the house,' Susie said. 'Can you find somewhere to stay?'

John nodded, but he wondered where he could go. He wanted to be alone somewhere dark and secret where no one could see him.

'You'll have to let me know where you are as soon as you get somewhere,' Susie said. 'I'll need an address for the lawyer to send the divorce papers.'

John had to pull over and stop the car outside a house with a dilapidated For Sale sign on the gate. The tears in his eyes made it impossible for him to see clearly enough to drive.

He blew his nose noisily and opened the window to take in some fresh air.

'Sorry,' he said.

Susie didn't say anything, and when he looked at her to try to see what she was thinking, he saw that she was crying silently, help-lessly, so that tears were dripping unchecked from her face on to her T-shirt.

'Best get back to the kids,' she said. 'They'll be thinking we've got lost.'

'Not likely,' he said. 'I'm a cop, and they know that anyone who gets lost has only got to ask a policeman and they'll be all right.'

'Well, I'm lost,' Susie said, 'but it's not done me any good asking you the way.'

37

Six months later, Susie left the farm early in the morning without telling anyone where she was going.

It was a hard-edged kind of morning, the ground clenched in the fist of frost. Across the water meadows towards the sea, great pools of water had frozen and gleamed black as polished coal in the light of the reluctant rising sun.

Susie strode out across the stunned ground. The old dog Benson had come to the back door with her, taken one look at the frozen yard, and gone back inside. Susie seemed to be the only live thing awake. No birds stirred, and even the seagulls had disappeared.

What am I doing? Susie asked herself. Why am I doing this? She didn't understand herself.

Much as she would have liked to turn back, to be cooking breakfast for Dad and the kids over the Aga in the warm kitchen, she carried on. This was something she felt compelled to do. She could see no point in it, but she knew that she could never face the coming Christmas unless she did.

The brambles, their few remaining leaves crisp with frost, put up a show of tearing at her jeans and old skiing jacket as she began to climb up the track to the top of the quarry. But the nettles which had been so thick and green in the summer now stood stark like the ruins of buildings after a bomb.

The quarry had looked so different the last time she was here. Susie came out on the plateau at the top, close to the quarry's edge. She remembered how Belle had stood there waiting for her to clamber up the last few yards of track. Belle had been outlined against the sky; she'd loomed like some malevolent, primordial creature.

And then Belle had moved forward, and the spell was broken.

Susie could not help looking for signs that she and her sister had ever been here. Surely the emotional intensity of that last meeting with Belle should be mirrored in some small sign that lives had changed for ever in that place? But there was nothing, only her own fresh footprints like bruises on the rime-covered grass. Six months before, Belle had thrown herself off the quarry edge and crashed to her death on the rocky, bramble-covered floor of the pit, but now it was as though the place had been undisturbed for years.

But then, as Susie knelt on the short, stiff grass to peer down into the quarry, she could feel Belle's presence. She shivered as she stared out into nothingness over the cliff edge. This was Belle's private haven, it always had been. Susie felt like an unwelcome guest.

Oh, Belle, what happened to us, why did you hate me so much? she asked herself. What did I ever do to deserve what you did?

Susie was suddenly overwhelmed with grief. Everything else, her anger and resentment towards her dead sister, her fear and incomprehension, were suddenly swamped by excruciating sorrow at the awful waste of both their lives.

We had such hopes, Susie thought, we were so sure we would be happy.

It probably wasn't true. She'd taken happiness for granted, but maybe Belle never had. But that did not explain the gulf that had opened between them as they grew up. Other sisters were close. They fought but there was a bond between them which withstood petty jealousies and disagreements. But that wasn't possible for Belle. Poor Belle, who'd never been able to value anything she had, only what belonged to others. And then, on top of everything, believing that she had Huntington's chorea. I could have helped you, Belle, Susie wanted to tell her, I could and I would, but you drove me away.

Susie found herself weeping for her dead sister, great rending sobs which wrenched the muscles of her stomach and forced her to bend double, clutching herself to stop the pain.

The sounds echoed from the quarry walls, but it wasn't the sound of sobbing that Susie heard; it sounded like a great gale of scornful laughter.

It's Belle, Susie thought, Belle's triumphal roll.

As the sound swelled in her ears and seemed to fill her head, Susie's instinct was to turn and run. This place filled her with fear, it wanted rid of her as Belle had wanted rid of her.

'No, no, no!' Susie was shouting and her cry swamped the fading sound of victory. 'No, you haven't won. You're dead, dead and buried. I won't let you live on in my life.'

She picked up a lump of stone from the track and hurled it into the quarry. She stood and listened as it rebounded off the cliff and then smashed into the undergrowth at the bottom of the old workings. Then there was silence.

Susie turned and walked back down the track. In front of her, the dregs of the sunrise were reflected in the far-off surface of the sea, so that the horizon seemed like a sheet of fire.

Near the foot of the track, the old dog Benson was waiting for her. He was panting with the effort of catching up with her, and when he saw her, he sat down gratefully and wagged his tail.

Back at the farm, Dad came out to meet her as she came into the yard.

'Where the hell have you been?' he said. 'I couldn't find you anywhere and I finished the milking ages ago.'

'I took the dog for a walk,' Susie said. She sounded impatient, and she felt guilty, but for some reason she didn't understand she knew that there was no time to waste.

'Well, you might have said so, it's no morning for that poor old dog to be out,' Dad said, but she knew that he was fussing because she'd broken his routine and he didn't know what else to do.

'If you finished the milking ages ago, I expect you've got breakfast ready by now,' Susie said, teasing him. She knew he was blaming her because she hadn't been there to do it.

Dad started to walk back into the house. He was grumbling under his breath.

Susie laughed and took his arm as she walked beside him.

'Don't worry, Dad, the world won't come to an end because breakfast's late.'

'It's time that daughter of yours did a bit more to help around the house,' he said.

'Dad, she's seven years old,' Susie said.

'Yes, well, your mother let you get away with murder when you were little,' her father said, 'and look at you now.' He sighed and then muttered, 'But no doubt you'll do as you please. You always did. No one ever listens to what I say.'

Susie thought, He's got so old, it's as though he's turned into a puppet of himself.

And again she felt a curious sense of urgency about something she had to do, but wasn't quite sure what it was.

38

It was Christmas Day and John was off duty. When the rota was drawn up, he'd been included among the married staff with children rather than the single men and women who tended to have to work over public holidays. It was assumed they wouldn't mind so much.

John felt a bit guilty that he hadn't mentioned his changed status, but he hadn't. It would have been too final, an admission that his marriage was over. Perhaps it was something to do with the time of year, but the loss of his family seemed to consume his life. The job he had loved now seemed like a daily process of going through the motions, and when he wasn't at work he wanted to be alone. His colleagues tried to break the shell he'd built around himself, but he didn't want to go down to the pub or out for a curry with the boys. He wanted to be alone.

Actually, that wasn't what he wanted, either. Being alone was too positive a description of his state. He was like a bird chick waiting inside the egg to be released to life; he was removed from that life, helpless and inert, helpless to break out while waiting to hatch.

He hadn't seen or spoken to Susie since the day she'd come out of prison and gone out of his life. He knew that he had hurt her, that she felt betrayed that he had doubted her. He didn't blame her, he blamed himself. He couldn't understand now how he could have been so stupid as to believe Belle. But although he tried to, he didn't blame Belle either. Whatever kind of monster Susie's older sister was, it was down to him that he had chosen to believe her jealous fantasies.

When Susie first took the children to stay on the farm with her father, John had spent long hours when he couldn't sleep wondering about Belle. He thought of how she had been those few days after her mother's death when they'd worked together on the land and how he'd wondered then how two very different but straight-forward, apparently happy, women, sisters, could have grown so far apart. Even their mother's death had not brought them together, if only briefly, in grief.

He'd liked Belle. She was the sort of woman who, if she'd been in the police, he'd have liked as a partner; big, athletic, intelligent and fiercely independent. He would have liked to be friends with her. But the relationship between her and Susie made that impossible. If he were being strictly honest, he had some sympathy with Belle on that score. Being Susie's sister must have made things hard for her when they were growing up. However Belle might have felt about it, he loved Susie's girliness, the ease with which she used her sexual wiles to exploit men, including him. She made him laugh: she always had. He let her manipulate him because he knew she was doing it. She made him feel protected and secure in the family relationship she built like an invisible nest around them.

How could his loving little Susie share Belle's parentage, her environment, her DNA, for God's sake? When he thought of Belle now, it was as though what in Susie was charming and warm-hearted had been distorted in Belle and become grotesque.

How could someone who'd done the things Belle had done show no sign of remorse or guilt? It wasn't only killing Ben, which might have been understood as a crime of passion. But what about the innocent stranger she'd stamped out like a cockroach because she was afraid he'd heard her talking in her sleep? What about the girl from work she claimed to have crushed under the girl's own car? Had that terrible disease had something to do with her callousness, altering her brain?

The police had looked into these deaths, and established that they had happened. But in spite of Belle's confession in her letter to John, there was no evidence that either of the victims had been murdered at all. There was no link between his sister-in-law and the young man who might have been from the North. There wasn't much more to connect Belle with the girl killed under the car, except that they worked in the same office. But the girl hadn't died at work; the accident happened miles out in the suburbs of North London and there was nothing to say that Belle had ever been there.

It was incredible to John that the vicious and perverted perpetrator of such crimes could come from the same family as Susie. And yet he had to believe it, because he knew at first hand what she had done to destroy Susie's happiness. Belle had planned a long, lingering, living death for her sister, that could not be denied or explained.

No, he couldn't hate Belle; Belle was beyond hatred.

He hated Christmas Day, though. Or he hated this Christmas Day. Once it had been the happiest time of the year, when he and Susie were at home together in front of a wood fire with the children squealing with delight as they opened their presents.

Well, all that was in the past. It would be different now, and perhaps it had never really been as perfect as he remembered it. More likely the kids were fighting and Susie going berserk in the kitchen because the turkey hadn't thawed properly and he'd drunk too much the night before and couldn't keep awake in front of the television.

He didn't know when he'd decided what he was going to do; it had been some sort of organic internal process but he'd known for days that he was going to try to spend this Christmas at the farm with Susie.

He hadn't rung to ask her. He knew she would tell him not to come. He hadn't even asked if he could take the kids to his mum's for Boxing Day, which she might not like, but could scarcely refuse point blank.

He set off early, before there was much traffic on the road. It was a cold, miserable day with flurries of sleet, nothing like those nostalgic magical Christmas Days he pretended to remember.

He'd almost arrived at the farm, well beyond reach of the nearest town or even motorway service station, when he realized that he hadn't brought anything with him: no presents for the children, no food, no drink, no festive flowers.

There was nothing he could do about it now. And maybe that was how it should be. This trip wasn't about Christmas, and if he'd come laden with gifts, Susie might have thought it was. He didn't want that.

He drove into the yard and stopped the car near the barn. For a few moments he just sat behind the wheel, remembering how it had been earlier in the year when he and Belle had cleared out all the old straw and she had taken him up into the hayloft to show him where Susie had seduced Ben years before. And then she'd tried to make love to him . . .

I shouldn't have come here, he thought. If Susie wanted to see me she'd have rung me up or e-mailed or something. She wants to be left alone, and she'll think I'm bullying her.

And then Susie opened the back door and walked across the yard towards him. She didn't recognize the new car that came with the job and she wasn't expecting visitors. He could see that much from the expression on her face. I shouldn't have come, he told himself again.

And then she recognized him and for one wild, wonderful moment he knew that she was happy he had come.

It was a fleeting reaction. Almost immediately her face looked guarded once again, curious but suspicious.

'What are you doing here?' she said.

Be careful, John told himself, what I say now could be a beginning or the end of everything.

'I haven't brought anything for Christmas,' he said, and he could hear how his voice was shaking. 'It's my day off and I came because I had to.' And then his voice broke and in spite of himself, he added, 'I've got to talk to you. Please, Susie, let me talk this through with you and after that I'll do anything you want and get out of your life if that's what you want.'

Susie was staring at the car and looking puzzled. She didn't look at him. Then she said, 'I put your name on the children's presents.'

'Susie . . . ?'

'You would come today,' she said. 'I've got a turkey to cook, and you want to talk.'

She would talk to him. John wanted to fling his arms around her in gratitude, but of course he didn't.

'I'm sorry, I forgot about Christmas. I've been in a sort of trance since . . . well, for months. And then this morning it was as if I came out of a coma and I knew I'd got to find out what had been happening in the real world and I had to talk to you. I can go away and come back another time, if you'll only say you'll talk to me.'

'Not here I won't, I'm getting soaked and freezing with cold. Come into the hayloft, at least it's dry. We can't talk in the house, not with Dad and the kids.'

'How are they?' he asked as he followed her into the barn. He could smell hay, and the clean dry scent of straw.

'They're fine. They'll be over the moon to see you. I told them you're working away.'

'So I can see them. You don't mind?'

'They're your children, of course you can see them.'

If he had ever stopped loving Susie, he would have fallen for her all over again as he watched her climb the ladder to the hayloft ahead of him.

When he pulled himself up over the top of the ladder, she seemed to him like some kind of sprite, sitting cross-legged on a bale of hay with her skirt halfway up her thighs showing her legs in thick black woollen tights. He had never imagined he would find his fastidiously fashionable wife allowing herself to be seen dead in anything so practical and unflattering.

She saw what he was thinking and said defiantly, 'At least they're warm.'

'You'd look good in anything,' he said.

Then he stood wondering what to say now that he was alone with her.

She spoke first. 'I d have been in touch with you before now,' she said. 'But I didn't have the guts.'

'I wish you had,' he said; 'you've nothing to be afraid of from me.'

'I know that now,' she said, 'it's Belle I was afraid of. It was almost as though after I found out what she did I felt she was possessing me.'

'I know,' John said. 'It was as though she was controlling our lives from beyond the grave. She poisoned me. I never stopped loving you but I couldn't stop myself from half believing her.'

He went and sat beside her on the bale of hay, feeling absurd in his formal dark suit and black city shoes.

Susie uncrossed her legs to make more room for him. 'I went up to her special place by the quarry the other day,' she said, 'and I know it sounds silly but I sort of had it out with her. Belle was my big sister and she always bullied me, all my life. I've never stood up to her. I didn't even mean it the time I cut her finger off, I was just pretending and the axe was too heavy, I couldn't stop it. She didn't try to take her hand away. Why didn't she move her hand?'

Susie looked down at her own hands, much rougher now than

when John had last seen them, and the nails broken. She said, 'I felt she was there, at the quarry, her spirit was there trying to claim me. But I refused to let her. It was like an exorcism. It's hard to explain.'

She looked at John to make sure he wasn't laughing at her.

'I know,' he said, 'I know what you mean.'

'It was the first time I really understood what she'd done to me,' Susie went on. 'Before, I'd always thought it must be my fault in some way. John, she planned and plotted and did all those awful things like killing those poor innocent people, and it was all so that she could get her revenge on me. It wasn't because I had sex with Ben, I wouldn't even have done that if she hadn't already sort of pre-ordained it. She wanted revenge on me just for being her sister and having to share part of her life.'

John took Susie's hand in his and she grasped it tightly.

Then she said, 'For as long as I can remember, she made me feel guilty because she thought my being born spoiled her life, she wasn't the one and only any more. But I didn't want to, I couldn't help being born or being me. She made me believe I was the malign spirit she thought I was, and I let her. I did actually believe it.'

John put his arm round her shoulders, and she turned to hide her face against his chest. He had to strain to hear what she was saying.

'That's why I was so angry with you when I came out of prison,' he heard her say.

'You had every reason,' he said, stroking her hair. It felt springier than it had before, she'd stopped having it professionally straightened.

'No,' Susie said, 'it was part of her plan. She worked on you. It wasn't your fault she made you doubt me, she made everything she invented seem so real.'

'Maybe it was real to her,' John said, 'it was other people who weren't real to her.'

'Up at the quarry the other day was the first time I knew Belle was dead,' Susie said. 'Before that she'd been alive inside me, and I was living the life she'd made for me. I thought I heard her laughing because she'd won, and quite suddenly I wasn't going to let her call the shots any more. She hasn't won. I won't let her. She is dead, and I'm not.'

She smiled at him. 'You came here to talk to me and I haven't let you get a word in edgewise. John, I've got Belle out of my system, but can you look me in the eye and not think of her and all those evil things she did? Can you separate me from my sister? Not just in your mind, but really?'

'Body and soul,' John said, and kissed her.

'I've got that turkey to cook,' she said at last. 'Let's go in to the kids.'

The kitchen window overlooking the yard was steamed up as they walked back towards the house. She opened the door and a rush of steam surrounded her in a romantic mist; it was almost theatrical, like in a ballet.

'My God,' Susie said, 'I'll never get the hang of that bloody Aga. Do you think it's blown up?'

'Wow, that smells good,' John said. 'I'd forgotten what real food smells like.'

Susie led him into the sitting-room, where her father was asleep in front of the television and the children were squabbling over some card game they'd been playing.

They jumped up when they saw John. They shrieked, rushing over to him and hanging on to him as though they would never let him go.

'Daddy, why are you crying?' Kim demanded to know.

'I'm not,' he said, 'it was all that mist in the kitchen.'

'Go and wash your hands before we eat,' Susie told the children.

She turned off the television and her father woke up.

'Look who's here, Dad,' she said. 'John made it after all.'

The old man got to his feet and came to shake John's hand.

'Good to see you,' he said, 'I'm glad you're here. If you've got time tomorrow there's a bit of fencing down on the twenty-acre field near the estuary which needs fixing. You could give me a hand.'

'I'd like that,' John said. 'I've missed the fresh air, to tell you the truth.'

Susie left them together and disappeared into the kitchen. Dad poured whisky for himself and John and made room on the sofa. He turned the television back on, then off again.

'We won't mention this again,' he said, 'but what happened about those poor people . . . ' He couldn't bring himself to finish the sentence.

John understood that he was talking about Belle's victims.

'The police reopened the cases and did all they could,' he said, 'but honestly, there wasn't a scrap of evidence she had anything to do with either of them. Only what she wrote in that letter.'

The old man poured more whisky into his glass and John's.

'It's good to see you, my boy,' he said, 'and good to see Susie looking herself again.' He looked confused, and then added, 'You know, when Belle was small, she used to bully poor Susie shamefully. We did everything we could, her mother and I, but we couldn't stop her. Her mother used to think she'd been swapped at birth. Mary often said that when we were wondering what to do with her.'

John thought in passing that that was ironic since it was Belle who had apparently inherited the dreadful curse of being born her mother's child.

The old man looked John straight in the eye and asked, 'Do you think she was born bad, or was she sick in the head?'

John shook his head. He couldn't answer and hoped that the old man didn't expect him to.

Kim and Jonty came running into the room to call them to lunch, then they rushed into the dining-room.

John got up and Dad reached out a hand for him to help him out of the sofa.

'Poor Belle,' the old man said, 'I don't think she ever enjoyed the blessing of normal family life.'

My father-in-law, John thought, is a master of understatement, but he didn't reply. There wasn't really anything to be said.